The Ice Factory

RUSSELL LUCAS

Mandarin

A Mandarin Paperback
THE ICE FACTORY

First published in Great Britain 1993
by William Heinemann Ltd
This edition published 1994
by Mandarin Paperbacks
an imprint of Reed Consumer Books Ltd
Michelin House, 81 Fulham Road, London SW3 6RB
and Auckland, Melbourne, Singapore and Toronto

Copyright © Russell Lucas 1993
The author has asserted his moral rights

A CIP catalogue record for this title
is available from the British Library
ISBN 0 7493 1806 6

Printed and bound in Great Britain by
Cox and Wyman Ltd, Reading, Berks.

The Ice Factory

Russell Lucas was born in Bombay and moved to Britain when he was sixteen. In 1952 he returned to India and worked there for three years, before coming back to work in the motor-car industry. In 1990 he published his first collection of short stories, *Evenings at Mongini's* and in 1991 his first novel, *Lip Service*, appeared.

For Eleanor, Florence and Joseph

Acknowledgements

To Elspeth Sinclair for her invaluable help,
Toby Eady my agent, Peter Shortland for his research
and, of course, Helena Petrovna.

PART ONE

Fram

Chapter 1

Banoo and Kety visited Fram on two afternoons a week. Around four o'clock on the days they were expected, he began to grow restless, straining his mind through the stillness of the sanatorium for the distant wasp-like hum he suspected would progress into the hoarse rumble of a Cunningham V-8 engine. He listened, anticipating the confirmation his clairaudient awareness sensed. Occasionally, an approaching buzz was devoured by painful silence and he was bruised by soundlessness. Yet, no sooner was he certain of the familiar drone he awaited than he grew restless and tense. Why had they bothered, he wondered querulously, biting a cardamom to balm his breath and giving his heavy-lidded, dark eyes, John Barrymore moustache and gleaming teeth a critical sneer in a hand-mirror. He was tall and slim, affable when given reasonable notice of company and capable of exuding a deceptive radiance that only more perceptive minds doubted. In reality, Framroze Chutrivala was consumed by restless insecurity and hostage to a psychopathic quirk that had consigned him to Dr Dilip Dilduktha's establishment.

For many, Dilduktha assured him, the enjoyment of a fetish remains a pleasant and private joy. Liberating even. But in Fram's case, it had become a tiresome inconvenience that required either restraint or urgent alleviation.

'Sanity has never been my problem,' Fram assured the psychiatrist.

'The definition of sanity has confounded the most complex and gifted minds,' Dilduktha chuckled, rubbing his crotch indulgently.

'My brother Soli,' Fram interrupted, 'thought some form of aversion therapy might be of value.'

'Aversion, perversion, we'll try everything, dear boy,' Dilduktha promised, staring past Fram's head at the young girl sweeping leaves by the steps. 'But let us start,' the doctor added, 'with your acceptance that it is not unusual for odours to become fetishes. These can be natural animal secretions or artificial aromatics. Let's face it, Mr Chutrivala, the perfume industry is founded on attractive smells.'

At first, the long-haired Dilduktha, with his grey, almond eyes, red lips and mocking smile, irritated Fram. He appeared to have an instant answer for everything. Fram much preferred solemn doctors with close-cropped heads, who scratched their noses, picked their earlobes and looked thoughtful for several minutes before opening their mouths. This fellow let you have it before you finished speaking. Like Fram's brother Soli, Dilduktha had been trained abroad, a factor that Fram suspected accounted for the psychiatrist's arrogance. Although Soli had escaped with just three years' contamination at the London School of Economics, Dilduktha had been subjected to a protracted process in London, Berlin and Vienna. Perhaps, Fram reflected charitably, after such an expensive educative experience, a man was entitled to be a little chirpy.

'Confidence still eludes me,' Fram complained.

'Self doubt,' Dilduktha assured him, 'is a common human condition rooted in an irrational fear of mortality. I would recommend the "Death is my fast friend" sutra.' He felt Fram's pulse. 'It is essentially a meditation upon one's own faeces.'

Fram shook his head. 'I would prefer to devote my thoughts to pleasanter matters,' he replied. Dilduktha smiled.

'Evasive strategies are not unusual. What about some Meade Lux Lewis?'

Fram looked puzzled.

'He's a honky-tonk pianist,' the psychiatrist explained. 'I'll have the ward boy fix up a gramophone beside you. I suggest you turn your mind to the more positive remarks people have made to you as you listen to the music.'

'Do you like English ladies?' Fram asked suddenly, aware that Dilduktha must have tried his hand with them when in London.

The psychiatrist shook his head.

'No,' he confessed. 'I'm more inclined to the Irish and Welsh. Also Viennese Jewesses. I find the English unfriendly.'

They watched a flying fox attach itself to an overhead fan.

4

'I have discovered English women,' Fram sighed, 'to be quite wonderful.'

'You have known many?' Dilduktha asked, a note of surprise in his voice. 'In Bombay?'

'I wouldn't go that far,' Fram conceded, not venturing to discuss the matter further.

A second flying fox joined the first on the fan.

'The sweeper girl has been in Mr Fazal's room for nearly an hour,' the psychiatrist murmured. 'He thinks I didn't see him smuggle her in.'

'How old is she?'

'Oh, at least twelve,' Dilduktha replied with a wave of assurance, hesitating before adding, with a malicious grin, 'He's a bugger, you know.'

'Literally!'

'Of course.'

Fram brooded for a moment on the prospect of fat Mr Fazal buggering the little sweeper girl. The thought darkened his mind. Dilduktha rose to go.

'There's hundreds of scorpions here,' Fram complained, brushing two off his pillow.

'Not poisonous,' Dilduktha cried, as he moved down the verandah, turning to call an amiable warning. 'But ring the handbell if the baboons arrive. They could be rabid.'

Later, Fram settled back on his pillow, having tried to exorcise the bleakness of his situation through the wistful tumble of 'Honky-Tonk Train Blues'. He wondered why Dilduktha hadn't made the most of his opportunities when in London, recalling a particular equine protection convention for the succour of infirm gharry horses. It was there that an English lady had remarked upon the brooding limpidity of his big, black eyes. Unfortunately, the observation had not been addressed to him but to her English companion. Although he never doubted the sincerity of the words, he regretted not being allowed the opportunity to respond to the unexpected compliment, for before he could articulate his gratitude the ladies had flitted on to the next guest. He felt at first like one of the spavined geldings that were the objects of the association's proposed rehabilitation but on further reflection concluded that Mrs Vanessa Beauchamp's intention had been unmalicious and utterly benign.

5

Mrs Beauchamp was the wife of Bulldog Beauchamp, a Superintendent of Police. Their daughters were schoolfriends but this in no way qualified the parents for even the most minimal social intercourse. Fram sighted her at charity bazaars, fund-raising committees and gymkhanas. And ever since her poetic allusion to his eyes, he had employed every available opportunity of approaching her, exercising the greatest discretion as he hovered around her. Nothing excited him more than these close encounters. He was enchanted by her auburn tresses, bright blue eyes, bow-shaped mouth and the brazen length of her red nails. Her bosom he could only imagine, as she had a virtuous predilection for full dresses. He had procured, through the paid services of her woman servant, ginger combings from her head and a few frizzy moults taken from the warmth of her morning sheets, Titian curls he never tired of examining under a magnifying glass. To his disappointment, these precious, kinky specimens were quite odourless, although on warm, humid days he imagined he detected the elusive aroma of mushrooms. He lusted for more personal smells but frightened the servant with a request for a piece of Mrs Beauchamp's soiled underwear or even a discarded menstrual cloth. A threat of exposure eventually quietened him and he settled for the souvenirs he had, keeping them in a silk envelope under his pillow.

However, two group photographs in which Vanessa Beauchamp appeared were nearly his undoing. Establishing that they had been taken by Bourne and Shepherd of Hornby Road, Fram asked them to provide him with enlargements of her. The Goanese counter-assistant reported Fram's order to the English manager, who came out of the office to investigate. He gave Fram a long and critical stare.

'Who are you?' he demanded sharply, looking from the photographs to Fram and back again several times.

'My name is Chutrivala,' Fram stammered.

'Well, Chutrivala,' the Englishman said, 'I'm afraid we won't be able to provide you with an enlargement of the lady in question without her express permission. Perhaps you'd care to tell me who she is.'

The power drained out of Fram's legs. He felt faint with terror.

'If the rules preclude you from taking my order, then let's forget it.' Fram reached out for his prints. But the Englishman had other ideas. He had already nodded to the chaprassie to restrain Fram if necessary.

'It's not as simple as that. I happen to know who this lady is. She's Mrs Beauchamp, isn't she? Superintendent Beauchamp's wife. I don't know what filthy idea you had in mind but I'm certain the Superintendent would not be happy if you possessed an enlarged photograph of his wife.'

After an unpleasant argument, Fram was arrested and taken to the police station in a victoria.

'I have my Cunningham outside,' he pleaded to the Anglo-Indian sergeant. The man sniggered and bundled Fram into the carriage.

Three hours later he was told that no charges would be pressed, and released. Jockey, his chauffeur, was waiting for him outside. Fram felt dismal with the humiliation.

The following month, an unexpected letter arrived. It was a short note from Mrs Vanessa Beauchamp with the two enlargements he had ordered from Bourne and Shepherd. For a while, Fram read the letter several times a day.

> Dear Mr Chutrivala,
> I sincerely regret the inconvenience you were caused by the unfortunate misunderstanding at Bourne and Shepherd. I hope you will allow me to settle the account as a modest token of friendship.
> > Sincerely,
> > Vanessa Beauchamp

He replied the following day, spending the night drafting his letter and settling on a simple, final version after he had scrapped several effulgent and dangerously ambiguous responses.

> Dear Mrs Beauchamp,
> Thank you. I will never forget your kindness and generosity. I remain your servant and well-wisher.
> > Ever in your debt,
> > Framroze Chutrivala

Despite this correspondence, Fram had never spoken to her, although he had raised his topee twice with as much charm as he could manage. On the second occasion, he was almost certain he detected a half smile of acknowledgement. But Soli derided Fram's abject behaviour, contemptuous of his regard for Mrs Beauchamp. He denied, however, that he was in any way responsible for incinerating the Hornby Road premises of Bourne and Shepherd.

'Don't insult me with your suspicions of petty arson,' he snarled at Fram. 'When I go for a target, it will be Government House or nothing.' It was a grisly threat Fram preferred to forget. Of Vanessa Beauchamp, on the other hand, he thought most nights, private reflections that were generally improper, dreams of unseen breasts and the caressing of her milky white skin when he was servicing Banoo.

Fram waited for the Cunningham's double declutch at the crest of the hill by the old Jain temple that was now infested by grey-faced monkeys. He held his breath at the unnecessary whine of deceleration around the final turn. He expected three. Fat Banoo, perspiring in the nearside rear seat, the glittery-eyed Kety drenched in perfume beside her and the saturnine Jockey, in his white, fan-shaped pugree at the wheel, pumping the pedals with leathery, bare feet, jerking the car forward at every gear change and ogling Kety slyly through the rear-view mirror. His sister's innocent mind probably didn't understand the true nature of those covert looks, but Fram was only too familiar with Jockey's cock-stiff glances.

Banoo waddled in, swathed in a pink sari, bearing a chatty of gulab jamuns. She set them on a table beside him and pecked him on the forehead.

'Where's Kety?' Fram asked, looking around.

'Washing her hands.'

'Why?'

Banoo shrugged. Fram took the opportunity to ask her to keep an eye on Kety.

'What about me?' Banoo demanded. 'I'm your wife. Who's to keep an eye on me?'

Fram frowned. Her spasms of coyness irritated him. It was quite ridiculous in a woman approaching fifty, who weighed two hundred and twenty pounds and even by the most modest standards was scarcely an object of desire. But he made emollient noises, declaring that her aura of dignified authority deterred speculative lechery.

'Kety, being unwed, is vulnerable,' he argued. 'A virgin with moist lips and breasts like melons is always in danger.'

'One cannot presume upon such things as virginity at thirty-five,' Banoo sighed. 'At least not in a celebrated table-tennis player.'

'What do you mean by that?' Fram asked miserably.

'It's no secret,' Banoo said, 'that since the age of twelve, she has spent a great deal of time in the company of the opposite sex. And I've never approved of playing mixed doubles with Charansingh.'

'They're provincial champions,' Fram protested vacuously.

'Fame has made her proud and devious,' she sighed. 'Besides, I've always been suspicious of men with hairy faces. It's like going around in a mask.'

Fram bit another cardamom. Banoo, he reflected, was jealous of Kety. He attributed her malice to a crooked eye and mossy, upper lip. His sister's sporting achievements were deeply resented. Also the fact that Roshan his mother and Kety had moved into Peccavi, the Wadia family home, after Banoo's parents' deaths.

'The house is full of bloody Chutrivalas,' she once hissed nastily, when she found Kety using the bathroom.

Kety was an imposing female. She was large-breasted, wide-bottomed, sturdy-thighed, with heavy accusative eyes, juicy lips and blue-black hair that, when unfurled, fell like a shawl to the cleft of her arse. It was an obvious vanity and she contrived a number of ingenious coiffures, embellishing her chignons, buns, pompadours, snail-whorls and plaits with jewelled kangas, pins, clasps, fans and silk-ribbons. Her nose, perhaps, was an incongruence, too small and beaked for her broad face, giving her the raptorial appearance of a fleshy owl. As a young girl, her mother had supported her interest in diversions like kite-flying, cycle-racing and tap-dancing. Table tennis seemed no more than a related frivolity. Roshan allowed her daughter extraordinary liberty from early age. She voiced concern, however, about Kety damaging her breasts.

'Keep them well secured, sweetheart. Too much movement can lead to cancers.'

And when Kety jumped her way to the top of the table-tennis tree, back-smashing the opposition into oblivion, nobody was prouder than Roshan, who'd had Kety's breast harnesses specially measured and hand-stitched by her own elderly tailor. Roshan insisted for the sake of decency that the tailor wore gloves when he touched Kety's skin and would not allow any measurements to be made unless she was present. The fact that he was a septuagenarian was also a comfort to her.

Banoo's reservations about Kety's doubles partner disturbed Fram. He had privately voiced the same concerns about Charansingh to Soli, but his brother, being a revolutionary Bolshevik, had eccentric ideas about the sanctity of women, caring little about who fucked whom. As for Jockey, Fram had heard the jingle of bangles and anklets from his room on more than one occasion. He suggested to Soli that Jockey was a womaniser, but his brother laughed. Jockey, Soli had assured him, was a casualty of proletarian servility, unable to achieve intimacy with anyone he perceived to be his social superior, rarely aspiring higher than ragged, bazaar-girls.

'Are you certain?' Fram asked.

'The only certainties that I recognise,' Soli declared emphatically, 'are the collapse of capitalism, the disintegration of the British Empire and the ultimate victory of international socialism.'

'What about the perilous situation of our unmarried sister?' Fram demanded.

'Apart from some ideological damage because of her membership, through your marriage, of a regressive mercantilist family, Kety's world view is not unsound. Her future gives me little cause for concern.'

'But Papa was a businessman too,' Fram pointed out.

'What business?' Soli laughed. 'Umbrella-repairing is not materially different from cobbling or shoe-shining. It is an essentially working-class occupation. Papa was never an employer of labour.'

'What about Jal and Jehangir?' Fram shouted.

'They were second cousins,' Soli replied, 'who wouldn't have been able to secure employment elsewhere, both of them being lunatics. It was more an act of philanthropy than genuine employment.'

Fram hated Soli's disparagement of the values he held dear.

'By the way,' Soli said, 'I have even persuaded Kety to become a regular reader of *Red Tiger*.'

Soli's remarks had done little to allay Fram's unhappy fears. And now Banoo had revived them with her comments about Charansingh. The bitch.

Chapter 2

'How's little Meroo?' Fram asked, turning his mind from trouble-some thoughts.

'Morose as ever,' Banoo complained, popping one of the gulab jamuns she had brought for him into her mouth.

'And my mama?'

'Still dying very slowly and with a great deal of noise. The doctor says that six months should see her out. The question is, how are you?'

'Dilduktha feels that I should be back in a month or so. We're trying a little meditation before the aversion therapy.'

'No straitjacket then?' she grunted, taking another jamun. Fram shook his head. He saw the little sweeper girl approach them. She handed Banoo a paper cone filled with hot chunna, and some change.

'I sent her to the shop for something to munch while I was here,' Banoo explained to Fram. The little girl accepted a small copper coin for her trouble and shot a grateful smile at Banoo and Fram. He noticed her usually light brown eyes and that her breasts were no larger than limes. She had a fierce, white cicatrice across the taut brown skin of her belly.

'What's that?' he asked, touching her with his forefinger.

'My brother knifed me when he was drunk,' she said, lowering the band of her red checked skirt to show the scar's jagged continuation down her groin.

'The little whore will undress if you give her half a chance,' grumbled Banoo.

The girl waited uncertainly for her dismissal.

'Shoo,' ordered Banoo, waving her away.

Fram watched her move down the verandah. She walked with

a jaunty hesitancy, like a vigilant chicken searching for millet. Banoo leafed through the papers scattered across his razai, checking the names at the top of each sheet.

'Who's this Emanual Lasker?' she enquired, waving a chess-notation sheet at him.

A wave of resentment engulfed him. He was irritated at her treatment of the sweeper girl and by the knowledge that she was as uninterested in chess as she was in most things. Yet here was the fat buffalo poking her nose into his affairs. Fram got out of bed and reached for his maroon dressing-gown. He slipped it on and stepped around to the back of Banoo's armchair.

'He's a German guy I play with,' he said, taking the sheet from her. 'Almost as good as your father was.'

Banoo stared at him wide-eyed.

'Here, a German?' she asked. 'In Kapoli?'

Fram nodded, determined not to elaborate. He didn't disclose that one of the junior doctors, a Punjabi called Ram Lashkar, had been nicknamed Emanual Lasker as a joke. He was not inclined to explain that to her. She took her third jamun, looking round at him guiltily.

'You have them,' he urged, managing a smile. 'I'm on a diet.'

The irony of his remark escaped her as she lifted the chatty onto her lap.

'I'll save the chunna for the return journey,' she decided.

There was a clip-clop of footsteps behind them and the sound of Kety's laugh. Fram turned towards his sister, framed in the doorway. He was surprised she was wearing a white dress and had so dramatically overdone the lipstick and eyebrow pencil. It made her look, he thought, slightly available. Her fifteen-minute absence had inexplicably rattled him.

'You look rather tricky,' he said reproachfully, sniffing the air which was drugged with a dark perfume.

Kety giggled, conscious of his morbid concern for her respectability.

'I'm trying to attract a husband,' she announced playfully.

'What?'

Fram had never seen her look so enticing. God help Charansingh, he thought.

'What's that stain on your skirt?' he asked, his eyes drawn to a wet patch just below where he judged her pubes would be.

Although he knew that the mark was not cockjuice, a fluid that mapped differently from any other, its location disturbed him. Kety responded with the ludic coquetry of an experienced fornicator. She blinked her lubricious, black eyes and smiled. And she held her breath as she spoke, stammering, then rushing her words as though she had been caught *in flagrante delicto*.

'I wet myself at the tap,' she whispered, slanting him a smile drenched with dark meanings.

Why, Fram wondered, were women so perfidious? Banoo was still eating the jamuns.

'Will you inform Jockey,' he said, addressing Kety, 'that it's quite unnecessary for him to keep the Cunningham in second gear coming down that miserable one-in-seven gradient. Third should be quite sufficient. I don't like to hear a decent motor car whine like a whipped cur.'

Kety came forward to be embraced. He kissed her dutifully on each cheek, conscious of her provocative water melons against his chest.

'There's little doubt,' she said as they faced each other, 'that you are on the mend.'

She attributed her certainty to the energetic gleam in his eyes. They had, she declared, looked burnt out when he was first admitted, barely three months earlier. Fram noticed Mr Fazal come out onto the verandah and walk to the far end. He leaned over the rail and made an imperious chuch-chuch to attract the sweeper girl's attention. Banoo twisted uncomfortably in the direction of the sound and scowled.

'Who's that?' she asked, polishing off the last jamun and licking her fingers.

'Mr Fazal, a barrister,' Fram murmured. 'The girl runs his errands.'

Later, Dilduktha confirmed that apart from a more aggressive respiration, a slightly enhanced pulse rate and signs of pupil dilation an hour after the two women had driven away, Fram appeared to be feverish with excitement. These, Dilduktha considered, were encouraging signs of recovery. But Fram did not disclose that he had been singing a mantra given to his late father-in-law by the legendary Kala Baba. It was an antidote for depression and even erased tiresome memories.

Kali, Kali, Ma,
Indra ki bheti,
Brahma ki pali,
Dho dho hath,
Bunjwani tali.

He sang to himself, thinking wistfully of Dr Friski Dalal and wondering whether he'd made a mistake in not registering at her clinic instead. Banoo would not have approved, of course, which in itself now seemed to be an excellent reason for the choice. Dilduktha bent closer to Fram and asked him whether he was aroused by the sweeper girl, who had started to sweep the compound again. Fram shook his head. He was still unsure of himself.

'Oh very well,' Dilduktha sighed, taking Fram's pulse perfunctorily, as he whistled at the girl. She glanced up and smiled. The doctor mouthed something behind Fram's back that appeared to amuse her.

'Think about it,' the doctor urged, giving Fram's wrist an encouraging squeeze.

'Do you know Dr Dalal?' Fram asked, trying to divert Dilduktha's interest from the girl.

'Friski Dalal?' Dilduktha's face fell. 'It's only a matter of time before she's struck off the Register. Several of her patients have suicided.'

'Really? My late father-in-law, the great Byramji Wadia, was treated by her. I found her a most attractive personality when I visited her ashram.'

'You slept with her?' Dilduktha enquired confidentially.

'Of course not,' Fram frowned.

Dilduktha shrugged.

'She calls her clinic an ashram,' he complained, 'giving it a quasi-religious status that makes prosecution difficult. But young girls have been compromised and there have been reports of unbridled sex.'

'Unbridled?'

Dilduktha nodded. 'Her Kuthagiri technique,' he declared, 'is hardly more than an excuse for villainy. You see, Friski's qualification is basically aryuvedic and she was undeniably the mistress of that arch-bounder, Kala Baba.'

'Kala Baba a bounder?' Fram asked. 'But surely he was a saint. A man who fasted continuously, drank his own urine, kissed lepers on their mouths and transported himself on a rusted bicycle.'

'The bicycle was certainly rusty,' Dilduktha agreed, 'but after dark Friski and he used to go hither and thither in a silver Lagonda, eating red meat, drinking foreign liquor and jigging to up-to-date American music.'

But despite Dilduktha's disapproval, Fram rather liked Dr Dalal. He recalled the jolly, grey-haired woman with bright, black eyes and protruding teeth who dressed in pink Punjabi trousers and smock. She twinkled with excitement and wore silver bells on her wrists and ankles. And if it hadn't been for his inhibition about nudity and Banoo's hostility to Mrs Dalal, he might have been a patient himself.

'Don't you realise that harlot was Daddy's mistress and contributed to my mother's death?' Banoo had cried hoarsely. It was an accusation that Byramji had always denied, wild-eyed with indignation at the charge. However, Zarina, his mother-in-law, was slightly cracked and notorious for her unfounded allegations.

'Friski's morals are beyond reproach,' Byramji had assured Fram. But Fram was aware that both Banoo and her mother could never be persuaded of Mrs Dalal's good intentions.

'Promise me that you'll never go near that man-eating charlatan again,' Banoo sobbed when she heard that Fram had visited the ashram.

It was expedient at the time to submit dutifully to his wife's wishes and respect his mother-in-law's feelings. He had never been a man to ignore a woman's tears or cause the family unnecessary distress. Female screams made him tremble and sweat profusely under his armpits.

Mrs Dalal throbbed with restless energy and tinkled her ornamental bells to emphasise her more significant dicta.

'Kuthagiri,' she advised Fram, 'is rather like dumb charades.' His ear not yet attuned to her high-speed articulation, misheard the penultimate word.

'Thumb?'

'No, dumb. It has its roots in Subudh, Tantra and Zen. The

patients are confined behind high walls and encouraged to imagine themselves to be dogs.'

'Dogs?'

'In other words, kuthas,' she laughed, 'hence Kuthagiri. It is inspired by the koan. "Has a dog Buddha nature?" '

She explained that the intensive three weeks of canine projection encompassed the simulation of quadrupedal status, prohibitions on the use of implements, the wearing of clothes and conversation. It prescribed the lapping of water, barking, snarling, licking, sniffing and gentle biting. Mrs Dalal declared that as a qualified medical practitioner she assumed the role of pack-mother. She dropped briefly onto all fours, darting her head rapidly from left to right and back again to demonstrate enlightenment, adding that she was also a legatee of Kala Baba's healing powers which were salivatory in nature. She growled, demonstrating her head movements again, poking out her tongue then panting and dribbling therapeutic spit onto the rush mat before rising to her feet.

She showed him the icons of Kala Baba, the pot-bellied sage with a long, black beard but waist-length, white hair. His photographs were displayed in every room. Byramji had earlier told Fram that Kala Baba never ate for the last five years of his life. Well-water and Gold Flakes was all he needed. He smoked a hundred and twenty cigarettes a day. And every day without fail he rode his rusted bicycle to Jogeshwari and back, a round trip of fifteen miles. Fram was surprised to see that rusted bicycle suspended from a hook, garlanded and exhalted by a chirag burning below the saddle dusted with ochre powder. It had become an object of spiritual merit.

'The bicycle is much esteemed for its alleviation of stomach ulcers, flatulence and impotence,' Friski said, 'the three arch-enemies of the great serpent, Cundalini.'

She pointed to the great sage's enormous paunch in the pictures along the wall.

'His belly was filled with sunlit ragas,' she said brightly, 'which can be heard quite distinctly on each anniversary of his death, if one stands beside the rusted bicycle.'

She explained that Kala Baba, when fasting, drew his energy from her.

'Through my yoni,' she declared, 'a simple lingam–yoni conjunction. Three times a day, just like normal meals.'

It was a point that Fram considered making to Dilduktha but realised that any matter illuminating Mrs Dalal's spiritual relationship with Kala Baba would have been greeted with derision. Dilduktha had even sneered at the attested fact that Kala Baba was one hundred and thirty when he died. There was abundant proof that he'd been born in Benares in 1791 and had joined the Universal Mind in 1921.

'The imposter was no more than fifty,' Dilduktha scoffed.

Friski Dalal had informed Fram that nothing saddened her more than the incredulity of educated people. Fram sympathised.

'As a man who is a prisoner of a smell, I have no right to be sceptical about anything,' he conceded.

'Its garam masala, isn't it?'

Fram nodded miserably.

'And given the correct proportions, the most potent aphrodisiac known to man.'

'I know,' Fram sighed.

'You're a sweet boy,' Friski murmured. 'Like your father-in-law, Bobby.' This was Byramji's nickname.

'If you hadn't been Bobby's son-in-law, an audience would have been impossible. Everyone wants to see me. Princes, nabobs, croreputties, ICS officers, film stars, yogis, even General Dyer.'

'*The* General Dyer?'

'Who else?' Friski cried, jingling her feet prettily. 'One of the most celebrated murderers of the Raj.'

She smiled sweetly, showing her teeth and dark gums. For a fair-complexioned woman, she had unusually dark gums. A deep purple. A black-faced baboon trundled through the door and helped itself to a banana from a tray of fruit in the corner of the room. It stared at Fram through small, lime-green eyes.

'General Dyer came here for forgiveness,' Mrs Dalal said. 'He was genuinely sorry about Amritsar. Kala Baba received him privately. It had to be an incognito job as he had many enemies.'

She did a little dance movement, raising her arms over her head in an arch. Fram remembered that Friski was the consultant choreographer to Amazing Films and taught dance in the State of Pinjrapore.

'Kala Baba forgave the general completely,' she said. 'He left here unspotted by his silly mistake.'

Fram raised his eyebrows. It was hardly more than a twitch.

'I know what you're thinking,' Friski said, 'three hundred and seventy-nine admitted dead is hardly a silly mistake. The silly mistake was to give the command to fire. Just one mistake. The three hundred and seventy-nine dead were the consequences of that mistake. The fact that the cause and effect were so close together merely dramatised his error. But in life, the effects of evil decisions are often never clearly perceived. In some instances, they are several incarnations apart. Pray for Reggie Dyer, Mr Chutrivala.'

Fram closed his eyes and lowered his head reverently. He felt constrained to follow her example, disturbed from his contemplative silence by a sharp, feline sound of pain from outside. Looking through the window, he saw the baboon, who had sloped out of the room, mounting a white cat on the verandah. He looked at Friski with alarm.

'There's no problem,' she assured him, 'they are lovers, like all my animals. Love is everywhere in the ashram.'

The baboon, having extinguished its need, lifted itself off the cat which crawled painfully away across the compound. The baboon returned and sat by the door before reaching forward to appropriate a mango. It eyed Fram coldly, not appearing to approve of his presence.

'He's jealous of you,' Mrs Dalal laughed. She made kissing noises and the beast edged nearer Fram.

'Is he safe?' Fram asked warily.

Friski Dalal made some more kissing noises and the baboon trundled over to her, thrusting its grey muzzle between her thighs.

'He's a scoundrel,' she fussed, bending down to press her lips against its wet nostrils. It now sat back on its haunches and bit solemnly into the mango.

'The purpose of Kuthagiri,' she said, 'is mortification, free expression, sensory awareness and spiritual enlightenment.'

She watched the clouded uncertainty of Fram's expression. The baboon's face and chest were now smeared with the orange pulp of the mango.

'Do you mix the sexes?' he asked quietly.

19

'Of course,' she said, jingling her feet. 'It's like life. Naked, quadrupedal life. You see, the rationale of the quadrupedal position is that the sexual encounters are not compromised by eye contact.'

The baboon had now returned. It nuzzled her crotch, soiling her pink trousers with mango juice.

'He's an absolute so-and-so,' she scolded, tugging the animal's ears. They walked out onto the verandah. Jockey the chauffeur, sighting them, opened the rear nearside door.

'Its dear Bobby's Cunningham,' Friski cried with delight, recognising the black limousine immediately. She touched a polished mudguard tenderly.

'We treated him for psoriasis,' she mused sadly, recollecting as an afterthought, 'also piles.' Her reference to his father-in-law's ailments had the effect of reviving Byramji's memory. Fram suddenly remembered the wet, pink patches on his face and hands and the air was filled with the smell of zinc, castor-oil cream and sulphur.

'Bobby is back,' Friski announced, confirming Fram's impressions as she sniffed assiduously. 'Can you smell the Lubafax?'

'My God,' Fram murmured, his body-hair kindling with apprehension, but excited by Friski's psychic powers. He was certain that Byramji's spirit moved around the ice factory, but he kept the knowledge to himself, often talking to his dead father-in-law when alone at night. He glanced at Friski, whose eyes were filled with tears.

'Love brings him to us,' she whispered. 'Look, he's sitting in the car.'

Fram's gaze followed the pointing hand but he saw nothing.

He had already decided against Kuthagiri, hinting to Mrs Dalal that his knees probably wouldn't be up to the quadrupedal demands of the discipline. The truth was that he was alarmed at the prospect of seeing the erect phalli of competing males. Extremely large cocks depressed him. At school in St Mary's, he hated using the doorless showers and was scrupulous in shielding his organ from the eyes of his curious peers. It was not that he was dramatically undersized or diminished by any sense of inadequacy from penetrating receptive vaginas, but he often wished he was better endowed and had the means of inspiring astonishment in his partners.

'Oh father, what a monster,' was an exclamation he had never heard and which would, if addressed to him, have inspired lascivious and sly pleasure.

Sometimes, as he strove to satisfy a woman, taking performance as a serious responsibility, he enquired hopefully, 'How was it?' The replies varied from 'OK' to 'Very good', but he was never sure, searching the face before him for some indication of the satisfaction he'd hoped had been delivered. Banoo, his wife, whose obesity was a problem when coupling, became extremely wet and cavernous when excited, invoking his anxious enquiries whether she could feel him.

'Of course I can,' she grunted, licking his eye-sockets, a joyous symptom of her ecstasy. Once, he even asked her whether she would not have preferred a larger cock. He was cast down for months with her reply that it was unrealistic to expect everything one needed, despite her addendum that love was not about penile mensuration, followed by wet kisses and a painful squeeze of his scrotum.

But the sensation that he was floating inside her contributed to the gradual disintegration of their love life. In the early days of the marriage, he felt more acutely that the provision of regular orgasms for Banoo was a contractual constituent of the bargain he'd struck with Byramji, her father. Each stroke repaid part of his share in Singleton's Hotel, the heritage of Peccavi, a three-lakh dowry and the ownership of the ice factory. These solemn considerations were never far from his thoughts as he ploughed the red furrow between Banoo's fleshy thighs, a diligent husband, lugubrious as a dog fretting busily away on the job.

It was with regret that he left the ashram. When Friski had hinted at the possibility of fair-skinned partners his thoughts turned wistfully and improbably to Mrs Vanessa Beauchamp. But the moment of weakness passed.

He offered Dr Dalal his hand, withdrawing it as he sighted the baboon's warning lurch forward. The beast uttered an intimidating snarl.

'It would be prudent not to touch me,' she smiled, nodding at the hostile baboon.

As the car swished past a pair of spotted deer and a flock of guinea-fowl, Fram saw the still form of the white cat under a thorn bush.

'It's dead, sir,' Jockey observed, noticing his master's fascination with the unmoving creature.

'That bloody baboon,' Fram cursed, thinking of the rapist with disbelief and horror.

'The monkey is like Valenchino, Sir,' Jockey said, trying to subdue a grin. 'A number one lover.'

It was nearly midnight when he heard the sweeper girl return from the direction of Mr Fazal's room. Her movement disturbed a myriad of fireflies that rose from the canna bushes by the trellis. The two pariah dogs that skulked below the verandah boards growled warily at the creaking above them. Fram hissed at her in the darkness, flashing his torch from his bed. She came to him stealthily and he caught her lip-biting apprehension in the flashlight. He had two rupee coins ready.

'What's your name?' he enquired softly, pressing the money into her outstretched palm.

Chapter 3

Fram's father-in-law Byramji was a big, substantially-built man who was rarely without a cigar in his mouth and a tumbler of whisky in his hand. One of his vanities was that he had been born on the same day as Mohandas Karamchand Gandhi and nobody would have guessed that by looking at them.

'Just consider that toothless old stick,' Byramji would shout at his wife Zarina, 'and then take a good look at me.'

Zarina, an admirer of M.K.G., deplored her husband's puerile vauntings.

'You're a meat-eater,' she'd sneer, 'whisky-drinker and, if the truth were known, a whoremonger.'

'Me? Me, a whoremonger?' Byramji would protest, his roseate chops twitching as he turned to his daughter and son-in-law for support.

Zarina's cursing was largely a joke but the simulated rancour never failed to alarm Fram.

'What I mean,' Zarina shouted, 'is that you're burning yourself out like a candle. Your face is flushed with drink, your body swollen with gluttony and the blood rushes to your genitals at the rustle of a woman's skirt. That toothless old stick, as you call him, will probably still be around years after the vultures have picked your bones clean.'

'Such vulgar observations are hardly matters for poor Fram and Banoo,' Byramji reproved, clicking his tongue. He lit a cigar with a defiant flourish.

At the time of these histrionics from his in-laws, Fram was thirty-five, and had just taken over the management of the ice factory. He was careful not to upset either of Banoo's parents, feeling privileged at the time to live under the same roof as the

Wadias. Had Soli been present, Byramji might have found an ally, for Fram's younger brother detested M.K.G., although it was less for his acetic ways and appearance than for the politician's lack of revolutionary balls. Soli, however, was in London, alarming his infirm mother with apocalyptic postcards from a commune in Canning Town.

'Why can't the bugger be decently suited and booted like us?' Byramji complained, cornering Fram in the drawing room. 'No one would believe that this bounder, who looks like a hamal, is an England-returned, a barrister of the Middle-Temple and somebody whose speeches are reported in the international press.'

Byramji disclosed to Fram that he'd written to Gandhi on several occasions but that the man hadn't the courtesy to acknowledge any of these communications.

He got up and, sliding open the drawer of a squat, mahogany davenport, he withdrew a file which he handed to Fram.

Fram turned to the first letter as he tried to make something of the cigar his father-in-law had forced on him. Sumatras always cut into his throat.

'What's the matter?' asked Byramji. 'You look pale.'

Fram smiled weakly. 'I've swallowed a little cigar-sap,' he confessed with shame. But he was determined to acquire a taste for Byramji's reeking tobacco.

'Read the first letter aloud,' Byramji said. 'It'll clear your tubes.' Byramji's requests always sounded like instructions.

'All of it?'

'Why not?' demanded Byramji, snapping his fingers.

Fram began in a low, tremulous voice that deteriorated to an almost inaudible quaver as he progressed.

Peccavi,
Wadia Ice Factory Compound,
Mazagaon.
11.12.1919

Dear Mr Gandhi,

    May I, as a fellow Indian and believer in progress, suggest where I suspect you have gone wrong. Firstly, your dress strategy is a miserable joke. I realise that by looking like a starving peasant you are trying to identify

with the inarticulate masses of our country. Don't. They
are not likely to respect you for pretending to be what you
obviously are not. Everybody knows that you can afford
to kit yourself out like a gentleman. And although
Indians, being good-humoured and tolerant people, may
put up with your ridiculous fancy dress for a while, the
novelty value will soon wear off. Such symbols may be
OK to make a debating point but are hardly the ticket in
the real world. A well-cut gaberdine suit, white linen
shirt, dark tie, silk socks, well polished black shoes and a
good quality pith helmet are what you need. Believe me,
Gandhi, you will be transformed. I enclose the address of
Naratamdas Shah, my personal dursi, who will provide
you with a respectable wardrobe at really cut-throat
prices, certainly far cheaper than you would have to shell
out at The Army and Navy Stores or even Whiteaway
Laidlaw and Co. Secondly, please consult a reputable
dentist about the maintenance of your mouth. A
successful politician needs shining teeth, dear Sir, for
smiles are the rupees, annas and pies of your business;
indeed it is what the unhappy masses expect from aspiring
leaders. And you have little conception, Mr Gandhi, how
ladies of all ages are susceptible to the occasional flirty
grin. Speaking as a man of some experience with the
opposite sex, let me assure you that for seduction, political
or sexual, a decent set of teeth is a prerequisite. As for
those half-moon, granny spectacles of yours: throw them
away. The up-and-coming modern executive tends to use
hornrims. Invest in a pair of strong, rectangular frames,
available at Popatlals of Apollo Street. They really make a
chap look more attractive than Nature seriously intended.
Thirdly, for God's sake, do not aggravate the British. You
must not presume upon their patience and restraint. A
nation does not conquer half the world to be fingered
indefinitely by somebody (no offence intended) of your
ilk. Every day, I expect to read that you have disappeared,
been found bayoneted in a ditch or accidentally shot
during one of your demagogic effluxions. Remember, the
British are your mother and father when it comes to
assassination. Do what you have been trained for. The

High Court of India will always need vakils with persuasive tongues.

Your friend and well-wisher,
Byramji Wadia

'Well, what do you think of it?' asked Byramji proudly.

'Masterly,' croaked Fram.

'Gandhi,' observed Byramji, 'is not the sort of man who'll have a long-term impact on the course of history and I'm rarely wrong about such matters. Politically speaking, I'd place Soli above Gandhi any day.'

'Our Soli?' Fram asked, pouting a plume of smoke sideways.

'It's not that I approve of Bolshevism,' Byramji murmured, 'but Soli at least possesses the low cunning to persuade some of the less perceptive English-language newspapers to print his seditious rubbish.'

'He confuses the editors with his complex syntax,' Fram mused.

'Acumen,' Byramji said, plucking a leaf off his thick, wet lip. 'The boy's got acumen.'

Byramji waited until young Meroo had flitted through the room.

'What about a grandson?' he winked, leaning forward to grip his son-in-law's arm.

'It's God's will,' sighed Fram.

'Listen,' Byramji wheezed confidentially, 'a great sage called Kala Baba gave me the secret of producing a male but it was too late. Zarina's womb was in shreds after Banoo's birth. Sixteen pounds is no joke.'

'Maybe Banoo took after her mother. After Meroo, we had no luck either.'

Byramji puffed at his cigar before speaking.

'Rub your scrotum with a paste compounded of equal parts garlic, coriander, fenugreek, cummin, ginger and tamarind with a sixth part chilli-powder, half an hour before congress.'

Fram looked mildly alarmed.

'A garum masala? It'll sting.'

'Do you want a son or not?' Byramji demanded.

Byramji's dramatic suggestion was the start of Fram's tribulations. At Banoo's menopause, the formula still hadn't produced a male heir. True, Fram found the application intensely aphrodisiac but all Banoo had to show for the messy practice was an irksome formication along her labia majora.

'I can't stop scratching,' she fretted.

It was Dr Dilduktha who discovered that the masala's sexually-stimulating effect on Fram was psychological rather than chemical.

'It is only fortuitous that Kala Baba's recipe had an effect on you,' the doctor remarked cheerfully.

'How can you be sure?' Fram asked.

'Because an aphrodisiac is a product of the human psyche and not something that can be bottled and retailed in the bazaar.'

'Kala Baba had supernatural powers,' Fram insisted irritably.

'Bullshit, Mr Chutrivala,' Dilduktha laughed. 'Kala Baba was just a rogue who exploited simpletons.'

And before Fram could question Dilduktha's arrogant assumption, his eyelids closed, responding to flashing lights and the psychiatrist's persuasive voice. As he lay on the couch, Fram resented the fact that Dilduktha always appeared to have the upper hand. The devious bugger often crept around behind him, making it difficult to see what he was up to from a supine position. Besides, Fram was undecided whether the sort of hypnosis the psychiatrist practised wasn't some insidious form of auto-suggestion. Banoo had concluded that only inferior wills could be subdued by real hypnosis, chickens being particularly susceptible. If this was so, he was less than a chicken. A cracked egg perhaps, for Dilduktha could fuck up his level of consciousness with no more than an authoritative clearing of the throat.

He was regressed to an incident in his pubescence. Fram recalled Jublee and trembled with the catharsis of realisation. She was the young woman who used to clean the kitchen utensils when he was thirteen. Jublee allowed him to straddle her back as she squatted in the draining-deck, scrubbing the brass and copper vessels with sand. His equestrian games encompassed the covert feeling of Jublee's breasts.

'Don't tug so hard,' she panted as he tweaked her nipples with juvenescent ardour. His pursuit of her progressed to visiting her sleeping area in the kitchen during the early mornings, waking her with the pressure of his body on hers as she snored unclothed beneath a cotton sheet. She grumbled at his precocity but allowed his fingers access between her strong thighs.

'You're far too young,' she scolded, capturing his thickening cock between her turmeric-stained fingers. Then, wearied by his persistence, she showed him how to use her correctly, holding his satin cheeks between her palms as they made love. It all came back. Dilduktha had tapped the source of Fram's problem with the facility expected of a Vienna-returned man.

The remembered perfume of Jublee's caresses provoked an instant bone-hard erection. Garlic, coriander, fenugreek, ginger, cummin and tamarind with a leavening of chilli-powder. It was the irresistible evocation, Dilduktha concluded, that had driven an itching Banoo from his bed and turned his mind. During analysis, following a short spell of Meade Lux Lewis, Fram revealed that his aberrant behaviour commenced at the time he detected that odour of venery on the old woman who mashed their masalas, ambushing her as she was leaving the house.

'Let me smell your hands,' he pleaded, drawing her urgently into a stall in the old stable-block.

'My hands?' the toothless hag gasped, astonished by the unexpected molestation.

She trembled as Fram savoured her orange-coloured palms and sniffed his way along her bony arms to shrivelled, vestigial breasts. But the initial anxiety about the preoccupation of a great master like Fram Chutrivala with her atrophied flesh was quickly dispelled by the bared unambiguity of a bloated phallus.

'I'm a dry old cunt,' she laughed apologetically, wriggling her way out of her tattered sari.

He waited indulgently. She spat on her fingers and dutifully moistened herself for his ingress. Passive in the dust below him, she avoided the presumption of touching his flesh or linen with her hands as he silently jigged to a jerking conclusion. Even her eyes were closed in awed deference. Fram dropped two rupees on the ground before leaving the stable. It was the equivalent of four days' employment. It had been a long time since she'd earned that kind of money for five minutes' work. After that rewarding encounter, the old woman looked for the master on her weekly visits to Peccavi, lurking around the stable-block until he appeared. And when the old masala-woman didn't turn up for several weeks, Fram asked Cessara, the servant girl who now did the grinding herself, what had become of the hag.

'She's dead,' Cessara informed him, blinking as the fumes from the condiments stung her eyes. 'Some goonda stabbed and robbed her in Gunpowder Lane where she slept under an old banyan tree.'

Fram murmured his regret but stood silently for a while watching Cessara at work. She looked up at him and smiled, suspecting his awkward presence.

'When you have finished doing that,' Fram whispered, 'I'd like to smell your hands.'

Predictably, his eccentric need to smell garum masala on the hands of females who worked in the kitchen ended badly. The fetish captured his mind and became, finally, a scandalous embarrassment involving the assault of strangers in the bazaar.

'Is he mad, Dr Dilduktha?' Banoo enquired anxiously.

'Not at all. Just a little out of control. A few weeks at my clinic at Kapoli should help.'

'I understand he has visited Dr Friski Dalal,' she said.

Dilduktha looked contemptuous. 'She consorts with monkeys, Mrs Chutrivala. Need I say more?'

'You need not,' snapped Banoo grimly, electing not to mention Friski's past association with her late father.

Soli, who had other ideas about his brother's problem, expressed his reservations privately to Banoo and Kety.

'I would prefer him to visit the Institute of Experimental Medicine in Leningrad,' he said. 'A man called Pavlov has done some very interesting work with dogs.'

'Dogs? It's not Kuthagiri, is it?' Banoo enquired with a frown.

Soli shook his head. But Kety was unconvinced about Pavlov.

'Who needs a veterinarian when we can afford Dilip Dilduktha?' she asked. 'A genuine, Vienna-returned fellow.'

'Pavlov's a physiologist,' Soli explained drily.

'Anyway, I don't think Fram would be happy in Leningrad,' Banoo decided. 'What would the poor chap eat?'

That night she put the matter to Fram, who agreed with her.

'It's Kapoli,' he said after some thought. 'I mean, what do they understand in Russia about garum masala?'

Chapter 4

Fram could scarcely remember his own father, who had been run down by a victoria when he was barely five, Soli just one and Kety a three-month embryo. Byramji Wadia had become the Chutrivala children's surrogate parent. He took a particular interest in Fram, who used to visit the ice factory as a boy to feed the pigeons. Not only did Byramji pay for their education, but he promised Roshan, their mother, that Fram would one day inherit the ice factory and have his only daughter Banoo's hand in marriage. At the time, Fram was barely twelve and Banoo already a young woman of seventeen.

'In another five years, the difference in ages will not be noticed,' Byramji predicted.

Fram was persuaded by his mother. Although he suspected that Byramji was a secret caller at their modest house that stood at the end of the lane leading to the ice factory, nothing was ever said to confirm this. It was the distinctive stench of Byramji's Sumatras that provided the clue. Soli discovered a burn on the nilgai skimmer beside his mother's bed.

'Its a cigar,' the twelve-year-old decided with a coarse grin, making a fricative sign to Fram, using the middle finger of one hand through the loop of the index finger and thumb of the other.

Roshan was extremely distressed at her younger son's suggestion that a cigar-smoker, and by imputation a male, had visited her bedroom. The matter was never discussed again.

Shortly after Fram's seventeenth birthday, the date of the marriage to Banoo was fixed. Fram, who knew what was expected of him, had always been fearful of the blubbery girl who was to be his bride. One evening, a few weeks before the ceremony, she cornered him in the sewing room at Peccavi. She pressed her mouth hungrily over his and, unbuttoning his flies, withdrew his cock. Holding him in a fearsome headlock, she masturbated him to a quick conclusion into a damascene table-runner.

'Its pleasant to know what one can expect,' she whispered, inviting him to feel her.

He groped her with assiduity, surprised at her hairiness and scope. It ended prematurely when they heard footsteps on the stairs.

When he suggested another visit to the sewing room, Banoo temporised.

'Once is enough,' she decided. 'Time enough for those games on the honeymoon.'

But she relented one rainy afternoon, the boredom of playing patience becoming unendurable when she realised that Fram was alone in the library. She agreed to expose herself for his inspection on condition that he didn't touch her. This ambition was contrived on a walnut bergère in which she wedged her arse, with meaty thighs stretched over the padded arms. To his disappointment, he was not nearly as stimulated by her pulpy labia, dark-red cavetto and puckered scut, as he had been with the mauvey-pink orifices of the servant girls he had poked over the years. And he was saddened by her admission that she had pushed large objects into herself for many years.

'It proves that I'm hot and ready for marriage,' she breathed, allowing him to suck her purple, plum-plump nipples.

Roshan could hardly contain her excitement over the match, disarming Fram's panic and last-minute reservations about Banoo's obesity, moustache and squint in her left eye.

'For one lakh,' she declared, 'it's bad form to quibble over a few maunds on a girl's belly; for two lakhs, even crazy cockeyes should be accepted with grace; for three lakhs, a boy should prostrate himself before Ahura Mazda in gratitude that all her vital organs are approximately in the right place. You, my son, will in the course of time have three lakhs, an eighteenth-century mansion, a twenty-five per cent share in Singleton's Hotel and an ice factory. Think of it. You have nothing to grumble about. Anyway, who seriously cares about such superficialities as physical beauty in the dark? Climb into her saddle and trot me out a clever grandson.'

But all Banoo and he could knock out was Meroo. Try as they would, nothing else took hold in her womb.

It would be a serious understatement to say that Banoo regarded her daughter as a disappointment. And Fram, who was itching to bestow his love, found Meroo somewhat indifferent about receiving it. To be truthful, her parents were never really big numbers in Meroo's life.

In the beginning, Banoo seemed more than content with her sex life, although three days into the honeymoon at Matheran she did enquire cautiously whether Fram had ever damaged his cock.

'Of course not,' he replied.

She pointed to the emphatic bend that gave his organ a leftward bias.

'The angle is almost twenty degrees,' she estimated.

'That's how I was born,' Fram said irritably.

Banoo disclosed that many years previously she had spied on her father, Byramji, bathing.

'His was long and thick, like a large cucumber,' she laughed.

Fram did not reply. Banoo said she suspected that the size of her father's cock probably contributed to his propensity to philander; just as men with powerful legs tended to become proficient cyclists and girls with pretty faces were more easily induced to take up whoring.

'I would much rather,' she reflected, 'have a husband with an average-sized penis who was faithful than one with equine equipment who lusted after every female he saw.'

Fram informed her frostily that he had enjoyed many women before his marriage.

'Servant girls don't count,' she declared, laying her head on his shoulder. 'I mean, they are hardly likely to complain about the size of their masters' dicks.'

Fram pushed her away, advising her that he was completely normal and sexually adequate. He suggested that she had probably eroded her sensitivity by poking foreign objects into her vagina. His irritation surprised her and she followed him onto the hotel verandah to give him a reassuring squeeze.

'I didn't mean to upset you,' she whispered, nibbling his ear.

'It's all right,' he murmured finally, taking her hand as they stood in their striped silk nightshirts, wondering at the radiance of the full moon that was the colour of an over-ripe marsh-melon and listening to the distant tinkle of the tongas from the town below them.

The source of Byramji's money had been the Wadia toddy-plantations and, later, liquor shops. Shrewd marriages had helped as well. But the main fortune had eluded Banoo's father, who was a younger son. He did, however, inherit Peccavi, an estate of ten acres that went with it and one per cent of the equity of the shipbuilders and engineers, Wadia and Mackenzie Ltd. He built the ice factory in the grounds of Peccavi in 1895 and five years before he died bought control of Singleton's Hotel at Cuffe Parade, a rambling mid-Victorian building that had once been popular with merchant-navy officers, junior civil servants, tea planters on furlough and younger engineers who were awaiting posting up-country. It was celebrated for the range of its wines, spirits and beers, thick beef sandwiches, twelve billiard tables and relaxed house-rules, male guests being allowed overnight, lady visitors who were entered in the register as their wives. By the turn of the century, Singleton's had decayed and was only used by Europeans as a last resort. After the war, nightly dances were its principal attraction, the concession lately having been given to a Mrs Dulcie Meredith who provided respectable young ladies as hostesses in the Horizon Room. The clientèle were now British other ranks, minor local businessmen, sailors in port for the night, and the more adventurous young foreigners. The city police called more often than the management would have wished but it was a not unpleasant place to take lunch or afternoon tea. A half-share in the hotel was sold within a year of acquisition to cover Byramji's debts at the card-table (Chemmy and Fan Tan) and meet a settlement on Dr Friski Dalal.

Fram recalled Zarina's hoarse screams and recriminations as his father-in-law, partially paralysed in those last days, sat propped up in an armchair by the window mumbling incoherently.

'Cards and syphilitic whores! That's the sum of your dirty life,' she sobbed, 'and now we are paupers.'

It was an exaggeration, of course. Zarina, envious of the wealthier Tatas, Jeejeebhoys and even Byramji's cousins, the shipbuilding Wadias, considered that she had been reduced to penury by her profligate spouse. She complained that where she had once travelled in a velvet-curtained clarence (once the property of Sir James Mackintosh), she was now expected to be transported about Bombay in a smelly automobile.

'Like butcher's offal,' she sniffed.

'This is 1924, Mama,' Banoo observed. 'Motorcars are here to stay.'

'Why must you be so pessimistic?' shouted the unhappy woman.

Fram found it difficult to erase the memory of his father-in-law's swollen face and dark, fearful eyes with tears streaming down into the tangle of the grey beard he had grown during the last weeks of his life. His words were difficult to apprehend although their ears had become attuned to the phrase he babbled again and again.

'Forgive me, Zarina,' he lisped, his cherry-ripe mouth flecked with frothy spittle. 'Forgive me, Zarina, forgive . . .'

Zarina tossed a sheaf of unpaid bills over Byramji's head, then struck him clumsily across the face with the heel of her hand. Blood spurted from a broken lip, dribbling through his beard onto a white chemise.

'Bastard,' she cursed. The word remained trapped in Fram's skull. He suspected that it would always be with him.

When Byramji died a few weeks later, Fram felt that Peccavi had crumbled in sympathy. The damp patch in the drawing room expanded, cracks he had never noticed before suddenly materialised and the purlin below the tiles appeared to sag like the spine of an ancient beast. But it was not an observation he cared to share with the rest of the family.

The widow, Zarina, never recovered. It seemed as though she was resentful that Byramji had slipped away. Death, perhaps, might provide her with her only opportunity to confront him once again. Indeed, her eyes lit with hope when the doctor advised her that she was inoperable and that recovery from her malignant tumour was unlikely.

'Wait until I catch up with him,' she whispered happily. They were almost her last words.

Apart from Fram, nobody appeared to care when Byramji died. Banoo seemed almost relieved at her father's passing; Soli sneered openly at Fram's allegiance to the Wadia dynasty and the rest of the Wadia family focussed their emotions on Fram, the principal beneficiary, regarding him with a mixture of contempt, hostility and envy, unhappy that a mediocrity, the son of an umbrella repairer, had swallowed in one gulp such a large portion of the family wealth as a reward for taking Byramji's unprepossessing daughter.

The loss of Peccavi, in particular, was the cause of much bitterness, and a private offer of two lakhs for the house and the ice factory was made to Banoo by two of Byramji's nephews. The two, who were both in the catering trade, perceived that the ice-factory was a natural extension to their activities and argued that Peccavi should remain in the ownership of a Wadia. Banoo referred the cousins to Fram, advising them that it was Byramji's wish that he inherited everything.

'You mean,' they asked with stunned incredulity, 'that a Chutrivala is now whole and sole?'

'Whole and sole,' Banoo confirmed, smirking.

After Fram's return from Dilduktha's clinic at Kapoli, there was every indication that his problem had been resolved. He told Banoo about a book he'd read called *Dead Souls* and his new interest in Dixieland jazz.

'Isn't that very noisy?' she asked.

'I have a device called volume control on my electric gramophone,' he informed her with a smile.

'My word, what will they dream up next?' she mused, sniffing at the glass on the table beside him. 'And what's this?'

'Malt whisky.'

Banoo frowned. 'Take care. That's the poison that gave my Papa his stroke.'

Fram nodded impatiently. Towards the end of his stay, Mr Fazal and he had taken a peg or two every evening to celebrate the arrival of the Petromax lights. Mr Fazal, a Gray's Inn man, had three wives and eleven children at home. Learning that Fram was in business, he advised him to try oil cakes, which he believed to be a very lucrative line of trade, two of his clients having made fortunes in that line. But, for the most part, they just sat watching the clustering of the flying foxes and listening to the ullulations of the jackals. On the last evening they spent together, Mr Fazal confessed that he'd been cured of acute melancholia.

'That's excellent news,' Fram murmured.

Then after a long silence, Mr Fazal informed Fram that Dilduktha had sacked Gungoo, the young sweeper girl.

'What for?'

Mr Fazal sipped his scotch solemnly.

'For gravely immoral conduct, Mr Chutrivala.'

'Little Gungoo?' asked Fram in dismay. 'Such a sweet child.'

'She is,' Mr Fazal confided gloomily, 'more than five months gone. Some bugger hasn't been playing the game.'

Chapter 5

Fram's discovery of a letter to M. K. Gandhi in a wormy copy of Macaulay's *Essays* evoked with haunting immediacy Byramji's breathless voice and singular obsession. He had for some time been considering the possibility of commissioning a statue of his father-in-law in white marble, of approximately the same size as the one in black marble of Sir Maneckji Wadia that had stood by the Peccavi fishpond for more than half a century. Initial enquiries revealed that James Muskie, a Scottish sculptor who was just completing a bust of Curzon for the Victoria Memorial Hall in Calcutta, might consider working on Byramji's effigy for forty thousand rupees. Banoo did not share Fram's enthusiasm.

'On horseback?' she enquired. 'I can't imagine Papa on horseback.'

'I was thinking of a standing job,' Fram mused, 'with his hands in his pockets.'

'I'm sure we can find a local man who'll do the job for a fraction of that price,' she declared.

The Bombay School of Art suggested several candidates and a Suresh Bhonsle, who'd done seven Shivajis, three Tilaks and a composition of a stallion rearing over a mare for the Manjri Stud Farm, was invited to call at Peccavi.

'How much do you want?' Banoo demanded after examining an album of photographs showing examples of Bhonsle's oeuvre.

The wizened old sculptor scratched his nose thoughtfully.

'It would be difficult to do justice to the subject for anything less than one thousand eight hundred rupees,' he said.

'As much as that?' Banoo boomed.

And so a price of fifteen hundred was finally agreed, payable in three equal instalments, the statue to be erected on a granite block before the entrance to the ice factory. Fram could think and chatter of little else. He showed Soli the plans and sketches when his brother came to lunch.

'Old Wadia was crazy, of course,' Soli yawned dismissively as he tossed the project folder back to Fram.

'What the hell do you mean, crazy?'

'You can't deny he was cunt-struck,' Soli replied, picking the shell off a partridge egg.

'There was much more to the man than that,' Fram said indignantly. 'He built this ice factory.'

'So what's an ice factory?' Soli mocked. 'The technology is fairly shit-grade. It's pretty basic stuff, Fram.'

'For God's sake,' shouted Fram, 'you're talking about the man who paid for your education. In London.'

Soli remained unimpressed. 'We all know why he did that,' he said, winking.

Fram chose not to revive any discourse about their mother's relationship with Byramji. It was especially improper to refer to the matter when she had so recently been transported to the Tower of Silence.

'Do you deny he had a first-rate mind? That he was probably the finest twenty-moves-a-minute chess-player in Bombay?'

Soli seemed to find the proposition that Byramji had a first-rate mind hilarious.

Banoo tried to calm Fram. She shot Soli a warning frown.

'Why can't we all talk about more pleasant things?' she asked, reaching out to stroke Fram's cheek. 'Dr Dilduktha has requested that he's not to be excited overmuch.'

Later, when they were alone, Fram observed that he was tired of Soli's cynicism.

'Sometimes I wish he'd scrounge his Sunday lunch elsewhere,' he reflected.

'In the long run he means well,' Banoo soothed.

'In the long run we'll all be bloody Bolsheviks,' Fram brooded darkly.

And Banoo, noticing that he was trembling, held his hands in hers until he had quietened down.

Fram stood framed by the arch of the drawing-room window looking down at the black marble statue of Sir Maneckji Wadia on horseback that stood beside the goldfish pond. It was where Byramji had always enjoyed being photographed: in a setting of familial oil portraits, marble pilasters, Kurdish wall-carpets, baroque furniture, mirrors, crystal chandeliers, cabinets of ceramic figurines, shelves of gilt-lettered volumes tooled in morocco, tiger-skins, buffalo-heads, assorted tusks, a clavichord, a gilt harp, Moghul shields, bronzes, displays of spears, swords, scimitars and flintlocks.

Like his father-in-law, Fram was comforted by the room. The wonder of possessions never failed to warm him, although he was careful not to show unseemly pleasure when Soli was around. Even Banoo complained that she would have preferred to live in a more up-to-date house.

'Its old fashioned,' she sighed. 'The dreary debris of past indulgences.'

Fram pointed out that the sheer size of the room imposed an obligation to fill the available space.

'It's like living in a museum,' she said.

But any criticism of Peccavi depressed him. Banoo sometimes expressed the wish that her father had arranged his affairs more sagaciously. With luck, they could have had access to the sort of money that could have purchased a baronetcy for Fram and procured the chairmanships of a few influential committees. The grey fact that they were living on their capital was rarely mentioned. Investment was needed for Singleton's Hotel and the long-term future of the ice factory seemed uncertain. The dreadful disclosure that Byramji had left more to Friski Dalal than he had to his own wife was, Banoo felt, a contributory factor in her mother's demise. And it didn't help when Soli dropped in for lunch and persecuted Fram with unwelcome advice.

'Why the hell don't you sell all this rubbish and move to a more fashionable address by the sea? Mazagaon has had its day, comrade. Frankly, it's a slum. Respectable families abandoned this scruffy neighbourhood thirty years ago. At a pinch you could afford something much smarter on Malabar Hill.'

'I am,' Fram advised him, 'the custodian of the Wadia heritage.'

It was a comment that Soli invariably greeted with snorts of derisive laughter.

'The place is rotting away with structural leprosy. Peccavi is infested with woodlice, beetles, bugs and cockroaches.'

Soli pointed to a damp patch on the south wall, then stepped closer to poke holes in the plaster with his finger.

'What the hell are you doing?' demanded Fram, tormented by the crater his brother had picked in a cherub's mouth. 'That's the Fragonard mural.'

'Fragonard's bollocks,' Soli scoffed. 'It was painted by D'Cunha, the old schoolmaster from St Peter's, and dates from eighteen ninety-five.'

'It's after Fragonard,' Fram observed grimly.

'A long time after,' Soli replied. 'A few more monsoons and that shitty pastiche will be in the compound.'

Fram turned away with a frown, cracking his fingers with annoyance. 'Damn your eyes,' he muttered to himself.

Soli had a brutish streak that Fram sometimes found difficult to endure. He was thankful that they lived apart. Soli's lumbering, bear-like figure was always foraging about in Fram's life. His long hair and yellow teeth made Fram ill. And his fingers were never very far from his nostrils.

'Would you care to borrow a clean handkerchief?' was a question with which Fram acidly countered the nose-picking.

But Soli, who regarded laundered linen as a bourgeois affectation, usually responded by flicking a symbolic pellet over his shoulder, a provocation Fram found it prudent to ignore.

'Morally,' Soli reflected, 'some of this garbage belongs to me. The woman Byramji was sleeping with was my mother as well. And if Kety is to be believed, she has an even greater claim than either of us.'

'Who says?' shouted Fram.

'Mama's death-bed confession,' Soli said.

He was referring to Kety's allegation that when she had taken her mother a cup of warm milk and almonds, the terminally ill Roshan opened her eyes and stared at her daughter. It was a look of penitence.

'Byramji was your father,' she whispered in a fearful voice.

'Mama?' Kety gasped, setting down the milk in alarm. But Roshan had sunk into her final sleep.

Fram was disposed to qualify Kety's evidence. His sister was always hearing voices and seeing ghosts. Psychic phenomena was all she cared about since she had given up table tennis. Her room was filled with books by Sir Oliver Lodge and Conan Doyle. And

Banoo had warned her about using young Theresa to conduct experiments with a ouija board, a practice that gave the Catholic maid nightmares.

Certainly, Fram considered Soli's claims to Byramji's estate ludicrous and manifestly unserious.

'I thought Communists didn't believe in inherited wealth,' he scoffed.

'A means to an end,' his brother replied. 'I have my eye on a rather nice second-hand lino-type machine. I desperately need to improve the quality of *Red Tiger* and increase the print-run.'

'What about the one I got you from Dilduktha when I was at Kapoli?'

'That was two years ago. Besides, it's hardly better than a duplicator. *Red Tiger* is an international magazine.'

Fram allowed himself a frosty smile.

'We have an editorial office in London,' Soli declared.

'I suppose you're alluding to that dharamsala in Canning Town,' Fram commented. 'The place where you hung out with that ganja-smoking Spanish anarchist who gave you the clap.'

'It's a commune,' Soli observed evenly, 'and Dolores, of whom you speak, is not only literate in four languages but was an associate of Malatesta himself and an authority on the class struggle from a feminist perspective. And I find the remarks about my clap rather specious in the context of your sexual exploitation of young servant girls.'

Fram stroked his moustache slowly, his face full of condescension.

'Prophylaxis is a first principle with me,' he murmured grandly.

Soli looked undisturbed. 'An upgraded paper,' he continued, 'should attract more prestigious advertisers.'

'Who the hell will advertise in your rag?' Fram asked. 'Have you forgotten the six months' rigorous imprisonment you got for that scandalous libel about the Vicereine being fucked by the Prince of Wales?'

'It was true,' Soli insisted.

Soli, Fram reflected, had been spoiled by the family. All his life had been spent biting the hands that fed him. If it hadn't been for Byramji's support, the waster would have been compelled to take a real job. But whenever Fram suggested that he join him in managing the ice factory, Soli articulated his moral reservations.

'You know my views on capitalist enterprises,' he said. 'Besides, I could be off to France any day now to interview Leo Trotsky for *Red Tiger*.'

'Five years ago, you were going to Russia to see that blackguard.' Fram reminded him.

'These things take time,' Soli muttered, picking his nose once again.

Chapter 6

Fram believed that, as Meroo was the result of a loveless conception, some astral component was absent from the critical spurt. Not that he didn't derive marginal pleasure from slipping into Banoo. For one thing, she was always warm and moist and therefore more acceptable than his closed fist or the proverbial loaf of freshly-baked bread. Indeed, even after the troubled days of the garum masala couplings, things went tolerably well. Sometimes, when they were doing it, he was ferociously passionate in his application, but excessive devotion often meant that his mind was elsewhere, usually between Vanessa Beauchamp's trembling, white thighs.

However, Meroo was all they had. Although she was undeniably brilliant, a Sanskrit scholar no less, she had a subversive disposition. After Banoo caught her with her hand up the mali's daughter's skirt, they kept an eye on her. Not long after this, when she was hardly fourteen, she was found in bed with Pilloo Bharucha, a schoolfriend. They were both unclothed.

'Perhaps,' Fram suggested, 'she's working too hard. When a child matriculates at twelve, the brain is over-stressed. I have always feared excessive learning in a female. Their nervous systems are not up to scratch.'

In Meroo's sixteenth year Banoo's discovery of a folder of continental postcards behind their daughter's wardrobe that brought matters to a head. Banoo was indignant that Fram spent an hour going carefully through the collection. He said he was impressed by the plasticity and athleticism of the young models with their shingled heads posed between each other's thighs, and astonished by the vivacity of the tableaux. It was a celebration in sunny smiles, popping eyes, unfurled tongues and parted pudenda, exhibited with cheerful immodesty.

'Do you believe,' Fram mused, 'that there's much vice in all this lighthearted nonsense?'

'Are you bloody mad?' Banoo screamed. 'This is nothing less than depravity of the first water. You have no alternative but to thrash the little bitch.'

'Thrash? How?' enquired Fram unhappily.

'On her bare arse,' directed Banoo.

'Dear God,' muttered Fram, sucking a hollow tooth. 'I think I'll take a turn in the garden and seriously consider my options.'

Banoo suggested that the punishment should take place the following day when she had gone to Crawford Market for the month's shopping.

'It's a man's job,' she declared grimly.

Fram procured a springy cane of the sort schoolmasters use. He decided to whack Meroo while she leaned over the cushioned scroll of a rosewood couch below a rather romantic, Scottish landscape by Waller Hugh Paton. The picture, he hoped, would take his mind off the unpleasant duty. He wondered for some time just how many strokes she merited and came to the conclusion that three was just about right.

When Meroo came in, Fram put the matter to her as clearly as he possibly could. But the situation became confused when he was confounded by a simple act of defiance. Meroo refused to remove her drawers and accept the caning that Fram suggested a dutiful daughter should. After a prolonged discussion, Meroo persuaded Fram that any transactions involving her naked bottom would have embarrassing, incestial implications. Furthermore, since she did not have masochistic tendencies, nor, she suspected, was her father a man of sadistic inclinations, the proposed experience would not have the merit of being pleasurable for either of them. Gratuitous pain, Meroo reflected, was hardly an appropriate response to the psychic integrity of her behaviour.

'What a complicated little pussycat you are,' fussed Fram, stroking her cheek gently. 'You really shouldn't cram your head with too many strange ideas.'

Meroo frowned, averting her pale, bespectacled face. Physical contact with either parent distressed her.

'Do you love your Mama and Papa?' Fram asked quietly.

'I would not wish either of you to come to any harm,' she replied evasively.

They were interrupted by the arrival of Theresa with tea. Fram detected an exchange of quick eye-movements between Meroo and the servant. More complicity, he brooded uneasily. Meroo dismissed Theresa with an intimate wink and, moving her ovoid form across the room to the trolley where the tea-tray had been laid, busied her close-cropped head over the silver service. Meroo was naturally clumsy. Lifting the pot too high, she was unsighted and poured badly, splashing the liquor over the brims of the cups. Fram disliked tea in his saucer and abandoned it to grow cold on the table beside him.

'I suspect,' Meroo confided, sipping her tea, 'that I will always prefer my own sex to the other. However, it is difficult to predict where my inclinations may lead me as an adult. Given my native curiosity, it is not beyond credibility that I may try a man one day.'

'You speak of men as though they were a brand of cigarettes,' Fram said.

Meroo shrugged. She informed him that it had not been her intention to be flippant but felt strongly that the formality of marriage was something contrary to her present inclinations.

'But you're still a child,' Fram laughed.

Meroo resented what she regarded as a patronising reference to her age and began to yawn and fidget. He recognised with alarm the signs of boredom. It was not unusual for Meroo to fall asleep when her parents were reprimanding her. At first, they thought that she was suffering from meningitis that was prevalent at the time, but as she was pronounced fit by their local doctor Fram drove her out to see Dilduktha. He astonished Fram with his diagnosis of the then eleven-year-old girl's condition.

'She's suffering from chronic ennui, Mr Chutrivala.'

Fram recalled that his mother had predicted that her granddaughter would inherit the Kaka (her maiden name) intelligence.

'Look at that bulging forehead and magnificent Persian nose,' she declared, when Meroo was a few hours old.

Byramji had been equally enthusiastic.

'Genius or madness,' he trumpeted, stamping around the bed, 'no compromises.'

But excessive intelligence, Fram reflected, was a nuisance and the cause of much unhappiness. He thought darkly of M. K. Gandhi, his brother Soli and his misunderstood father-in-law. It was preferable, he concluded, to be slightly stupid.

Meroo gave Fram an undertaking not to give the family further cause for anxiety by indulging in anything scandalous when living at home. But when he began to lecture her on the inadvisability of familiarity with the servants, he was alerted to his prolixity when she closed her eyes and produced a characteristic snore. He clapped his hands loudly. Meroo awoke with a jump, goggling at him through bewildered eyes. He ruffled her hair and comforted her with a kiss.

'I'm sorry I startled you, pussycat,' he murmured gently.

Although the talk was hardly satisfactory from a narrow, disciplinary point of view, Fram considered it was the only feasible conclusion. Banoo, on her return from shopping, was less sanguine.

'The cunning bitch has manipulated you,' she accused angrily. 'Does she imagine that we're idiots?'

'Keep calm,' Fram soothed.

'You're a moral eunuch,' Banoo accused, jabbing a menacing finger at his face. She came towards him, shouting. Fram ducked. Anticipating her blows, he raised his hands and fended her away. She fell heavily against the wall, striking the back of her head. Fram comforted her as she sobbed, flinching at the unexpected smell of raw liquor on her breath. He decided not to mention it but suspected that she was more than slightly intoxicated.

'There's no need to distress yourself,' he coaxed.

He hated to see Banoo cry. It made her uglier than she really was. Some women seemed prettier when they wept. But not Banoo. Her puffy and blotchy face, with mucus streaming from a swollen, red nose, distressed him. And such panting and heaving, as though each breath would be her last.

The affair of Meroo was more serious than Fram suspected at the time. Mother and daughter scarcely spoke to one another again. And two years later, on the eve of Meroo's graduation, Banoo succumbed to liver failure. Fram was astonished to learn that she had been an alcoholic, consuming a litre of gin a day. It was Kety who led him to the store of bottles in Banoo's sewing room. He hadn't been in that part of the house since Banoo had exposed herself in the rattan armchair.

'Why didn't you tell me?' Fram asked tearfully.

46

'You've had your share of troubles,' Kety replied.

'But this?' Fram breathed, unable to believe the magnitude of the secret she'd shared with her brother and sister-in-law.

'She couldn't face life anymore,' Kety disclosed.

Fram suspected that he was the cause of her death. He had recklessly betrayed, he reflected, Byramji's faith in him.

'Banoo committed suicide,' Fram confided to Soli.

'She was killed,' Soli observed, 'by the feudal system that sold her into a marriage of financial convenience to a man who could hardly disguise his aversion to her body. She would have been far happier with someone whose mind was not corrupted by delusions of romantic love. Like old Jockey the chauffeur, perhaps.'

'Jockey?' Fram shouted. 'How dare you insult a Wadia's memory?'

But when he clenched his fist to strike Soli, his brother reminded him that it was only Fram's assumptions of class that had been questioned and he was quite prepared to defend himself if assaulted. Had Kety not thrust herself between her brothers, there is little doubt physical violence would have ensued.

When Banoo died, Fram and she had been married twenty-five years and nine months. He was now forty-two, and, although he had started to use Hennol on his greying temples, was still young in mind and body. Dilduktha had taught him that cold showers, a white-fish diet and regular press-ups were indispensible to his highly-strung constitution.

'All that twitching and blinking indicates a very sensitive temperament,' Dilduktha pronounced. 'You could have been trained as a classical violinist or even a halfway decent googly bowler.'

And when Dilduktha heard of Fram's loss, he called around within hours. 'It is time,' the psychiatrist advised, 'to cut yourself free from the past. Your union, by your own admission, was never complicated by love. Don't allow your memories to be compromised by remorse.'

Fram nodded solemnly. Dilduktha was right. And less than forty-eight hours after Banoo's death, the comforting sounds of jazz jangled through Peccavi. It was, he reflected, a honky-tonk valediction.

Later that evening, fortified by scotch and a Sumatra, he instructed Jockey to drive him to Singleton's Hotel, a place he had only visited for the occasional business lunch.

He was surprised to find the foyer filled with magnolias and potted plants. It had, he thought, a rather mischievous ambience, with coloured lights, and overcrowded with red-faced European males and giggling Anglo-Indian girls. And although the faded notice in the hall unambiguously stated that the establishment was out of bounds for NCOs and other ranks, there appeared to be a profusion of tattooed men in khaki who clearly were not gentlemen.

Fram sipped his whisky, listened to the swish of broken ice in shakers and inhaled the spicy perfumes exuded from female bodies. He looked around the room and counted seven blondes, although not all of them were fair-skinned. The sudden thought that he owned twenty-five per cent of this boisterous place elevated his spirits and he acknowledged the passing Mrs Dulcie Meredith with a genial nod. She returned a smile that could have passed for recognition and edged towards his table.

'Mr Wadia?' she enquired, peering at him myopically.

Fram rose courteously, extending a hand.

'I'm Chutrivala, Bobby Wadia's son-in-law.'

'Ah,' she murmured, examining him carefully, 'you look so much like him.'

Dulcie Meredith was a plump forty-year-old with flat, Nepali features, slanted eyes and a snub nose. Fram noticed that she had tinted her bobbed, chestnut coiffure and flirty frisette with henna. Her vermillion lip-paint and purple eye-shadow were no less theatrical statements than the creamy, pancake-smooth mask that was several times lighter than her peaty neck. She was delighted to hear that Fram now owned the Wadia ice factory, remembering a visit she'd made there as Bobby's guest some years previously.

'I knew Bobby extremely well,' she slurred, sheening her lips with a practised suck.

She noticed his critical stare at a party of raucous Englishmen in white shorts and bush-shirts. They were all blond, robust and unusually hairy.

'An up-country party of planters from Ooty way,' she murmured. 'Nice boys and no trouble at all.'

Mrs Meredith explained that entrance to the Horizon Room was fifteen rupees, but that meant he could dance with any lady of his choice during the evening.

'Perhaps I'll listen to the music,' he suggested as they went in together.

'The air-conditioning has failed,' she frowned, dabbing her face apprehensively and flapping the gauzy sleeves of her blue georgette dress as perspiration trickled down her wrists. Then, before he could escape, she captured him.

'It's a foxtrot,' she invited, offering him her fleshy arms.

He hesitated for a moment, but sensed the futility of resistance. They scraped into the jigging assembly, their clasped hands tackily warm. There were damp patches under the raised arms and along the corseted bulge he held as they sombrely sweated their way through 'Avalon'.

Meroo went her own way. After a First in Sanskrit Studies from Wilson College when she was only nineteen, she took up with a poet called Benazir Gulabi, going off to Lahore to edit a Sanskrit literary magazine. Fram thought it quite inexplicable. All that brain power dissipated in arcane whimsy. In the last year Meroo spent at Peccavi, she had taken to wearing men's clothes and smoking a pipe. Although he found her appearance in a jacket and trousers disturbing and the stink of her oily cheroots nauseous, Fram was desolate when she vanished from his life. Whenever he passed Bori Bunder, the gothic cragginess of Victoria Terminus reminded him of the day she left Bombay. A fat, perspiring Meroo, wearing a twisted black tie, solar topee and crumpled cotton suit that bulged at the hips and thighs. She looked fairly ridiculous, crazy even.

'If you need any more money,' he mumbled, his eyes clouded with tears. She allowed him to embrace her for the last time, kissing him unexpectedly on the mouth. A sort of final benediction. He sometimes awoke at night, dreaming that he could hear her voice downstairs. But she never returned. An occasional postcard in an indecipherable scrawl. Nothing more.

It was Soli who suggested a reason for Meroo's deviance. It started, he felt, at St Monica's Convent, the school she attended. He laid the blame on the English Mother Superior.

'Mother Marie-Céleste?'

'She forces the girls to share a communal bath after netball.'

'So?'

'Think of all those curious fingers under the soapy water. Not only is the practice culturally provocative but it's really another insidious variant of imperialist humiliation.'

Fram frowned. 'Are you telling me that Mother Marie-Céleste is politically motivated?'

'Sure. I'm doing an exposé in *Red Tiger* next month. We should never underestimate the sheer diversity of neo-colonialist strategies, comrade.'

Chapter 7

The gloom that had engulfed Fram following Meroo's departure persisted, despite his weekly visits to Dulcie Meredith's Horizon Room and involvement with the proposed refurbishment of Singleton's Hotel. He now spent more time at the ice factory, manifesting a new diligence in his supervision of the production and drayage of the blocks, replacing the four bullock-carts with an Albion truck.

The initial economies effected by the improvement in transportation did little to improve the profitability of the business, as the four reduntant bullock-cart drivers were retained on the payroll and redirected to the largely emblematic tasks of cleaning and repainting the scabby building. Since their duties precluded the destruction of the pigeons that perched above the water-pipes girdling the outer walls, or even the removal of nests, their Sisyphean labours, negated by the unending drip of columbine excrement, amused Soli enormously. He had now not only taken to dining at Peccavi daily, but often stayed the night, bringing Kety parcels of used postage stamps he alleged were procured from a disposal bin at the General Post Office where he had taken temporary employment. On his arrival each evening, he walked around the factory rattling the pipes with shots from a catapult to disturb the pigeons. Up they rose in a mist of feathers, a dark umbrella of fluttering birds.

'Death to all vermin,' he'd shout to Fram through the office window.

'They're God's creatures,' Fram would reply, conscious of his brother's teasing ways.

'Then send them to Mexico City to be with him,' Soli would laugh, alluding to Leo Trotsky's presence there.

The bullocks, now without their usual employment, were set free in an improvised paddock, where their grazing on rather marginal pasture was supplemented by hay and paddy husks. Financial inducements from local butchers to translate the gluttonous kine into four undemanding carcasses were politely declined, for Kety had declared an emotional interest. She visited the beasts every morning to kiss their wet snouts and gorge them with jaggery and sugarcane. This indulgence produced unforeseen dividends, for so fat, glossy-sheened and bright-eyed did the bullocks become that they began to be hired out for weddings, political processions, religious festivals and other celebrations. The income not only covered the cost of their maintenance but also supported entirely the wages of their former drivers. Accustomed to being photographed, garlanded, daubed with paint, stroked and generally admired, the bullocks became visibly melancholic if deprived of excessive attention for any length of time. Brass plates with their names – Motee, Hera, Sona and Chandi – were attached to their horns, and silver bells were hung around their velvet dewlaps.

'Bhagwan has blessed our master,' the old bullock-cart men agreed among themselves, pressing their palms together whenever they passed Fram and embarrassing him by dropping to their knees to kiss his brown and white co-respondent brogues when he was with important customers.

'It's difficult to know what to do with persistent foot-kissers,' Fram said to Soli and Kety over dinner one night.

'Kick them,' Soli replied instantly. 'Foot-kissers are traitors to their class and enemies of the revolution.'

Kety looked concerned. 'Would you like me to speak to them, Fram?' she asked.

'Perhaps defilement may be more appropriate,' Soli suggested. 'Piss on the buggers.'

He laughed at the look of horror on Fram's face.

'Soli's joking,' Kety declared quickly. 'He has a quirky sense of humour.'

Fram frowned. 'Are you suggesting that I urinate on my friends?' he asked Soli with quiet disgust.

Soli lay back in his chair and rocked with merriment.

'Since when have those coolies been your friends? That's typical middle-class hypocrisy. When did you last invite the bullock-cart drivers up to Peccavi for a meal, a drink or even a conversation?'

'I have known most of my employees since I was a child,' Fram observed. 'I am incapable of doing anything that would hurt, humiliate or confuse them. An invitation to Peccavi might do just that. Anyway, I can't imagine how kicking or pissing on decent people is a civilised response to what is no more than a demonstration of excessive respect.'

'Have you considered,' Soli asked wide-eyed, 'kissing their feet? Now that would be a Gandhian response.'

'I thought you didn't approve of Gandhi,' Kety said to Soli, raising a reproving hand to inhibit further flippancy. He acknowledged her disquiet with a solemn wink.

Fram did not reply but busied himself with his meal. He was suddenly overwhelmed by a black despair. He wished he could spend an evening talking to Byramji again. Or see his Meroo who was living in a distant city among strangers. He knew that Soli wasn't serious about kicking the coolies but wondered why he and Kety treated him like a simpleton. For some time now, he suspected that they were both laughing at him behind his back. Neither of them was an unkind person. Yet they treated him like a crazy outsider. He shuddered, brooding on the darkness of his life. Ever since Kety had given up competitive table tennis, she had begun to spend more time with Soli. This pleased Fram, for it had quietened Soli down and kept Kety at home in Peccavi. He didn't much approve of the ouija board and her talk of spirits, but he liked to think of them all under the family roof together. Aware that his eyes were filled with moisture, he hesitated to draw attention to his emotional state by wiping them, allowing the tears to trickle down his cheeks and splash on the table. Soli and Kety glanced at each other gravely. Fram sniffed and finally dabbed his face with a serviette.

'How did things go with Mr Bhonsle the sculptor?' Kety asked brightly.

'It's the wrong size,' Fram replied in a low voice. 'Hardly five foot six, instead of Byramji's heroic six.'

'Didn't you specify life-size?' enquired Soli.

'I imagined I did,' said Fram, 'but Bhonsle insisted that there was a scaling-down condition that he could invoke in the case of a flawed block.'

'As long as it's in proportion,' reflected Kety.

'The head,' murmured Fram sadly, 'is much too small. Hardly larger than a pomegranate.'

'Apart from the fact that he didn't have much in it, Byramji was a big-headed fellow,' agreed Soli.

Fram told them that he and Bhonsle had agreed a revision to the upper body which would be resculpted and fitted to the lower half. He had been assured that the join would be almost invisible.

'I saw Byramji pass my bedroom this morning,' said Kety. 'He was wearing a black coat and a mitred hat. He looked straight at me and nodded in exactly the way he used to. And then I heard the baby crying.'

'What baby?' asked Soli.

'I've heard the baby as well,' Fram confirmed. 'Sometimes it seems as though the sound comes from the ice factory.'

'That's exactly where it comes from,' said Kety. 'Although I have heard a sobbing noise by the stable block.'

Soli suggested it was an acoustical trick. He believed that the sound was carried below the ice factory by an underground stream.

'It used to keep Banoo awake when she was a little girl,' Fram said.

They did not speak again until they'd reached the conclusion of the meal, seemingly content with the silence. It was as though they were listening for a crying child. It was not heard. Theresa cleared the table and Fram reached into his jacket at the back of the chair and found a Sumatra. He had persisted with the detestable cigars in memory of Byramji, hoping that one day he would master their offensive taste. When Theresa returned briefly, Kety asked her the question that was on their minds.

'It's a dead baby, Miss,' the servant said, 'buried in the ice factory. The old woman who used to grind our masalas told me so.'

'Do you mind if I smoke?' Fram asked as coffee was served. The other two murmured that they did not.

'I would like to stay the night,' Soli said as they rose to leave the table.

It was the third consecutive night he had asked to stay, occupying Banoo's old sewing room on the second floor.

'Why don't you move in permanently?' Fram asked suddenly. 'It's a big enough house.'

Kety shot Soli a look of encouragement.

'I'm trying to find suitable accommodation for *Red Tiger*,' Soli said, smiling at Kety.

'There's plenty of room in the stables,' Fram said.

'Perhaps I could help you,' Kety suggested cautiously to Soli. For a while nothing was said. Soli had always found it difficult to express his appreciation in a direct manner.

'I've picked up some interesting stamps for Kety,' he ventured finally.

'Soli has found me a half-anna Scinde Dawke,' Kety babbled with a sudden gush of liveliness.

'Rare?' Fram enquired, when shown the scarlet specimen.

'It was issued in eighteen fifty-two under the authority of Sir Bartle Frere,' Kety explained.

'That's old,' Fram agreed.

They made their way to the drawing room, Soli and Kety taking up positions around a table on which lay Kety's albums and the packet of stamps Soli had brought for her. Fram watched them sitting at the table, their lamplit faces examining stamps. Stamp collecting, Fram reflected, was one of Byramji's passions. Kety had only involved herself seriously after his death, on the inheritance of his substantial collection. And Soli seemed to enjoy foraging around the city for her, delighting her with unusual finds.

After a while, Fram announced that he was going out. The other two scarcely looked up, emitting grunts of acknowledgement. Fram went downstairs into the compound, walking slowly towards Jockey's quarters. It was a hot, airless night, filled with the tumult of frogs from the pond.

Upstairs, Theresa paused as she entered the drawing room, warned by low sobbing and murmurs of endearment. From the shadows of the hall, she watched Soli and Kety with pulsing trepidation through the partly opened door. They had risen from the table and were embracing fiercely, shielded partly by the walnut screen of chinar leaves and antelopes that cut off a corner of the room. They were exchanging tongues, wet and eager-jawed, then rubbing their open mouths together in protracted and noisy slurps.

'Please,' Kety panted, in between kisses, writhing with the progress of his hand up her skirt. 'Please.'

Theresa stood for a moment transfixed, hardly breathing, before escaping silently down the dark stairway.

Jockey, sitting on his sisal bed, stringing a bead necklace, was surprised to see Fram.

'For a girl?' asked Fram with a smile.

The chauffeur nodded, dropping the beads into a tray and rising. He reached respectfully for his turban.

'I'd like to go,' Fram said, 'to Singleton's Hotel.'

'There is little reason to believe,' Dilduktha had advised Fram, 'that your impotence is anything more than a self-inflicted punishment for your wife's death.' He was alluding to the two unsatisfactory experiences Fram had consulted the psychiatrist about.

'Be patient,' Dilduktha counselled. 'Find a woman with the right chemistry and your confidence will return. Try love if you can. It's cheaper.'

Fram had been searching for somebody like Mrs Vanessa Beauchamp, but had settled for two white girls, whom he imagined might serve his purpose. The first was unwilling to allow him to chew her nipples, always a bad sign, and the second refused to allow him to get into bed until she'd inspected the rubber over his cock.

'What make is this?' she demanded, as he wilted.

'The best,' Fram assured her.

'It's not made in India, is it?'

'They're French,' Fram said.

'I'm afraid I only do it with British Chubbys,' she said loftily.

'Chubbys?'

'Imperial Chubbys,' she sighed, 'the ones with a Union Jack on the packet.'

She explained that she had some in her handbag. By the time he had changed rubbers, he felt crushed by her look of bored resignation.

'I'll have to tuck it in,' she fretted, glancing at her watch.

She was a great disappointment, despite the promise of ultramarine eyes, crimson talons and fluffy, carroty hair.

But Fram knew Dilduktha was right about chemistry the first

56

time he saw a certain girl dancing to 'Tangerine'. She was in the arms of an elderly Parsee with a limp and a leather stump-glove on one hand. But despite his disability, the grey-haired man was a tricky mover, using his uneven step in an ingenious, dancing shuffle that looked quite natural. Fram managed to catch her eye, signalling his interest in a dance as the quartet was preparing for the next number. They exchanged smiles across the room and, from her, an acknowledgement of his reservation with a flappy wave. She was as unlike Vanessa Beauchamp as any woman could be, a startling indication of the complexity of a man's libido. She was diminutive, copper-skinned, a shade on the skinny side, dressed in a light cream shantung skirt and a matching sleeveless blouse that revealed her lean stomach. She loped towards him, a swayer of axial fluidity, pelvis proud, the high-heeled wobble giving her physical brevity altitude. She had frizzed, marmalade hair, the black velvet eyes of a chinkara and plump pouting lips, clumsily painted. Her slightly Negroid nose had the suspicion of a break across the bridge but the damage furnished her supple femality with a feral wariness that only vanished when she bared her teeth in a diffident smile. A gentle creature, he imagined.

The musicians started up with 'Bei Mir Bist Du Schön', and she was in his arms. He sensed a sadness in her person but was uncertain whether this perception emanated from the manner in which she moved, inclined her head or was transmitted through some psychokinesis from her saurian body brushing his. He noticed that she had a barely visible hare-lip and a provocative lovebite low on her neck. She floated in his arms, accepting the frotting of his bulge against her pliant groin and he was teased by the friction of smallish, uncontained breasts each time his guiding knee pivoted her yoke through a leisurely turn.

'What's your name?' he asked, dazed by an urgent need to fuck her.

'Xenia,' she replied, in a voice darker than he imagined she would produce from such a slender throat.

'I like you very much, Xenia,' he whispered, through the tangle of her hair, inhaling the piny tang of recent lavation.

And so their affair started with an urgently scribbled cheque. It was first consummated on a spongy bed in a narrow, airless room, hardly more than a coffin of mirrors with flickering blue lighting, the ghostly sibilations of a tired air-extraction pump and the overpowering smell of cinnamon, vanilla and yeast percolating through the vent-grilles of the patisserie next door. For a while, Fram could not smell a zimonet-kuche or a Viennese pastry without a stiffening of the flesh.

Dilduktha was exultant. He declared that Fram's new olfactive allegiance represented significant progress, for in Bombay, a man was less likely to be betrayed by the smell of continental confections than he was by garum masala. Not only did the pastries provide an instant solution to Fram's temporary impotence but the aroma was socially exclusive and susceptible to control. He advised Fram to place a regular order with Felice Carnaglia and Sons.

Xenia charged between twenty-five rupees for a straight ejaculation and one hundred and twenty-five for an all-night carouse. There was an extra twenty-five for fellatio or buggery but cunnilingus was on the house.

On the third occasion, Fram took her back to Peccavi.

'I prefer doing it on my own bed,' he informed her, showing her the baroque monstrosity the Wadias had been using since 1800 or so.

It was a perfect eight-feet-by-eight square with the hypotenuses of two right-angled triangles parallel to two sides of silver isosceles solids at the head and base. On the upper isosceles were inscribed the names of all the male Wadias who had made love upon it, sixteen in all, and on the lower one, the female Wadias who had made similar use of the bed. There were eighteen. Fram pointed to Banoo's name.

'My wife,' he said proudly.

'You're married?' she asked anxiously.

'A widower,' he said.

'Where's yours?' she asked, peering at the list.

'I'm only a Chutrivala,' he explained sadly.

When they were in bed, Xenia told him that she was the sole support of her widowed mother and young sister who was a boarder at the Convent of Jesus and Mary.

'How long have you been doing this?' he asked as she rested on his shoulder at cockcrow.

'A year or so,' she said.

'Then you must stop,' he decided. 'I'll give you a job as my secretary at the ice factory.'

'But I can't add up or do joined-up writing,' she said.

'We have an Underwood typewriter,' he said. 'All one has to do is to hit the right keys to produce a very decent letter. As for adding up, we have an abacus that my brother Soli will teach you to use.'

'I'm only a Standard Three girl,' Xenia laughed, reaching for his cock. Fram covered her mouth with kisses and moved towards her skinny thighs. He slipped into her instantly, taking her for the fifth time with a rampant bravura, exhilarated by the way she trembled below him.

'Why do you shake so?' he asked her when they'd finished.

'It's my style,' she confessed coyly, as though he had discovered the secret of her life.

They splashed together in a hot tub before breakfast, Fram bathing Xenia's lower body with particular diligence.

'You don't have much pubic hair,' he observed, placing his lips on her soapy notch.

'I take after my mother,' she murmured, shaping a gorgeous grandee's beard for him.

He slipped a finger into her again, confessing that he was happy.

'And you?' he asked.

'I'm tired,' she admitted, drawing his hand gently away.

'I've made you tired?' he cried triumphantly.

Xenia reminded him that they hadn't slept all night, having talked a great deal about Banoo's obesity, Byramji's generosity, Meroo's cleverness and his psychiatrist friend, Dilip Dilduktha. He reminded her that he'd asked her if she went with soldiers and she had evaded the question.

'I've asked you three times,' he said sternly.

'Why do you worry about such silly things?' she asked.

'Have you?'

Xenia nodded. She slipped out of the tub and dried herself. Fram watched her from the water.

'How many?' he demanded, as she slipped into a pair of black silk knickers, then wriggled into her brassiere. She towelled her hair which stood up like a frizzed halo of auburn before returning to the bedroom to seat herself at the toilet-table.

Fram rose from the bath and followed her into the room. She noticed him in her mirror, holding his cock provocatively in his right fist.

'Has anyone told you that you're like John Barrymore?' she teased.

'I want to do it again,' he insisted, pressing his erection against the nape of her neck.

'I'm tired,' she said flatly, brushing her hair quickly into shape.

'I'll give you another twenty-five,' he promised.

Xenia leaned towards the mirror, painting her lips, then running a pencil over her brows.

'Maybe tomorrow,' she said, getting up and walking to the cupboard to take out her clothes. She slid a sheeny black dress off the hanger and over her head. Fram, having drooped a little, went back to the bathroom to towel himself. When he returned in his dressing-gown, Xenia was dressed for the street. He came slowly to her and kissed her gently on the lips.

'Like I said: another twenty-five for a quick one.'

'You look shagged out yourself,' she observed wanly, turning away to spray herself and dab her armpits with perfume. Fram noticed specks of morning stubble in her mauve hollows.

'Where did you learn to use the expression "shagged out"?' he asked. 'It's the sort of thing Tommies say. Did they shag you out?'

Xenia hung her handbag over her shoulder and lit herself a cigarette. 'OK, Fram honey. I'm on my way,' she murmured.

'But I've asked Theresa to serve us breakfast on the terrace,' he protested.

Xenia stared at him solemnly.

'What do you want from me, eh?' she asked in a throaty voice, tearful with resignation.

He went to the drawer of his bedside table and withdrew a clip of ten-rupee notes.

'You had one hundred and fifty last night,' he said, 'and here's another thirty for a quick one.'

He threw the notes onto the bed. Xenia did not say anything. She dropped her handbag to the floor, kicked off her shoes and, with an exasperated gesture, reached up her dress to pull her knickers down, stepping deftly out of them. Laying the still smouldering cigarette on the ashtray of a dumb-waiter, she slithered eel-like out of her dress, unfastened her brassiere and settled herself on the bed. She was naked, supine and vulgarly accessible. He disrobed and mounted her but found entry difficult. She helped him. It took some time before he finished and lifted himself off her body. Xenia returned to the bathroom to wash before dressing again. They had not spoken throughout the transaction.

Xenia was only too familiar with the arbitrary behaviour of clients stimulated by a need to dominate women. It was, she had learned, an infantile dénouement to what men imagined was priapic success – multiple penetrations, like rape, revealing a seething cunt-hatred and revenge against that dehiscent Alpha and Omega of male existence upon which their fragile self-esteem depended. Her own dignity reposed in silent submission and the knowledge that his invasive thrusts had not provided her with the merest flicker of fulfilment. She smiled wearily at Fram as they went out onto the terrace.

Theresa brought them breakfast. They sat in the morning sunshine at a table below a wall smothered in bougainvillea. Fram had instructed Jockey to collect a box of fresh pastries from Apollo Street but Xenia took no more than a sliver of toast. They watched Kety cross the compound to feed the bullocks.

'That's my sister,' Fram muttered.

Xenia did not reply.

'I'd like to meet your family,' Fram said.

'Why?' Xenia asked, staring at him.

'Because I'm interested in you,' he smiled, squeezing her hand.

'We're not your sort of people,' she said finally, lighting another cigarette.

'What about tonight?' Fram asked.

Xenia shook her head. 'Not tonight.'

He waited, playing idly with the silver ring on her little finger. 'Tomorrow night?'

'Maybe,' said Xenia, rising. 'I'll see you in the Horizon Room.' And before he could change her mind, Xenia had escaped. He remained on the terrace, sampling a pastry, a little surprised at her abrupt departure, waiting for her to cross the compound to the drive that led to the road. He had earlier offered to send her home with Jockey, but she'd declined. Now he watched her walking shakily towards the entrance, remembering the firm-ness of the drum-like arse under the dress. She would have to skirt the bullock paddock where Kety was and he had little doubt that there would be a mildly deprecatory remark from his sister later that day. Bringing a whore back to Peccavi was not quite up to Wadia standard or even a Chutrivala's for that matter.

Half resolved never to see her again, he changed his mind a dozen times before he'd dressed for the day, phoning Dulcie Meredith from his desk before he could start work. He asked her to reserve Xenia for him that night.

'She's not in tonight, Mr Chutrivala.'

'Tomorrow night then,' Fram insisted. 'It's an all-night job at my place.'

'My, my,' Mrs Meredith laughed. 'Little Xenia appears to be in great demand these days.'

The unsurprising hint that he had a rival or rivals so disturbed him that he took the afternoon off, to sulk miserably in a shuttered room, wearing an eye-shield for his disabling migraine.

Chapter 8

Although the Board of Singleton's Hotel claimed credit for a remarkable renaissance of the business in 1927, their principal contribution was the appointment of a new General Manager. And even that choice wasn't based on any respectable principles of selection, but on the fortuitous circumstance that Jerome Patcheco was Francis Cabral's nephew. Motivated by the nepotism of one director and an irresolution to confront it by two of the other three, the Board struck gold.

Friski Dalal, the new chairman of the Board with a forty-nine-per-cent interest, had profound reservations on whether they could afford the proposed salary, let alone the projected capital expenditure. The Raja of Pinjrapore however, who held his single share to give the Board prestige, was in broad agreement with Cabral. He was an incredibly handsome young prince, the proprietor of Amazing Films, a company he'd inherited from the Dowager Rani.

'Things have to change or we're cooked,' he warned.

Fram, like Cabral a twenty-five-per-cent stockholder, was undecided, but his support was crucial if the proposed reconstruction was to become a reality. Friski, who had used the extensive gardens of the Kala Baba ashram (of which she was the trustee) to accommodate a factory that manufactured portable urinals, had been the victim of a serious fraud. Protracted litigation and injudicious investments had drained her once-considerable resources. The Kala Baba Foundation, a charitable trust for the support of blind animals, was not attracting the level of sponsorship that it had in earlier years.

'Blind animals are no longer fashionable, darling,' she complained to Fram.

Her Kuthagiri Institute had been the subject of a sensational exposé by the gutter press and its activities were now restricted to members who were recommended for health reasons by their medical practitioners. Friski herself had, advancing towards middle age, become three stones heavier and significantly greyer.

'I swear by Hennol,' Fram discreetly advised her.

But Friski, who was a serious woman, abjured artificial aids to beauty. As a theosophist, celibate, teetotaller, non-smoker and vegetarian, subsisting on a few sprigs of bhaji and a cup of rice a day, she told Fram that her decayed appearance could not be attributed to either age or diet.

'There are evil forces directed against me,' she confided. 'A woman of God is surrounded by enemies.'

It was instantly obvious to Fram, when he saw Patcheco, that the man was unsuitable for the job. The applicant's youth, inexperience and bumptious manner disgusted him. He appeared to be too clever by half. But Friski Dalal and the Raja of Pinjrapore listened attentively to Cabral who had correctly predicted the decline of Singleton's over the previous five years.

'We have to prevent a certain kind of person using the premises,' he declared. 'Singleton's has become little more than a sleazy pick-up bar. Mrs Meredith and all she represents must be swept away.'

Fram took a contrary view, pointing to the trade Dulcie Meredith brought the hotel, but he was not supported.

'The Horizon Room is just a very noisy brothel,' Friski observed.

In the end, when Mrs Dalal, who was converted by Patcheco's bright-eyed optimism, supported Cabral, Fram went along with the choice of the ex-international hockey player.

'We'll have to spend money, of course,' Mrs Dalal warned, echoing Patcheco's demands.

The grey-haired chairman seemed impressed by Patcheco's advocacy, pleaded with expressive hazel eyes and articulated from a mouth filled with flawless white teeth. Patcheco's lips, Fram reflected unhappily, were unnaturally rosy, a matter he raised privately with the Raja of Pinjrapore, whose response was dismissively unsympathetic.

'So what?' the young prince snapped, before walking out of the room.

The figure of two lakhs that Cabral moved depressed Fram, who had just started improvements at the ice factory, adding a modern cold-storage section for the preservation of meat and fish.

'Two lakhs seems far too much,' he said doubtfully.

But once Patcheco had got into his stride, the two lakhs became three and then, largely because of the loss of revenue when Singleton's closed down for six months, escalated to four and a half.

'I'm afraid we're going too fast,' Fram grumbled, when the directors were guided around the hotel. They were shown the new lifts with Edgar Brandt-style decorative doors, yellow bathrooms inspired by Rateau, a reconstructed foyer with a ten-foot clock in azure glass, palmette, shell and swag motifs around the walls, a restaurant of chrome and mirrors, an ebullient facade in black and orange tiles, a flashing neon sign and an underground swimming-pool.

'We shall have to ban Tommies from the water,' Fram suggested, fearing their obscene language and horseplay would frighten respectable customers.

'That would be a political blunder,' Cabral warned.

'Is all this really necessary?' Fram brooded, dazzled by the transformation.

'No change is mange,' the Raja of Pinjrapore declared blithely.

'What does he mean by "mange"?' Fram asked Friski Dalal quietly.

'I think it's French,' she murmured. '*Manger* means to eat.'

'Eat what?' muttered Fram unhappily.

'Most of the work has been produced by local craftsmen from Chor Bazaar,' Patcheco boasted with a self-satisfied grin.

He told them that he'd also hired a ladies' band to play four times a week in the Pigalle Pavilion.

'What's that?' asked Fram nervously.

He was informed that the old Billiards saloon, Palm Court, Turkish Sweat and Horizon Room were being rearranged into a more cost-efficient area with creative lighting, abstract murals, modern furniture, music, cocktails and dancing.

'Didn't I tell you that my nephew was a genius?' said Cabral to Fram as Patcheco escorted them up to the planned roof-garden. Fram voiced his reservations to Friski when he was alone with her. She confided that, although she approved of Jerry Patcheco's energy, she felt he should be restricted to a short-term, comprehensively-defined contract of employment, adding that there was something sinister about his character.

'I'm speaking with the intuition of a psychic and, of course, a woman.'

Fram nodded. 'There's no doubt that below the charm he's an unpleasant sort of chap.'

Mrs Meredith had moved to premises on Lamington Road on the margin of the red-light district, recreating the Horizon Room in a former rice godown where the only horizon was the Bombay, Baroda and Central India Railways' shunting-shed. But the bedrooms were more spacious than they had been at Singleton's and there was little trouble with the police.

'We are licensed now,' Dulcie Meredith explained. 'The City Police much prefer dealing with legitimate houses. We pay the Deputy Commissioner a thousand a week and he takes care of his minions.'

Fram was surprised to learn that Bulldog Beauchamp was the senior officer concerned, the name producing a frisson that made his body-hair rise. His pulse quickened and he held his breath in wonder.

'I'd always imagined he was incorruptible,' Fram remarked.

'Almost,' Dulcie said defensively.

'And does he come here?' he asked, genuinely curious.

Dulcie Meredith, an inveterate gossip, shot him a look of sly cognisance that fell a little short of disdain.

'Bulldog is an old friend of mine, darling. Vanessa and I used to be telephone operators in Calcutta.'

Fram received this information with incredulity. At first, he suspected that Mrs Meredith was lying. It seemed remote from possibility that the genteel Vanessa was acquainted with this khaki-coloured brothel-keeper. But there was such assurance in her mischievous face that he concluded that there must be some substance to what seemed to be an outrageous claim.

'Isn't she English?' he finally asked.

Mrs Meredith assured him that, like her, Vanessa was from the northern hills and reminded Fram of Vanessa's daughter's distinctive appearance.

'Vivien was in class with my Meroo,' he recalled. 'She was almost as beautiful as her mother.'

'I was alluding to her Kalimpong eyes,' Dulcie said, pointing to her own with coy pride.

At Lamington Road, Fram took care not to use Xenia exclusively. He also resolved not to entertain her at Peccavi too often. Kety, he sensed, was unhappy about whores sitting on the toilet seat, ordering it to be replaced the day after Xenia spent the night there. But Xenia and he developed a more relaxed relationship, often dining together at restaurants in Grant Road and going to the late-night movies together. He no longer saw her as his personal woman, accepting that her business involved sleeping with other men as well. And he resisted asking questions about what she did when they were apart, and with whom, how many times, and where. Sometimes, when he was feeling down, he spent a night with her at a hotel, content to sleep chastely in her arms, a practice that disturbed her. She insisted that they did it just once, gently fellating him when he refused to fuck her.

'I feel cheap,' she confessed, 'taking your money and not making you happy.'

'I'm happy,' he smiled, burying his fingers in her springy hair. But Xenia, who had spent many nights alone with strange men, had a sixth sense about happiness.

Fram now felt he was obliged to visit Singleton's Hotel more often, if only to keep a wary eye on Patcheco's radical ideas. He was agreeably surprised when he saw and heard the Shalimar Swing Sextet for the first time, buying them an expensive round of cocktails during the evening. It was the trumpet player who really interested him. She was a short, chubby girl with bobbed, blonde hair and, from what he could determine through the fullness of her shimmering, silver gown, a rounded figure. He listened to the Shalimars playing 'Am I Blue?' with the chubby girl taking a long solo. Fram applauded ostentatiously, catching the trumpet player's eyes when he continued clapping long after everybody had stopped. Patcheco told him that her name was

Rosie Sweetwater and that she lived with her father, the groundsman at the Cooperage Football Ground, not far from the hotel. Fram scribbled her a note, asking her to have dinner with him when she was free. She did not reply.

When the Shalimars next appeared, he sent her flowers and a giant box of chocolates, and sat by the rostrum, tapping his feet to every note. Rosie Sweetwater's trumpet strutted its way through 'Baby Face', 'Button Up Your Overcoat', and 'Dinah'. But it was the dreamier numbers like 'Carolina Moon', 'After the Ball' and 'Am I Blue?' he loved best. Particularly 'Am I Blue?' He made a special request for that one and she played it twice. On the second occasion, the Shalimars swayed in twinkling blue stage-lights, while Miss Sweetwater did the business using a poignant mute. What, Fram asked himself with a shiver of delight, could be bluer?

He wrote yet another note, pleading once again with her to meet him and included his telephone number. However, at the end of the evening he was dismayed to learn that the plump trumpeter was not to be found. Wendy Rodrigues, the elderly pianist with a face scarred by burns, informed him that Miss Sweetwater, who was feeling indisposed, had gone home. Fram sought Jerry Patcheco's assistance. He explained that all he wanted was an opportunity to meet the chubby trumpeter.

'I admire her musical ability,' he declared solemnly.

'She's a respectable girl,' Patcheco said.

'Don't I know that?' Fram cried irritably, offended at the manager's tone.

He advised Fram that Heloise, the bass player, was probably more easily available. Heloise Wordsworth was a tall, cheerful girl with shingled, ginger hair, spectacles and a white freckled skin.

'Dinner, an inexpensive piece of jewellery and fifty bucks should see you home,' Patcheco mused.

'I'm not interested in such things,' Fram snapped.

'No?'

Eventually Patcheco promised that he would try to effect an introduction. Fram, detecting uncertainty in the manager's eyes, reminded him that he was speaking to a gentleman and a parent, with a daughter of his own. 'A prodigy,' he added. 'A Sanskrit scholar.'

But Fram realised that such vanities as scholarship were

beyond Patcheco's mind, which he suspected was a simple piece of equipment, suited to running about a hockey field or tarting up an old hotel, but not quite up to the complexities of an ancient language. Patcheco, he felt, probably didn't know what Sanskrit was. And the impertinent implication oi the bass player's availability rankled. Cabral's nephew was clearly getting above himself. Still, he reflected privately, fifty bucks for the red-haired Miss Wordsworth was a bargain by any standards.

It was Friski Dalal who casually mentioned one day that Miss Sweetwater was generally to be found at the Cooperage in the evenings, watching football. 'She is particularly keen on the King's Regiment.'

'I didn't realise you knew about such coarse things as football,' Fram said.

She told him that Rosie and the drummer, Grace Mumford, also known as Motherbunch, were taking dance lessons with her with a view to getting some film work.

'And Jimmy has promised to help,' she enthused.

'Jimmy?'

'The Raja of Pinjrapore,' Friski replied. 'He owns Amazing Films.'

'Yes,' snapped Fram. 'I know.'

The prospect of sitting in a crowded stand watching sweaty Tommies kicking a piece of leather around did not appeal to Fram. But despite his misgivings he arranged for Jockey to drop him at the bandstand in the new sky-blue Chrysler he'd just had delivered, walking with some trepidation the last hundred yards or so to the ground. He purchased a ticket in the best part of the stand and looked around for Rosie, spotting her with a group of Europeans in the Members' Club, a roped-off area, dignified by cane armchairs and peg-tables. She was in white, with a pink-ribboned straw hat that she unpinned and slid below her seat. There was a great deal of shouting, standing up, then sitting down around him. The King's Regiment appeared to be an extremely rough lot of men, nudging and kicking their barefooted Indian opponents out of the way. Their heavy boots, Fram thought, gave them an unfair advantage, enabling them to trample the toes of the Mohammedan Sporting players, who appeared to be more skilful. But Fram spent almost as much time looking back at Rosie as he did at the match, noting that she cheered whenever a Tommy kicked the ball and looked passive when the Indians demonstrated their intricate dribbling abilities. But, try as he would, he failed to attract her attention. It seemed that she did not see him wave or, if she did, pretended otherwise.

Apart from the pleasant smell of freshly mown grass, the geometrical white patterns on the green and a brass band of kilted Scotsmen who marched and played in formation at half-time, the evening had little to commend it. He learned as he was leaving the ground that the King's Regiment had won 4–0, a result that seemed to be a travesty of justice. If points had been awarded for cleverness, the barefooted boys would have won fairly easily. He left the ground in a stream of noisy Tommies, planning significant revisions to the rules of Association Football.

The suspicion that Rosie Sweetwater had seen but deliberately ignored him festered as he drove back to Peccavi. He felt sick with the need to meet this wonderful girl and the following morning wrote her a note saying how he'd seen her at the football match and hoped she was pleased with the result. He temporised for a time about posting it, then, around lunchtime, tore it into pieces and telephoned Patcheco. He had thought of taking Friski into his confidence but feared that, as a woman, she might let the cat out of the bag. It was, he reflected, a man's assignment. His best recourse was to arrange for Patcheco to introduce them before the Shalimars went on stage.

He went through the envisaged meeting in his mind. Miss Sweetwater, this is Mr Chutrivala, one of our directors and the proprietor of the Wadia Ice Factory. He remembered a book on etiquette by the Marchioness of Willingdon. It stated that it was polite for persons of the opposite sex, when introduced, to bow and not shake hands. Still, given half a shout, he'd risk offending convention to clasp Rosie's hand. The need for Patcheco's assistance became increasingly obvious. Tilting a shot of malt into a glass, he swallowed it and dialled Patcheco at Singleton's Hotel. There was no reply. He tried the reception desk but was informed that, although Mr Patcheco was in his room, he was not taking any calls.

'But I'm a director,' Fram announced stiffly.

He was outraged when they replied that Mr Patcheco had given specific instructions that he was not to be disturbed by anyone.

Fram put the receiver down. The young bastard, he seethed, needed a sharp stick up his arse. He summoned Jockey and was driven to Singleton's at speed.

'Blow the horn,' he ordered, 'several times.'

Jockey glanced up at the mirror. He had never seen his master so agitated. DO ME SO TEH the electric horn went. Again and again. Other cars, uncertain as to the meaning of the noise, moved to the side of the road and allowed Jockey to race through.

Fram ran up the steps and strode through the foyer with the authority of a director. He went up in one of the new lifts to Patcheco's room. Fram considered that if he could get Friski Dalal on his side they could squeeze some much-needed deference out of their manager. Nobody appreciated the improvements more than he, but Patcheco, wonderman or not, was only an employee. He rang the bell several times. After a minute or so, he heard voices and the soft pad of approaching feet. Patcheco, in a chequered bathrobe, opened the door a cautious few inches. He did not appear to be wildly pleased to see Fram.

'I'm taking a bath,' he snarled and blocked the door so that Fram could hardly get his nose in. Fram looked at his watch.

'It's three in the afternoon,' he announced.

'I make it a point to bathe three times a day in the hot season,' Patcheco said. 'When I first rise, after lunch and before dinner.'

The young manager did not appear to be at all contrite about the time he spent on his ablutions.

'I need to talk to you about a personal matter,' Fram explained, inclining his head as he heard a sound inside the room.

Patcheco promised to join him in the lounge in half an hour. As Fram turned to leave, he noticed the freak reflection of another person in the yellow bathroom skylight. It was, he perceived, a woman, unclothed upon the bed in the alcove which could not be seen from the door. Because of the distraction of pendant breasts and bushy pubes, Fram did not instantly identify her, only coming to a definite conclusion after the door was closed and he had commenced his descent in the lift. The realisation that what he'd seen was the reflection of Friski Dalal gave him an indefinable jolt and an unhappy feeling that Patcheco was less vulnerable than he once believed.

PART TWO

Rosie

Chapter 9

Fram's pursuit of Rosie Sweetwater was now almost undignified. The bouquets of flowers became grander and his scribbled notes expanded into several hundred words, with cribs from Keats, Elizabeth Barrett Browning and Ella Wheeler Wilcox. His appearances at the Cooperage Football Ground in a cream tussore-silk suit, floral tie, buttonhole and topee were considered as mildly eccentric by the regulars and provocative by Rosie. Her friends, Heloise and Motherbunch, were intrigued by the ardency of the unwanted suitor, but while Motherbunch, a voluptuous, dark-haired girl with large breasts and sleepy eyes, considered Fram Chutrivala repellent, Heloise thought him quite sweet.

'He's becoming a nuisance,' admitted Rosie.

'The guy only wants to fuck you, sweetheart,' said Heloise.

But when Rosie replied that she would only do things like that for love, the other two dissolved into uncharitable laughter, Heloise because she didn't believe in love and Motherbunch because she fell in and out of love with Tommies several times a week.

'Ask him for money,' Heloise advised.

'And then?' Rosie enquired.

'Ask him for some more.'

At that, they all laughed again and Motherbunch suggested that if Rosie was willing to compromise herself with this elderly lecher, it would be sensible to demand an extraordinary price.

'A thousand maybe,' mused Heloise.

'I wouldn't let him in for twice that,' growled Motherbunch, 'but think big if you do. You know, a new car, a racehorse, crap like that. But in my book there's no substitute for big, pink, regimental ones; young, springy and full of sap.'

'Do you think he's a little mad?' Heloise mused.

'He has a strangely vacuous stare,' agreed Motherbunch.

'I think he looks a bit like John Barrymore,' Rosie murmured playfully, a remark that provoked more levity.

Rosie complained to Friski Dalal about Fram. She told her about his claustrophobic attention and wondered whether it was a matter for the police.

'Oh, he's quite harmless. And probably wealthier than anyone suspects,' Friski said. 'He inherited all Byramji Wadia's money, being, like his brother Soli and sister Kety, Byramji's bastard. But if you've got something the blighter wants, play hard to get. You'll be surprised how that often pays off with silly men like him.'

When the Shalimars now played, Motherbunch and Heloise watched Fram with amusement while Rosie avoided his attentions. The cocktails he sent up to her remained ostentatiously undrunk and his special requests were never played. Indeed, when playing her solos, Rosie gazed soulfully over Fram's head to a point just below the fretted, silver drums of the droning ceiling fans. Occasionally, Heloise winked wickedly at him and Motherbunch made an ambiguous sign with a drumstick but Rosie's eyes never met his, although she waved and smiled to other men who raised their glasses to her.

One night, Fram was sufficiently desperate at being so sedulously disregarded that he drove out to Dulcie Meredith's place on Lamington Road and found Xenia. Eliciting that she didn't have a sleeping engagement, he spirited her into his waiting Chrysler.

'Singleton's Hotel,' he instructed Jockey.

They caught the last half hour of the Shalimars' act. He was particularly pleased they danced to 'Am I Blue?'

'How pretty,' Xenia exclaimed, enthralled more by the shimmering blue light than by the melancholy mute of Rosie Sweetwater. 'It's like fairyland.'

'I prefer dancing here to Dulcie's place,' Fram admitted, rubbing his bulge against her pelvic crest.

'It's expensive when you take me out without a reservation,' Xenia warned. 'Double all-night rates.'

'Double?'

She giggled at his moment of consternation before the shrug of resignation.

76

'It's only money,' she reminded him, as he radiated a spurious smile in Rosie Sweetwater's direction.

He was mildly elated at the response. A freakish glitch as the trumpeter missed her breath, provoking an involuntary musical fart and wild-eyed angst as a glittering Chutrivala sauntered past with his exotic partner. Nobody could deny they danced well. Even Dalal who had taken the floor with Patcheco for the last number was agreeably impressed with Fram's style if not the identity of his partner.

'She's a well-known whore,' the young manager hissed balefully.

'I know,' Friski murmured. 'I once treated her for the clap.'

For a while, Xenia was seen with Fram at most of the dances in the Pigalle Pavilion. And Rosie noticed that they even attended the occasional match at the Cooperage. He now wore an open-necked shirt and grey flannels while Xenia, heavily painted and poignantly conspicuous in flowery beach suits and floppy straw hats, attracted excessive attention from the young soldiers. For the most part, they were ill-mannered and unchivalrous, making fucking signs with their fists, pointing in the direction of their cocks and offering her four annas for a quick one behind the grandstand. This debased behaviour was endured with stoicism by Fram and his friend.

'These are low-class Englishmen,' Fram informed Xenia in a whisper, 'uneducated slum-dwellers who would be sweeping the gutters in their own country.'

He was careful, of course, to make these comments in a low voice and never met their insolent and challenging stares lest he was knocked down.

'Violence is part of their imperialist culture,' he declared pompously when they were safe in the Chrysler. On reflection, however, the remark made him feel uneasy. It was the sort of Bolshevik cliché that would have come easily to Soli's lips.

'Men tend to behave badly in crowds,' Xenia suggested. 'Tommies are no worse than our people.'

'I am told,' Fram said, looking sideways at her, 'that the English have extremely big ones.'

'Oh yes,' she smiled, 'and only the boys with twelve inches or more are allowed to serve in Bombay.'

*

Fram was mildly surprised when Kety questioned him about his relationship with Xenia. Apparently she had asked Jockey about the heady aroma that seemed ineradicable from the Chrysler, and which she suspected inflamed her sensitive eyes.

'It's a Baluchi attar,' Fram said, 'that persists for many days in a confined space. Perhaps you should take a taxi if you're distressed.'

'Are you serious about this black girl?' Kety enquired.

Fram, who had never thought of Xenia as black but as a warm, Mediterranean brown, frowned. He informed his sister that Xenia cost him a hundred and fifty rupees a night and on average two thousand rupees a month.

'My God,' Kety exclaimed. 'Can you afford her?'

He shook his head and confessed that he had taken an overdraft at Grindlay's as a short-term measure but this could be attributed as much to recent capital demands as to his personal extravagance. But the enormity of the sum he spent on Xenia could hardly be comprehended by Kety whose subsistence allowance was a tenth of that sum.

'Why, Fram?' she asked. 'Why?'

'Because,' Fram replied simply, 'she makes me feel like a real man.'

Kety took her brother's hand between hers.

'You should get married again,' she urged.

'What about you?' Fram demanded. 'You're still a virgin. At thirty-eight that can't be much fun.'

Kety did not reply. The pinched look in her face made Fram suddenly uneasy. He felt that he was not up to unwelcome confessions, certain that one was hovering in the air between them.

'There is somebody,' Fram confided finally, 'but she has no interest in me.'

'Send her flowers and a box of chocolates,' Kety suggested.

'I've done that,' Fram sighed.

'Speak to her father.'

'I suspect,' Fram said gloomily, 'that he is not that kind of father.'

Fram's brief conversation with Kety turned his mind to one last attempt to win Rosie Sweetwater's attention. He sat down and

78

drafted what he knew must be his final letter to the cuddly trumpeter.

Dear Miss Sweetwater,

I must by now be an object of ridicule in your eyes. But being ridiculous is my principal weakness. There are others; like drinking whisky, neglecting my inheritance and going with whores.

You already know the effect your reluctance to acknowledge my existence has produced in me. But my public appearances with a well-known prostitute are no more than a scream for help. A simple advertisement of my madness. The truth is, Miss Sweetwater, I want to marry you. Isn't that a crazy admission to somebody who has already made known their repugnance for me? But madness is like that.

If I can't marry you, may I be your friend? If friendship is denied, I'll settle for being an acquaintance. But for the present, I ask no more than sharing a dinner with you.

I will even risk degrading you by making you an offer during this proposed dinner that will take your breath away. Please accept this insult of a promised fortune as no more than the last throw of a madman in love.

Framroze Chutrivala

Fram considered showing this letter to Kety but changed his mind. It was not a letter any reasonable man would send to a stranger of the opposite sex. It lacked subtlety and was full of unpleasant revelations. He wondered whether he should have confessed that he'd had several spells of pyschiatric treatment but decided against it. Friski Dalal had probably disclosed as much to Patcheco, who he suspected would have passed on the information to Rosie. He had at least conceded madness. Need he say more? He slid the letter into an envelope, stamped and addressed it in his rather loopy and spidery handwriting. Soli always derided his hand and said it looked like a message from the other world.

It had started to drizzle when he left Peccavi. He decided to walk over the bridge towards Byculla, rather than take the car. The letter to Rosie was wrapped in a manilla cover and secreted in the pocket nearest his heart. Putting on gumboots, a raincoat and a waterproof hat, he set out, splashing through the brown rivulets

79

that ran down the hill as he used to do as a boy. He hoped the warm moisture of his body would make the ink sweat a little, as though the words had been invested with his humanity, remembering how he enjoyed receiving letters during the monsoon that indicated they had been consigned by damp hands, bearing the stains and stigmata of their watery transmission.

Two days later, Fram received the phone call he had scarcely dared hope for.

'Mr Chutrivala?'

'Speaking.'

'This is Rosie Sweetwater.'

At first, he imagined it was Xenia. The voice had the same dark quality, but the articulation was clear where Xenia's was hoarser and a little tired. He found himself trembling uncontrollably as he spoke, stammering when he tried to control his excitement. He invited her to dine with him at Peccavi.

'I'll send my chauffeur in the Chrysler for you,' he suggested.

She declined politely, advising him that it would be improper for her to visit his home, but agreed to take coffee with him one afternoon at Singleton's Hotel. He proposed dinner instead but once again she refused, informing him that if he particularly wanted to share a meal with her, lunch would be preferable. And she assured him that a car would not be necessary as she lived within walking distance of the hotel.

'In the meanwhile,' Fram promised, 'I'll send you some flowers.'

'No flowers,' she laughed. 'Maybe some fruit and a bottle of scotch for Daddy.'

'He drinks scotch?' Fram asked happily.

'And how.'

Fram told her that he had never heard the trumpet played so expressively before. This Miss Sweetwater did not believe.

'You sound like one of those black guys on the records.'

She laughed again, which pleased Fram, and confessed that she was thinking of giving up the trumpet for a career in films.

'Hollywood?' he asked, although he knew the answer.

'No,' she giggled, 'Indian movies. I'm brushing up my Hindi and Dr Dalal is giving me dancing lessons. Do you know she used to be a dancer? She's the consultant choreographer to Amazing Films.'

'A very versatile lady,' he agreed.

Fram had always admired Friski Dalal but her apparent duplicity about young Patcheco had persuaded him to modify his belief in her character. Yet the idea that Patcheco was her lover was so incredible that the memory of the naked woman whose reflection he'd glimpsed haunted him. What puzzled him was that there were no clues about their intimacy. If anything, Friski was more overtly critical of the young manager than before but Fram's suspicions persisted. He was puzzled, however, by the implications of her subterranean nature and the recollection of Byramji's high estimation of her probity.

'You have no idea how happy you've made me,' he chattered, anxious to talk forever.

'You're easily pleased,' she replied, a note of alarming disinterest changing her inflexion as she addressed somebody who had apparently entered the room. Then a blur of voices was followed by her urgent, 'I'll have to go.'

'Go?'

'Bye.'

He stood for some time holding the silent instrument to his ear, feeling that in some way that brought her closer to him. When he put the receiver down, he poured himself a stiff malt and tossed it down his throat, then paced the room like a wild beast, trembling with anticipation. He wanted Rosie Sweetwater more than he had wanted anyone before.

He left the factory in charge of Dagroo the mistry and went off with Jockey on a shopping expedition, picking up a shot-silk maroon tie, striped socks and pearl cufflinks for himself, French toiletry for Rosie, and a case of Black and White for her father. At Crawford Market, he bought two large baskets of fruit, a presentation tin of halva and a box of Russian cigarettes. The gifts were despatched with Jockey to the Sweetwaters' house on Wodehouse Road. On the accompanying card of a black shire in a wintry English landscape, above the word SINCERITY in italic glitter, he neatly inscribed his name.

It is doubtful whether Fram would have been able to sustain his state of manic elation had he known that the caller at Rosie's who had truncated their telephone conversation was male; or the nature of his subsequent transactions with her. He was a tall, lean man with grey hair and two Leicas dangling from his neck, who demonstrated a degree of easy familiarity with Miss Sweetwater that would have chilled Fram's heart. She was posed naked on a crumpled, red satin spread, compliant as he kissed her affectionately on the mouth, stroked her bare skin and patted her bottom. And as Fram was shopping for tokens of his professed sincerity, this man walked around the unclothed object of his esteem, clicking, brooding about angles, light and the aesthetics of his doubtful art. Fram might have been even more disturbed had he overheard a snatch of their lighthearted but coarse exchanges.

'You'll have to lose some fat off that arse, Piggy.'

'Oh, Shush, don't be an absolute bastard.'

'We could fuck it away.'

'Piss off, you dirty old sod.'

Fram reserved a table in a corner hidden by potted palms and a bamboo screen, overlooking the rocks along the breakwater of Cuffe Parade and the grey-green turbulence of the Arabian Sea. The rain had fallen without remission since dawn and cascaded down the deserted promenade, swirling in white whorls around the coconut trees into the purling waters of the gutters. Rosie Sweetwater arrived in a floral blue and white dress, a petalled azure cloche and pipeclayed shoes. The sides of her fair hair had been dressed close to her head and her lips had been painted a deeper red than he'd seen before. They shook hands and he was careful not to detain her softness a moment longer than propriety allowed. He was, however, so engrossed in her person that he forgot to draw her chair out to allow her to be seated, did not ask her if she'd like an aperitif and knocked over a vase of magnolias before scraping into his place.

She had, he noticed, a slight indentation on her upper lip where the trumpet was placed, large even teeth, lively grey eyes and dark eyebrows that contrasted with her blonde hair. And although the neckline decorously concealed a cleavage, her breasts appeared to be large and well balanced. Her snub nose, square jaw, strong downy arms and robust build hinted at audacity and athletic diversions: a thrower of discuses, javelins or cannonballs. Miss Sweetwater had a steel he hadn't suspected when he'd seen her on stage. Yet he couldn't imagine her as a dancer, particularly an Indian dancer, and the thought of that aspiration made him eager to see her legs, thighs and buttocks. Fully clothed, she didn't appear to be too heavily haunched or broad-beamed for sudden movement, but dancing hardly appeared to be within a natural competence.

His mind flitted away, diverted by the possible colour and conformation of nipples, swell of bottom and belly and floccu-lence of pubes. He placed mental bets on these weighty matters even as they talked in pretended awe about the extraordinary violence of the monsoon and exchanged banalities about floods in unlikely places. A glimpse of the pinkness of Miss Sweetwater's open mouth articulating an 'Ah' was enough to undo him. He was subsumed in vanities of erubescence, intoxicated by dreams of her flowering, sensing the plump cornelian tongue, folded modestly in a moist anemone, that prospered under their table, no more than a yard from his waiting fingers. It was the moment, he later recalled, when he realised that he would rather suicide than not ultimately penetrate her.

Miss Sweetwater told him that she did not take alcohol in any form, rarely smoked and generally preferred fish and fresh fruit. Her weight she attributed to a thyroxine deficiency and natural indolence. She disclosed that Motherbunch the drummer and Heloise the bass player had been her classmates, and, at twenty-three, they were still inseparable friends.

After a moment's silence, Fram admitted that he was forty-three. She peered at him closely, having believed him to be considerably older, on account of his dyed hair and pale, puffy skin. Heloise had estimated sixty but Motherbunch made him ten years younger, suggesting that he was a shade too spritely for a sexagenarian, reflecting that his wasted appearance indicated drink, venery or even pulmonary problems. Heloise reminded her that tubercular people were sexually insatiable, citing the example of her own father, who, not content with a wife and several mistresses, tried to mount his own daughters.

'He spat blood all over the house,' Heloise recalled with a shiver.

'Jesus Christ,' Rosie sighed.

These were the gloomy thoughts that she had brought to the lunch with Fram Chutrivala.

'You're a good dancer,' she said.

'Maybe we can dance together sometime,' he declared.

'Not here,' she said emphatically.

'Mongini's perhaps,' he said.

'I've never been there,' she replied almost wistfully.

Her response seemed as near an acceptance of his invitation to go to Mongini's with him as he could have wished. He decided, however, that it might be inappropriate to press the matter.

'I don't want soup,' she decided, glancing at the menu.

'No soup?'

Rosie Sweetwater shook her head.

'They do a very nice Country Captain here,' he said.

She shrugged and made a face.

'Ugh. That's full of meat, isn't it?'

Fram nodded apologetically.

They settled for a prawn molee with saffron rice and spinach. Fram allowed himself a seltzer water while Rosie took an iced soda. She accused him of being very shy as he screwed his bread roll into a debris of crumbs and he confessed that he suffered from nerves when confronted by important decisions.

'Do you drink much whisky?' she asked.

'Too much,' he admitted sadly.

'Daddy does as well,' she said. 'He's a person of your generation. You know, fiftyish.'

Fram reminded her with a wry smile that he was forty-three.

'Am I too old?' he demanded suddenly.

She noticed that he was trembling and had to clasp his hands under the table and bite his lower lip. He was not, she decided suddenly, really unhandsome; indeed, there was something of the matinee idol about his profile but he seemed disagreeably twitchy and miserable.

'You look quite young,' she said kindly. 'You should smile more.' They were on the guava kulfi before he got down to the offer.

'If you marry me,' he whispered quickly, 'I'll settle one lakh on you before the ceremony and another half a lakh on the birth of our first child.'

Rosie had never been able to evaluate large figures. To her, any sum over ten thousand was grotesquely prodigious. But the other implication of his offer dazed her. She leaned back in her chair, looking slightly horrified.

'Do you really expect me to have a child?'

Her reaction alarmed him. 'It's the natural outcome of a marriage,' he stammered.

'You mean, we'll have to sleep together?' she asked.

He attributed her disingenuousness to modesty. She at last had to confront the intimate implications of his remarks. He lowered his voice and spoke tenderly.

'Consummation is what a marriage is all about.'

Miss Sweetwater looked glum. 'Perhaps,' she suggested, 'we're moving too fast.'

Fram's eyes filled with tears. He started to shake once more.

'You mustn't cry,' she reproved with owlish surprise.

'I love you,' he proclaimed, averting his head.

She left most of the guava kulfi, toying with it until it melted. He watched her, his face clouded with a brooding sadness.

'I could use a coffee,' she said quickly.

'Coffee,' he hissed loudly to the waiter who stood sentinel by the door.

'What about your whores?' she asked finally.

'I'll give them up,' he promised.

'Daddy and I will have to sort this out,' she said, pouting thoughtfully.

'It's still raining,' he observed as they rose from the table.

She did not decline his offer to drive her home.

Chapter 10

Although the lunch was in many ways a disappointment, Fram was confident that some progress had been made. He spoke to Soli and Kety of his plans at dinner that evening.

'I have proposed marriage to a young lady,' he announced.

Kety rose and kissed his cheek. Soli smiled affably.

'Congratulations,' he said.

'Who is she?' Kety asked.

'Her name is Rosie Sweetwater. She plays trumpet with a group called the Shalimars and her father is the groundsman at the Cooperage Football Ground.'

'Sweetwater?' Soli murmured. 'What is she?'

'A human being,' Fram snapped, 'one of God's creatures.'

'She's not that black woman you knock about with, is she?' Kety enquired nervously.

'No, that's Xenia,' he said flatly.

'What I meant,' Soli explained, 'is, to what community does she belong? I asked as a matter of information, not as a criticism of your choice. As a revolutionary Bolshevik, I do not admit to any of these arbitrary divisions between people.'

'Her father,' Fram said, 'is English, but Rosie and her mother were born here.'

'An Anglo-Indian?' Kety asked.

'I suppose so,' Fram said. 'English, at a pinch.'

'There are fine lines in this sort of thing,' Soli observed.

Kety nodded sagely. 'Extremely fine lines,' she agreed.

'Of course,' Fram said, 'there is no certainty that she'll accept me.'

Little more was said at the table, but as Fram lit up a Sumatra in the drawing room, the phone rang. It was Bert Sweetwater, Rosie's father.

*

The following morning, Bert Sweetwater arrived at Peccavi in a green bull-nosed Morris, dressed informally in khaki shorts, a bush jacket and open-toed sandals. A large man with thinning, close-cropped fair hair, he was red-faced, big-nosed, genial and comprehensively tattooed. He crushed Fram's hand in a cheerful handshake and, after the third double scotch, got down to business.

'You're younger than I was led to believe,' he said.

'Indeed?' Fram smiled.

'To a young girl, anybody over thirty is a fogey,' he grumbled.

Sweetwater stamped up to a rack of flintlocks, lifting them out of their frames for examination.

'Love guns,' he enthused, squinting down the barrel and stroking the decorated stock of a Boutet.

Fram informed Sweetwater that his father-in-law, Byramji Wadia, was a great shikari and had left a large collection of rifles and shotguns.

'Do you shoot?' Sweetwater asked.

Fram shook his head.

'I'll teach you,' Sweetwater offered. 'Farhad Shushtary my friend and I do quite a bit. Although he's more interested in photographing the friggin' animals than killing them. Tigers are my thing. And buffaloes. A man has never lived unless he's faced a charging buffalo.'

'I'm afraid I don't like harming animals,' Fram admitted.

Bert Sweetwater gazed at him with surprise.

'What's the matter with you?' he grunted. 'Man is a natural hunter. The English aristocracy are always slaughtering birds and beasts. Like your maharajah types. It's not just a mark of manhood but of class as well.'

Sweetwater gratefully accepted his fourth scotch and tried one of Fram's Sumatras. He seemed taken with the drawing room, walking about to peer at the objects on view. Going to the window, he gazed down at the statue of Sir Maneckji Wadia.

'Who's that?' he demanded.

Fram told him. Sweetwater seemed impressed by the fact of Maneckji's knighthood. He stood framed by the morning light, puffing the cigar, asking after a thoughtful silence whether Fram had a title of any sort.

'I'm just a plain Chutrivala,' Fram murmured.

'That's a hell of a gobful to go to bed with,' Sweetwater laughed. 'It means umbrella man, doesn't it?'

'My family had an umbrella-repairing business,' Fram explained.

'Rosie's mother was half Parsee, you know,' Sweetwater confided. 'She was a Wadia too, like the old johnny on horseback downstairs.'

'It's a large family,' Fram reflected.

'They wouldn't have anything to do with her after she married a quarter-master sergeant in the Royal Scots, like.'

'Prejudice is an evil thing,' brooded Fram.

Sweetwater enquired about the profitability of the ice factory and was surprised to learn that it was not a gold mine.

'You probably don't have the right contacts, sonny,' Sweetwater said. 'What you really need is somebody who can fix you up with all the European clubs, military messes, gymkhanas and hotels.'

Fram's eyes lit up. 'That would be nice.'

Sweetwater offered to manage the ice factory for him, suggesting a figure of four hundred a month and free petrol. 'Peanuts,' the Englishman said.

Fram told him that he didn't think that the present income could stand any additional expense, but Sweetwater pointed out that it could if the turnover was trebled.

'There's the matter of capacity,' Fram countered.

Sweetwater went to the drinks trolley and poured himself a fifth whisky. He regarded Fram critically and advised him that nothing in life was impossible, reminding him of the motto of the King's Regiment. Fram stared at him blankly.

'Nec Aspera Terrent,' exulted the inebriated Englishman. 'It's Latin for "Nor Do Difficulties Deter", like.'

He admitted to Fram that he was basically a businessman and, had he gone into land reclamation after demobilisation, he would now undoubtedly have been a millionnaire with the kind of money that would have changed Rosie's life.

'Now take my mate Farhad Shushtary. He went into property speculation and has never looked back. Shush is friggin' loaded.'

Being a Ground Manager with the Western India Football Association had, he reflected, its rewards, but there was a limit to what even a first-rate mind could do with grass.

'I was very impressed by how green it is,' commented Fram.

'You can't touch English grass,' boasted Sweetwater, excusing himself as he made for the lavatory.

'It's the second door on the right,' said Fram, guiding him to the door.

Sweetwater returned, walking unsteadily. He complained that the floor was uneven, as he eyed the whisky decanter with genial intent. Fram assured him that his late father-in-law had informed him that the Peccavi corridor had sloped for fifty years or more and that the house was inspected regularly by a qualified surveyor.

'You wouldn't want the bugger to fall in, now would you, son?' Sweetwater demanded, accepting another scotch in his hairy fist.

Fram considered the beefy ex-soldier anxiously. He noticed the words 'They Shall Not Pass' tattooed over crossed swords on his right forearm and a wonderful, diamond-backed serpent that started at his left wrist and disappeared somewhere up his armpit.

'You may as well know,' Sweetwater confessed, 'that it is my intention to eventually return to Blighty.'

Fram learned that Rosie's father's ancestral home was in Liverpool.

'When were you last there?' enquired Fram.

'Eighteen ninety-five,' Sweetwater sighed.

'That was the year the ice factory was built,' Fram reflected.

'I was a soldier of the Queen,' Sweetwater said. 'Now there was a woman. The present hairy Herbert's not a patch on his old nanna, you know.'

'Who?'

'George the friggin' Fifth,' Sweetwater sneered. 'He'll give the lot away if he had half a friggin' chance.'

'What?' gasped Fram, finding it increasingly difficult to comprehend Sweetwater's adenoidal accent.

'The friggin' Empire, son,' the Liverpudlian replied, pushing his empty glass across the table.

There was an awkward silence after Fram had topped Sweetwater up.

'About Rosie . . .' Fram murmured.

'A lovely girl,' her father reflected, 'quite unlike her Mam.' He shot Fram a wild and bitter look. 'She was a right toe-rag. Buggered off with a lance-jack in the friggin' Somersets when the kiddy was in nappies.'

'Rosie?'

Sweetwater held his drink against his chest, rocking very slowly in his chair, conscious that he had at last come to the crucial part of his visit.

'It's important I fix things up for her before I leave,' he muttered. 'A lakh and a half is what we need. Straight and simple in one lump on the morning of the marriage.'

Fram nodded, trying to calculate how he could get the sum together.

'And if you want,' Sweetwater promised, 'I'll organise the ice factory for you as a bonus.'

Sweetwater swallowed his drink and rose. He held out his hand which Fram, getting to his feet, grasped.

'I'll have to think about this, Mr Sweetwater,' he said.

'Call me Bert,' Rosie's father invited.

'Bert,' murmured Fram weakly.

'Grasp the nettle, Fram,' Sweetwater urged. 'Grasp the friggin' nettle.' He punched his puzzled host playfully on the arm. 'It's an English expression,' he explained, laughing. 'In your lingo, "make it juldee".'

'Had you any marriage date in mind?' Fram asked, still bewildered.

'Your call, wacker. Money, marriage. One thing follows t'other. Like night and day, eggs and bacon, dogs and friggin' bitches. We could fix you two lovebirds up tomorrow if you're despy like.'

Fram accompanied Bert Sweetwater to the door.

'There's just one more piece of aggravation, Fram,' said the swaying Englishman. 'You'll have to change your name, lar. My little Rosie won't consent to be known as Mrs Chutrivala. Know what I mean? Eh?'

Fram looked at him aghast.

'Change it to summat that won't embarrass the kiddy.'

'What?'

Rosie's father gave Fram a parting squeeze around the shoulders.

'Well, in my book there's nowt much wrong with Sweetwater.'

Events moved faster than Fram imagined they would. An hour after Bert Sweetwater had left Peccavi, Rosie rang. She was bubbling with suggestions. Her father, she said, had agreed that she could go on motorcar rides with him as long as they made up a foursome with two other responsible people. She disclosed that Farhad Shushtary, her father's friend, and Heloise Wordsworth were prepared to accompany them.

'The ginger-haired bass-player?'

Rosie Sweetwater laughed.

'Fancy you remembering who she is. You're not keen on Heloise, are you?'

Fram assured her that he had no interest in Miss Wordsworth.

'He's prepared to let us visit the cinema on the same conditions.'

Fram, suddenly depressed that he was being swept along at a pace that confused him, felt the threat of a migraine behind his nausea and eidetic flashes. And the quantity of whisky he'd ingested so rapidly in the morning made him lust for an untroubled sleep in a dark cave. The first suspicion that the price being exacted for the girl he wanted was beyond his psychic resources flickered painfully at the margins of his mind. He needed more time than the Sweetwaters were prepared to allow, more money than he could easily raise and more strength to negotiate his advantage than at present he possessed. He perceived that the menace of Bert Sweetwater had less to do with the man's Anglo-Saxon muscularity and brutish assumptions than his offered camaraderie and claustrophobic friendship. Sweetwater appeared to be already retreating from the pre-emptive demands laid down that morning. If the man was willing to sell his daughter with such alacrity for one and a half lakhs, Fram's original suggestion of one down and the balance on the provision of a child seemed more than sufficient to clinch the transaction. The prospect of Bert Sweetwater running the ice factory chilled his blood and he knew that he must summon the resolution to reject the red-faced Englishman's generous offer. Certainly the ridiculous demand that he change his family name to Sweetwater was unacceptable. He had, he remembered, once considered changing it to Wadia or even Chutrivala-Wadia, but the insult to his father's memory was too much for his sensibilities to endure. It would do no harm, he concluded, to court Rosie Sweetwater for a while, before he disclosed his hand. He needed an emotional response from the girl he was certain he loved. He was reluctant to enter a marriage without some hand-holding, kissing and discreet embracing. Chaperones had never been on his agenda. In his abject proposal to Rosie, he had been prepared to concede everything. Now, realising that the Sweetwaters had come to trade, he took comfort in the fact that trading was a skill with which he was not entirely unfamiliar.

Fram arranged a drive to Juhu Beach the following evening.

'We could paddle in the water and eat fresh coconut,' he suggested.

'And watch the snake-charmers,' she enthused.

When he picked Rosie up at the arranged time, he took the Chrysler himself, hoping that he would have Rosie all to himself on the front seat. She looked particularly cool and attractive in white. He was pleased to see that she was hatless and wore sandals through which her toes, with crimson painted nails, were visible. Fram was entranced by the pinkness of her fubsy feet, thinking how he would not be averse to feeling their pressure on his stomach, chest or even his face. They were feet that could be kissed, licked and sucked.

'Where,' he asked, as she settled on the passenger seat beside him, 'are the other two?'

'I've arranged to meet them there,' she croaked in a congested voice. 'Shush is taking Heloise in his new Duesenberg,' she said. 'It goes at over a hundred and fifteen miles per hour. He's promised to drive me back.'

'What about me?' Fram asked miserably.

'You can take Heloise,' she said, surprised by his petulance.

He told her that he was concerned for her safety in this man's fast car. And the prospect that they wouldn't be together on the return journey wasn't a pleasant one.

'You men are never satisfied,' she pouted, sliding closer to him. He swelled with desire as he glanced down at her brazen décolletage and the outline of her nipples under her blouse. He resisted an impulse to place a palm on her right thigh. She blew her nose with difficulty, reeking of eucalyptus and clove oil.

'You've got a bad cold,' he murmured, looking sideways.

'You mustn't come too close,' she warned.

'We must stop before we get there,' he said, switching on the windscreen-wipers as the rain slanted down suddenly.

Fram was giddy with happiness at being alone and unchaperoned with her. He drove the Chrysler with dash, using one hand on the steering wheel, and rested the other on the space between them, almost touching her thigh. The car swished imperiously through flooded streets, travelling faster than he would have chosen to go had he been by himself. He sensed that she was alive to his driving skills as she tensed, peering past the singing wipers into the approaching darkness.

Rosie gave a husky laugh.

'We won't be able to paddle in this,' she said, flinching as he narrowly missed a victoria. He slid around a corner, through a pool of water that cascaded over them. She made an appreciative noise that Fram acknowledged by lifting his palm and pressing it down on her thigh. There was a slight but indecisive reflexion as she twitched away from him, but her submission to his restraint did not require immoderate resolution on his part. Fram turned left into a narrow lane that led to an open space fringed with distant palms. He directed the car along a track that led to the centre of a flooded field. Stopping, he switched off the engine and lights. It was now quite dark.

'Where are we?' she asked, staring out into a black wilderness.

'Not far from Juhu,' he replied, moving to her and kissing her on the lips.

'I can't breathe,' she whispered, as he took her mouth again, slipping a hand into her blouse to caress her breasts. She pushed him gently away and informed him that she had a problem, pointing to the water all around them.

'What?' he asked anxiously.

'I need to pee,' she frowned, 'rather badly.'

He started the car and drove carefully through the rising monsoon water to the road that led to Juhu.

Shushtary and Heloise were waiting for them at Dacosta's Beach Hotel. A long, low building made of palm leaves and built on sand, it had a bar, two billiard tables and four love cabins, with recessed washstands and towels. The sanitary arrangements comprised a latrine block that housed a cess-trench and four compartments with bridging planks for the support of the occupants. It was serviced by Mrs Dacosta's pigs. The beasts had learned to thrust their snouts through the damaged palm walls to scavenge the excrement as it arrived, surprising the squatters with unexpected and terrifying nuzzles.

'It's not suitable for a lady,' Shushtary decided instantly, when he learned of Rosie's needs.

'Oh Shush,' she said, looking pitiable and helpless.

And before Fram could devise an alternative arrangement, Shushtary had led her to his red Duesenberg and driven her away in the driving rain.

'Where has he taken her?' Fram asked Heloise irritably.

'I wouldn't be surprised,' she replied, 'if Rosie uses the car.'

'A brand-new Duesenberg?' Fram asked in horror.

'Shush is that kind of guy,' she said with a quiet smile.

Fram knew that there was something he disliked about the gangling, grey-haired Iranian. A cocky assurance, perhaps, or maybe an almost indecent familiarity with Rosie; the conspiratorial glances between the girls whenever the bastard's name was mentioned. And those Leicas dangling around his neck. Forever clicking at everything that moved. Besides, what self-respecting man likes his fiancée pissing in another guy's car?

Rosie and Shushtary were back within ten minutes or so. The girls laughed, Fram ordered three Cognacs and a milkshake for Rosie, and Shushtary took several dozen photographs, mostly of Rosie. There were no snake-charmers or dancing monkeys to be seen. Shushtary decided that Rosie was not well enough to sit around in the damp bar. He put his coat around her shoulders and offered to drive her home.

'I'll take you,' suggested Fram, as Shushtary popped away two flashes of him advancing on Rosie.

'I want a spin in the Duesenberg,' she pouted, reminding him of the earlier arrangements. Fram gave Rosie's hand a gauche shake as she left with Shushtary. He ordered another two Cognacs for Heloise and himself.

'The Duesenberg does a hundred and sixteen miles an hour,' Heloise declared.

'I thought it was a hundred and fifteen,' Fram snapped.

They drank in silence for a while.

'How old is that guy?' Fram asked, brooding about events.

'Old. Real old. Forty-five, fifty maybe. He's got a wife and six kids in Tehran.'

They took another Cognac apiece, and sat at the window looking out into the blackness of the howling storm. Heloise told him that she sometimes sang solos while playing the bass and that she'd been engaged three times before her eighteenth birthday. Fram noticed that she seemed pleasantly inebriated. She took off her spectacles and put them away.

'Just in case I fall down,' she giggled.

Mrs Dacosta, a plump, white-haired lady who was never seen without a knitted skullcap, came over to them and placed the Cognac bottle on the table. She told them that she was going to bed and asked them to leave the money in the drawer on the serving side of the bar. She left them a hurricane-lantern on a hook.

'Do you want to hire a love cabin for the night?' she asked.

Heloise looked at Fram, raised her eyebrows and shrugged.

'I'm easy,' she murmured.

But Fram decided that, in the circumstances, it was not a good idea.

They didn't talk much on the drive back to Heloise's place. And when he tried to kiss her goodnight, she gave him her right ear to peck before escaping. He sat thoughtfully in the car for a while, then drove past the Sweetwater house on Wodehouse Road. The red Duesenberg was parked in the drive and the drawing-room light was on behind the blue curtains. He checked his watch. It was nearly ten. Starting the Chrysler, he made for Lamington Road, getting to Dulcie Meredith's place before the half hour.

'Hello, stranger,' she said, offering him a pair of friendly lips.

Chapter 11

Fram appropriated Xenia in between dances, rushing her out of the door into his car.

'Where are we going?' she asked, bemused by his hyper-activity.

'To Peccavi,' he said, trying to subdue a facial spasm.

'I'm hungry,' she shivered, staring bleakly at the rain.

They stopped at Sarvi's in Nagpada and he bought her sheekh kebabs, mogul-rotis and green chutney.

'It's leaking all over me,' she complained with disgust, as the food dripped over her skirt.

But the promise of a new dress, lingerie and a bottle of imported perfume lifted her spirits and she had devoured the kebabs before they got to Peccavi. Fram scolded her for not eating at the proper time and suggested that she was probably too preoccupied with entertaining Tommies.

'I've had no customers all day,' she protested, licking her fingers.

She went into the bathroom and on her return found him in the drawing room. He was reclined on an Empire-style fauteuil covered in silver and blue brocade. Xenia took off her shoes and approached him cautiously.

'What do you want me to do, Sir?' she mocked lightly.

'Kneel between my legs,' he said.

She did as she was instructed but noticed that his eyes were closed and his entire body was shaking. He appeared to be having a mild fit, something she had seen in other highly-strung customers. She placed the sole of her discarded shoe against his face and he began to recover.

'You've bitten your lip,' Xenia fussed, dabbing the blood from his mouth with her handkerchief. He appeared to be alarmed by the news, struggling to his feet to examine his face in a mirror.

'I look like a monster,' he cursed.

She prescribed ice and he went out in the pouring rain across the compound to the factory, returning after a while with a small block of ice in a hessian bag.

'You're soaked,' she squealed in childlike wonder, following him into the bathroom, where the ice was packed in a blue ceramic basin on the floor.

'Press your mouth against it,' she urged.

Upstairs, Soli, in his vest and drawers and holding a lantern, peered over the balustrade.

'Fram? Are you alone?'

'No,' Fram grunted.

'Kety and I are playing chess,' he called.

Fram failed to detect the ironic ingratiation in his brother's voice, pitched a tone higher than usual. It was as though the ice had anaesthesised his perception. He instructed Xenia to wait for him in the bedroom. When she had gone, he returned to the drawing room and, as the clock struck twelve, dialled the Sweetwater number. He did not have long to wait. Rosie answered, husky and concerned.

'Hello?'

He held his breath, listening for other sounds. Nothing.

'Hello?' she said again.

Fram replaced the receiver. When he returned to the bedroom, Xenia was drowsing. She opened her eyes as he mounted and attempted to occupy her, listening to his coarse breathing, intermittent barks from the banjaras and the comforting plash of rain on the trout pond. He came quickly, baptising her belly, then rolled away to curl behind her, brushing his lips against her neck in contrition. She nestled her warm rump against his moist pliancy, preparing to be taken again.

'Fram?'

He grunted, stiffening a little.

'Take it easy. You've had a fit, for God's sake.'

'I'm OK.'

'I don't want you dying on me, do I?'

'I'm just a little tired.'

'Fram? Can you hear a baby crying?'

'It's the dead baby from the ice factory.'

'Holy Mary.'

They lay, stealthily awake for a while, before he prospered sufficiently to tup her flowering tail. Xenia's awareness, shaped by an experience of attenuated sounds in dark places, encompassed muted creakings from another room. She recognised the unmistakeable piano carillons of love. The music was, however, beyond Fram's percipience, distracted as he was by the sibilance of hot kisses and the fricative pleasuring of viscous flesh.

Fram kept away from Singleton's Hotel for a week. He found it difficult to sleep, work or eat, drinking significantly more than usual. He considered abandoning the whole idea of marrying Rosie, but wept uncontrollably when he reached that decision. Kety, unable to persuade him to discuss his problems with her, arranged for Dilip Dilduktha to call.

'Who asked you to come here?' asked Fram, when he saw his long-haired friend rise from the chesterfield and greet him as he came in.

'Your sister thought you might need help,' Dilduktha said.

'I don't,' snapped Fram, pouring himself a drink.

'Would you care to spend a week at Kapoli?' the psychiatrist asked.

'I don't require treatment,' Fram said, explaining that he was in love.

There was a long silence before Dilduktha spoke.

'I am informed you want to get married again. A film star, I understand.'

Fram shook his head sorrowfully, poking about in the thermidor for a Sumatra. He informed Dilduktha that Rosie was a musician who had ambitions to become a film star. Dilduktha smiled.

'Where will that leave you?'

'God knows.'

'A Parsee girl?'

Fram looked irritable. He wasn't up to the psychiatrist's cat-and-mouse games.

'Hasn't Kety told you that she's only one quarter Parsee?' he demanded.

Dilduktha shook his head.

'One quarter is not to be sniffed at,' he conceded, before asking, 'And the rest?'

'English, I suppose. Local as oppose to expatrial, of course.' Fram lit his cigar. 'There are contractual complications, money settlements and other conditions,' he sighed miserably.

'I see.'

Fram regarded his friend glumly through a cloud of smoke.

'Do you remember old Fazal, who was a patient the same time as you were?' asked Dilduktha.

'The bugger?'

'Was he one?'

'You told me so yourself.'

There was an awkward hiatus as Dilduktha, rubbing his forehead with a forefinger, tried to recall his alleged slander.

'Anyhow,' he continued, 'Fazal is the trickiest vakil in the business. I would recommend him as a negotiator. I use him myself.'

'I'll think about it,' Fram promised.

They talked pleasantly about old times before Dilduktha left. The doctor was particularly animated by the report that Friski Dalal's lavatory ceramics factory was in the hands of the receiver.

'She's a crook,' Dilduktha warned on his way out.

Fazal worked with extraordinary speed. He gave Fram an appointment at his chambers overlooking Flora Fountain, squeezing him into a tiny room packed with briefs from floor to ceiling. He introduced him to a Khoja youth with soft facial hair and an insane grin.

'This is Mr Dossa,' Fazal said. 'He's the solicitor who is instructing me. Kindly answers all his questions truthfully.'

Mr Dossa inscribed Fram's answers in shorthand on a long roll of paper. Fazal floated in and out of the room from time to time, disappearing long before Mr Dossa had completed his questions.

'Where's Mr Fazal?' Fram asked.

'Who?'

'Fazal.'

'Ah, Gulamhusein Sahib,' the youth smiled. 'He's gone to court.'

'Isn't his name Mr Fazal?'

The boyish Mr Dossa nodded and gave Fram a vacuous grin.

'Yes, that's his name.'

Fram regarded the youth suspiciously.

'Are you really a solicitor?' he asked.

Mr Dossa nodded. 'Indeed.'

Three days later, Fram received a marriage settlement contract. It specified fifty thousand on the conclusion of a civil ceremony, fifty thousand on the birth of the first child, a one-lakh policy on Fram's life with Miss Sweetwater as the beneficiary and a twenty-five thousand rupee payment to Major Bert Sweetwater, the bride's father, within a month of the marriage.

Fram phoned Fazal's office and asked to speak to him. He recognized Mr Dossa's voice.

'Ah, Gulamhusein Sahib. He's gone to court.'

'I see,' Fram said, 'that the contract is signed by a Major Sweetwater on behalf of an infant Rose Ursuline Sweetwater. Doesn't she have to consent to this arrangement?'

'No.'

'How old is Miss Sweetwater?'

There was a pause as Mr Dossa shuffled through the papers.

'Eighteen years and three months.'

Fram replaced the receiver, trembling at the prospect of marrying a girl who was three years younger than his daughter. He was on the point of ringing Bert Sweetwater when Theresa came in to announce the arrival of his prospective father-in-law, hardly two paces ahead of him.

'Your man Faz drives a very hard bargain, Frammy,' he declared, pumping Fram's hand.

'I've hardly had time to study the details.'

Sweetwater strode across to the drinks trolley, lifting out a bottle of malt. He waved it cheerfully at Fram.

'No objection to me tickling my tonsils with a celebratory tot or two?'

Fram shook his head.

'Join me,' invited Sweetwater.

'No thank you.'

He watched the ebullient Englishman down a large one and provide himself with another.

'I thought Rosie was twenty-three,' Fram said bitterly.

'She lies about her bloody age, son,' Sweetwater said. 'Tries to push it on a bit. For professional reasons, you know. But she's old enough, if you know what I mean.'

He beamed a conspiratorial smile at Fram and, gripping his glass, made an arc across his chest to describe female development.

'It's all there, you know. And they've got snouts on them like Cocker friggin' Spaniels. They'd be the pick of any litter, old son.'

Fram already had profound reservations about Sweetwater. Now, quite suddenly, he despised him and considered that marriage was a way of saving the girl from this loutish man. He informed Sweetwater that he would be phoning Rosie to arrange a date before the wedding. Sweetwater rubbed his nose thoughtfully.

'I'd have to organise a chaperone, son,' he reflected.

'No chaperone,' Fram snapped.

Sweetwater frowned for a moment, then beamed wickedly.

'It'll have to be scout's honour then,' he warned cheerfully, putting on his topee. 'But hands off the old Blackpool front. OK?'

Fram saw him to the door. He looked out of the window and watched the Englishman handle-start the Morris. It backfired several times, setting the banjaras off.

'Monsoon friggin' damp,' Sweetwater shouted, filling the compound with oily smoke as he accelerated the engine.

Fram watched the car lurch forward and bump slowly down the drive past the ice factory. Its explosions disturbed a multitude of pigeons from the eaves of the factory building. They rose, flapping noisily, wheeling away in a dark phalanx against the grey, morning sky in a moult of feathers before they returned to shiver and shelter as it started to drizzle again.

Shortly before Fram's date with Rosie, he received an urgent message from Princess Street Police Station. His brother Soli had been arrested, was being charged and being held overnight to appear before the magistrates the following morning.

'What's the charge?' Fram asked in dismay.

'Theft.'

Fazal was phoned and in due course Mr Dossa arrived to visit his client. Two hours passed before Kety and Fram could see Soli.

'It's a political frame-up,' Soli assured them. 'The British government is moving against all enemies of the Raj. The frontier defences have been strengthened to prevent a Russian incursion and naval craft have been deployed in the Arabian Sea and the Bay of Bengal to prevent a surprise attack.'

'From whom?' Fram demanded impatiently.

'A revolutionary alliance supported by at least two national governments is suspected.'

'But what exactly are you accused of stealing?' Kety asked aghast.

'Stamps,' Soli murmured quietly.

Kety burst into tears. She reached through the grille to hold Soli's hand. The sepoy on duty shouted at her.

'Take care,' Soli warned, 'he'll shoot if he believes you're passing me a weapon. Remember, I'm a dangerous subversive according to these lackeys of imperialism.'

'Are you innocent?' Fram asked, staring at his brother.

'Of course,' Soli replied blithely. 'the only guilty party in this affair is the fucking Viceroy of India.'

'Keep your voice down,' pleaded Kety.

'I understand that they've taken Gandhi as well,' Soli hissed. 'That is, of course, a standard counter-revolutionary diversion, M.K.G. being, as everyone knows, an agent of the British Secret Service.'

'After they'd left Soli, Fram tried to have him released that night, but was informed that nothing could be done until he'd appeared before the magistrate in the morning. Instead of returning to Peccavi, Fram and Kety drove to the Sweetwaters' house, where Bert and Rosie were having dinner.

'I'm sorry we've disturbed you,' Fram apologised, explaining why he hadn't appeared for his arranged date with Rosie.

It transpired that Bert Sweetwater knew a superintendent at the station where Soli was being held and suggested that a personal visit by him could do no harm. Fram told Sweetwater that Mr Dossa was handling the case and it would be prudent to keep him advised of any initiatives. Sweetwater was not impressed. Rising from the table, he made for the door.

'Take the Chrysler,' Fram offered, instructing Jockey to drive the sahib to the police-station. Kety and he stayed with Rosie.

'I had no idea,' Fram said, sitting on the settee beside his fiancée, 'that your father was a major.'

Rosie laughed. 'Oh, he's just a groundsman at the Cooperage. He used to be a company sergeant-major in the King's Regiment. He occasionally calls himself major as a joke.'

'Joke?'

She raised her hands and made a face in an attempt to find the appropriate words.

'You know. To impress the natives.'

Bert Sweetwater returned an hour later. Soli was with him. Kety rushed to the door to embrace her brother.

'What happened?' Fram asked.

Sweetwater advised him that the charge had been dropped and Soli was free to return home.

'And he doesn't have to appear before the magistrates tomorrow?' Kety enquired happily.

Sweetwater shook his head.

'It was a political decision,' Soli explained, lighting a cigarette. 'The government were warned that it would be advisable to delay the crack-down against subversives until after the monsoon.'

'What's he talking about?' Sweetwater demanded.

'You wouldn't understand,' Soli said. 'Your friend, Super-intendent Gillespie, had instructions to release me anyway.'

Bert Sweetwater looked incredulous. 'Bollocks,' he shouted, glaring at Soli.

Fram intervened, stepping between them.

'Let us not forget,' he soothed, 'that we're soon to be one family.'

Kety drew Soli away and led him out of the house to the car. Sweetwater turned to Fram after they'd left the house.

'Is your brother all there?' he asked.

Fram nodded. He informed Rosie's father that Soli was inclined in certain extreme emotional states to think in terms of unlikely plots and possibilities.

'He told me that the Vicereine was sleeping with a leading member of the Congress Party,' Sweetwater complained.

'Soli,' Fram confided, 'is not to be taken literally. Sleeping for him is a very racy metaphor that really implies conspiratorial association.'

'He used another word,' Sweetwater declared grimly.

'He has,' Fram mused, as he thanked Sweetwater and took his leave, 'a notoriously abrasive vocabulary.'

Chapter 12

There was a last-minute financial hitch before the ceremony. Grindlay's would only provide an overdraft of twenty-five thousand rupees on the wedding day, a further twenty-five thousand rupees being available subject to their evaluation review of Singleton's Hotel, unlikely to be completed before the end of the month. Fram offered Friski Dalal ten per cent of his Singleton's stock for the balance but she didn't feel that able to do much better than ten thousand rupees in cash and suggested that the Raja of Pinjrapore might be induced to give him another fifteen thousand rupees for a lien on the ice factory.

'I already have a first mortgage of ten thousand rupees on that,' he said glumly.

'What about Peccavi?'

Fram explained that he could not encumber a property that morally belonged to Byramji's seed. Friski Dalal gave a bitter laugh.

'I think,' she said, 'that it is time for us to have a little talk.' She suggested visiting Peccavi. 'It's a long time since I've seen the old place. Do you know that Zarina actually pushed me down the stairs? I sustained a double fracture of the left ankle. That put paid to my career as a professional dancer.'

Fram declared that it was time the quarrels and passions of former times were forgotten now that most of the protagonists were dead. And he was hardly disposed to rake over the past, three days before his wedding.

'And there was another, even more unforgiveable consequence of Zarina Wadia's uncharitable assault,' Friski said balefully.

'What?'

She did not reply but informed him that she would like to call at Peccavi later that afternoon, after she had supervised Jerry Patcheco's therapy.

'By all means,' he murmured courteously.

But he trembled as he put the phone down. He suspected that he was not robust enough to receive scandalous news. Unpleasant disclosures gave him palpitations and diarrhoea. And, unnerved by what was to come, he succumbed to a serious fit of farting.

Friski arrived driving a showy yellow and black Velie. She was dressed in a pink trouser suit with a black lace shawl around her shoulders. Although she had thickened with age, Friski was still an attractive woman, despite the protuberant teeth and dark pouches below her large and lustrous eyes. She jingled as she came in and Fram remembered her fondness for wearing silver bells around her ankles.

'You've got dry rot,' she announced, looking at the door posts and lintels.

'A little,' Fram agreed.

She advised him that it made sense to demolish Peccavi and sell the land for industrial development; but sensing the unhappy look in his eyes, kissed him generously on the cheek.

'I suppose you've had your suspicions about dear Bobby,' she said, kicking off her sandals and making herself comfortable on the carpet with her feet tucked beneath her. She declined his offer of a chair with a self-deprecatory laugh.

'Since when have humble Indian women perched their arṣes on genuine Aubusson chairs?'

'This?' enquired Fram, staring at the chair. 'Is it valuable?'

Friski shrugged and moved her head from side to side in an enigmatic dance movement. The blackness of her thick eyebrows and extravagant lashes contrasted dramatically with her ash-grey hair.

'I bought it for Bobby as a birthday present. It was made by a Frenchman called Foliot around seventeen seventy. Without the woodworm, it would make about fifty guineas in a London showroom. However, I paid two rupees for it in Bhendi Bazaar.'

Fram admitted that his knowledge of period furniture was limited.

'This place is a gold mine,' reflected Friski, looking around.

Fram reminded her of his need to raise an additional twenty-five thousand rupees within the next seventy-two hours.

'Bobby had five children,' she declared. 'You, Soli, Kety, Banoo and Ardeshir.'

'Hearsay,' Fram protested with a frown.

She reminded him that Roshan his mother and Bobby were friends of hers and disclosed that Fali Chutrivala was an accommodating homosexual.

'What sort of accomodation is that?'

'He went for a long walk whenever Bobby called,' she explained.

'Why are you telling me all this now?' Fram cried. 'Can't you see that I have enough trouble?'

'Because,' Friski said, 'you are marrying a very tricky girl. Rosie will need plenty of everything. And unless you can provide her with it, your proposed marriage is doomed. Preparing you for what you are about to face is the least I can do for Bobby. Hopefully the knowledge that you are really a Wadia may help you to act like a Wadia. Remember, Fram, you are the whole and sole of this estate.'

She stared grimly at him. 'Did that charlatan Dilduktha cure you of your fetish?' she enquired.

Fram nodded. His darkest suspicions had been fulfilled. The news that Banoo his first wife had also been his half-sister loosened his bowels. He informed Friski that if what she said was true, Meroo was the product of an incestuous union.

'Think nothing of it,' Friski said. 'In small communities there is often some overlapping. And knowledge often helps us to avoid compounding our offences too outrageously.'

Friski had, Fram recalled, mentioned Byramji's five children. There was one name however, that remained a mystery. Who, he asked her, was Ardeshir?

'He was Byramji's eldest son by yet another woman.'

'Not my mother?'

'No.'

'Who?'

'Let the dead keep their secrets,' she sighed. 'Ardeshir only lived for a few hours.'

'I've never heard of the blighter,' Fram admitted with a nervous twitch.

Friski Dalal rose to her feet and shuffled on her sandals. She suggested that he send along the Peccavi deeds to the Raja of Pinjrapore's solicitor and that she would fix up the rest.

'He's a man called Mr Dossa,' she recalled. 'You'll find him in the directory. Although he's unqualified, he's the great Gulamhusein Fazal's son. All the solicitors in the practice are.'

Fram was standing by his guest's revving machine when he remembered that Rosie had asked Shushtary and Patcheco to be witnesses. Friski's earlier mention of the therapy Patcheco was receiving prompted a solicitious enquiry as she released the handbrake.

'What's Jerry's problem?' he asked, raising his voice above the resonant burr of the three-litre machine.

The fact that the Velie had wheeled away in an arc and was already rolling down the drive made it necessary for her to turn and match her nasal pitch against the triple exhausts and booming Lycoming straight-eight.

'He's impotent,' she screeched.

In the end, Friski had no problem in persuading the Raja of Pinjrapore to supply the short-term deficiency. The money was passed, documents signed and a cheque for fifty thousand in Rosie Sweetwater's name was uttered and folded into Fram's wallet. The contentment of having successfully organised the money and the relief that all impediments had been finally removed was slightly diminished by a bill that arrived before Fram, Soli and Kety left Peccavi for the Registry Office. It was a statement of account from Smithers, Bourne and Limpard, the partnership to which Mr Dossa belonged, for three thousand rupees.

Kety wore her late sister-in-law's turquoise sari, a yellow satin choli with blue embroidered trimmings, gold sandals and two diamond combs in her shining jet hair. Fram and Soli arrived in cream silk suits, black and white striped shirts, and red satin ties. Fram wore Byramji's sapphire tie-pin and matching cufflinks. Bert Sweetwater, redder than ever, sweated in a grey cashmere with a regimental tie while the bride appeared in a simple, white taffeta and a swansdown hat the size of a modest soup-plate. And apart from Heloise Wordsworth, Motherbunch, Jerry Patcheco and Farhad Shushtary, there were no other guests present at the ceremony.

'What excitement,' giggled Heloise.

Curious onlookers imagined that Kety, who looked like a maharani, was the bride and Jerry Patcheco, in his shiny pink suit, the groom. Bert Sweetwater grumbled that there were not enough flowers and Soli, who had undone his collar-stud before he had alighted from the car, told Fram that he had a premonition that the government might use troops to arrest him during the ceremony as a gesture of contempt for civil rights.

'Do up your fucking collar-stud,' ordered Fram with Wadia-like authority.

But Soli did not comply. He informed his brother that it was the very least he could do to demonstrate solidarity with the studless masses of India.

'Choothia,' Fram cursed, his mordacious snarl evidenced in the definitive exposure that Shushtary flashed of the wedding group posed around the ostentatious white dentures of Carioca Alvares, a bald-headed dwarf who dignified the office of Deputy Registrar with radiant hauteur.

An evening meal was waiting for Mr and Mrs Chutrivala when they arrived at 'Cheelchinar', a bungalow set on a lonely spur of the Western Ghats. It belonged to Dilip Dilduktha who had provided its use for a month as a wedding gift. But there appeared to be more servants lurking around the seven rooms than Fram imagined there would be. He counted seven, not including the elderly mali, two sices and a sweeper girl who stood on the rear verandah grinning and cupping her hand playfully over her pubes.

'Who are all these people?' Fram enquired unhappily of the old butler in a white utchkan with a green cummerbund and matching turban.

'We are sixteen,' the old man, who wore Dilduktha's imprimatur in gothic brass, announced. He took pride in identifying the staff and describing their functions. 'Inside,' he said, 'there are two boys for fetching and carrying water from the well; two ayahs for Memsahib, one for hair and body and the other for clothes. There is one cook and his mate, one boy for dusting, one girl for sewing, washing and ironing, one table boy and I, who am in charge. Outside, there are two sices, two malis and two sweeper girls.'

'What are they doing around the bungalow after dark?' demanded Fram. 'And where do they sleep?'

The old butler smiled. 'Here and there,' he said, waving a hand crippled with arthritis around the room.

'Let them sleep outside,' Fram ordered sternly.

'There are leopards,' the butler protested. 'Outside, there are leopards.'

'What about the servants' quarters?' asked Rosie.

'Servants' quarters are in Lonavla,' the old man explained, 'four miles away.'

'I thought this was Lonavla,' Fram said.

The butler shook his head. 'This,' he said smiling, 'is Tiger's Leap.'

'Are there tigers here?' Rosie enquired.

'Only small ones,' the butler said hopefully.

'I wish Daddy was here,' Rosie sighed. 'He loves killing tigers.'

After dinner, Fram called the old butler.

'What's your name?' he asked.

'Madhu.'

'Look here, Madhu. See that all the servants sleep on the lower verandah. OK?'

'There are snakes there, sir,' he muttered.

Fram looked him straight in the eye. 'I don't care about snakes.'

The butler shuffled his feet.

'Can Sir talk to Doctor Sahib tonight about our sleeping arrangements?'

Fram told him that he did not intend to drive down the ghats to discuss the matter with Dilduktha. The butler observed that if the servants were excluded from the bungalow, they would have no recourse but to return to Lonavla for the night. Rosie looked anxious as the menials prepared to disappear.

'I need a bath, Frammy,' she pleaded.

Fram raised a peremptory hand. He explained an immediate requirement for two hot tubs. This need, old Madhu observed, necessitated the presence of the bath boys and the sweeper girls for at least another hour or so, a situation that ended in negotiated settlement. It was agreed that all four verandahs be reserved for servants sleeping accommodation, the two ayahs occupying the second bedroom, while the sweeper girls were left on the snaky, rear verandah with a protective lantern, considerations of caste precluding all four women from occupying the same room.

After they had both bathed, Rosie complained to Fram that she had caught the sice with the broken nose peeping at her through the skylight.

'I feel that we're being watched all the time,' Rosie fretted. She asked Fram whether it occurred to him that their bedroom had no curtains and an unlockable door that led to a verandah where four men would be spending the night.

'They can't see through mosquito nets,' Fram soothed.

But that night, desire had to be caught by the tail. After three fretful and nervous hours of whispered endearments, nipple rubbing and discreet frotteurism, Rosie troubled by an inconvenient cystitis and visiting the privy on half a dozen occasions while Fram monitored the verandahs for any suspicious movements by the staff, the marriage still unconsummated at two o'clock in the morning, they escaped from 'Cheelchinar' and its suspected voyeurs to Peccavi. Jockey, wearily aware of the seriousness of a transit down the ghats in the loving hours of his master's marriage, screamed homeward through the moonless night, kindling the lovers with the violence of vertical and lateral motion.

They passed scudding herds of wild pig, startled hyaenas and mysterious green eyes that watched their progress. She lay across his lap, looking up at him as he caressed her breasts.

'Have you had many women?' she murmured, conscious of the tumult of his flesh below her.

'Not many,' he confessed, lowering his head to kiss her mouth.

'Would you mind if I bought a racehorse?' she asked, taking his hand in hers.

He found the idea shocking and obscenely profligate but held his breath before replying.

'I'm not sure whether we have the sort of money at present to sustain that sort of ambition,' he said gently.

She struggled up.

'I was thinking of my fifty thousand,' she explained. 'Shush has nine in training and knows all about the game. I might even go into partnership with him.'

'Ah,' he said, biting his lip. She sensed the sudden flatness in his voice and felt him subside against her.

'What's the matter?' she asked.

'Nothing,' he replied, playing with her hair.

It rained intermittently. They huddled together in the steamy car, listening to the rhythmic swish of the wipers and the slither of the tyres through the wet scree. He gently rolled a rubbery nipple between his forefinger and thumb as their lips met in discreet silence.

'Will you get hard again for me?' she whispered.

'Of course,' he said, stiffening responsively.

They stopped briefly on the outskirts of the village to allow Rosie to squat behind a tumble of rocks. Restless monkeys jabbered from the dripping trees and on the hill above them a jackal sobbed. Fram waited for her. They embraced in the shadows behind the car before he helped her in.

'I love you,' he breathed as the Chrysler accelerated away.

She reached down and for the first time placed a hand over his crotch.

'It's like a crazy dream,' she said, giving his cock a gentle rub. 'I mean, being wealthy all of a sudden.'

'I don't regard myself as really wealthy,' he said cautiously.

'Rich men rarely do,' she murmured.

They arrived at Peccavi before first light, slamming car doors, arousing dogs, encouraging the clamorous remustering of crows and provoking a cockerel's strangled vaunts. A row of pigeons fluttered below the stable eaves and the intrusive croaking of the pond frogs ceased in trepidation. It was a warm, damp morning that smelled of fresh earth, smouldering cow-cakes and the astringency of closely-confined buffaloes. They did not make their entry in a particularly stealthy manner. They came laughing, talking and switching on lights as they made their way to the great Wadia bed. It was occupied.

The pair on the bed, apparently too exhausted to hear their arrival, did not stir as Fram and Rosie stood over them. They were both naked. Rosie was sickened by the musky aroma of the hot and airless room.

'It's Soli and Kety,' she declared, turning away in disgust.

'Yes,' said Fram glumly, trying mentally to evade the implications of the discovery.

Having asked Rosie to leave the bedroom in the interests of decency, Fram, unable to contemplate the shame of his brother and sister, opened the terrace door and, standing with his back to the bed, wept abuse across the terrace in a trenchant vernacular.

Soli and Kety, awoken and then terrified by the apocalyptic sounds of Fram's weeping litany of curses, dressed and left the room without a murmur. When they had gone, Fram summoned a trembling Theresa and instructed her to change the linen, clear away any debris associated with the recent tenure of the room, open all windows, burn an agarbutty and ask Soli to see him.

It was some time before Soli, uncharacteristically contrite, appeared. Fram could hardly contain his emotion. Addressing him in a halting voice, he ordered his brother to leave Peccavi immediately, undertaking to pay for his support and accommodation elsewhere.

'You're not to come anywhere near this place,' he said sorrowfully. Soli nodded.

Fram told him that the printing press in the stable would be crated and forwarded to any address he provided and hoped that as a matter of honour he would not attempt to communicate with Kety ever again. He would arrange for Jockey to transport him and his possessions anywhere he chose.

'I have no job,' Soli said miserably.

'I'll provide you with two hundred and fifty rupees a month,' Fram declared. 'You should have little difficulty in finding a room in Gowalia Tank for about fifty, so life will not be unendurable.'

'I understand your feelings,' Soli said tearfully, 'but we are hostages to outdated bourgeois values. Kety and I are in love. Furthermore, she is not a full Chutrivala but a Wadia, being Byramji's daughter.'

'Whatever the truth is,' Fram said, 'what you have done is an insult to your mother.'

'One can't insult the dead,' wailed Soli.

Fram slapped his brother across the face.

'Hit me again,' Soli cried unhappily, his face wet with weeping.

'God forgive me,' said Fram, considering his hand in disbelief, for it was the first time he had ever struck his brother.

'May I say goodbye to Kety?' Soli mumbled.

'Do what you want, but go,' Fram said, turning away.

After Soli had left, the sounds of Kety's screams filled Peccavi. Her hoarse cries of despair lasted most of the day and did not abate until nightfall.

Chapter 13

Rosie was waiting for Fram in the drawing room, visibly apprehensive at the noise Kety was making, a pattern of wailing punctuated by desperate screams.

'Perhaps you should see her,' she suggested.

Fram shook his head despondently. He unfastened the silver humidor, extracted a Sumatra and, half turning to Rosie, asked her if she'd like a cigarette.

'It's bad for a saxophone player,' she said flatly, walking around the room to inspect the smoke-darkened portraits, threadbare silk drapes, the clutter of ugly furniture and the faded spines of cloth-covered books on the shelves. There was an assortment of company reports, family histories, a set of twelve volumes on the criminal tribes of Bombay, a treatise on equine diseases, Wellington's campaigns, a binder holding the detailed drawings and description of the Tower of Silence erected by Framjee Cowasjee in 1832 and some wormy, romantic trash from the 1890s.

'Who reads French?' she asked, examining a much thumbed copy of *La Vie d'une femme d'amour* by Michaud.

'The Wadias, my first wife's family, all read French,' he said. He was on the point of adding that Soli also understood the language but hesitated to utter his name.

Rosie turned back to the plans of the Tower of Silence, noting that there were separate beds for men, women and children. But she was fascinated by the steps for the escape of those who were presumed dead but were only in a trance.

'How terrible,' she reflected, imagining the nightmarish awakening as one lay naked on a grille under a burning sun, surrounded by vultures.

'It would be more terrible,' Fram reminded her, 'if the steps were not there.'

Fram rang for Theresa. He instructed her to bring up a cooler of ice and a jug of pressed sweet limes for Rosie. In the meanwhile, he endured a warm whisky topped by soda water, watching his bride with covert desire. He swelled at the sensual warmth of her youth and the carnality of her movements. Then suddenly, desperate to penetrate her, he enquired casually whether she was ready for bed. She shook her head and, lifting the lid of the clavichord, partly eaten by weevils, picked out a few jangled bars of a blues number.

Rosie stared down at the keyboard, willing Kety not to scream again. She could not erase from her memory the vision of a supine woman: the placid mask of a dreaming face, pneumatic, prune-nippled breasts and shaggy black pubes, silvered with cock-dribble; and her man: prone, face averted, cylindrical as a dugong, well-fleshed, hairy, snoring with bestial resonance.

She looked up at Fram, who gave her a heavy-lidded stare of need as he puffed at his cigar. But there was a darkness in the lust that encircled them. Even the room, that she had imagined was full of enchantment and baroque magic when she saw it briefly before the marriage, now looked like a junk shop. The keys of the clavichord were split, the inlaid ivory had been picked away from its spindle legs and its gilt-inscripted provenance was just less than legible.

A barefooted Theresa hurried in with the ice bucket and a jug of sweet-lime juice, setting them nervously on the table. Upstairs, Kety screamed.

The skinny servant girl chilled a long glass and filled it with orange liquid before bearing it to Rosie on an electroplated tray, embossed with the Kutab Minar. The girl looked haunted, squinting warily at Rosie as she placed the tray beside the clavichord. She bent down, exuding a whiff of onions and stale fish from her grubby skirt.

Fram hid petulantly behind *The Times of India*. The smoke from his cigar curled around the paper.

'What are the bathing arrangements here, Frammy?' Rosie asked.

'There are no problems,' he murmured without looking up. He sounded a little disappointed.

The bathroom at Peccavi was mid-Victorian. It was robustly plumbed in burnished copper pipes and decorated with blue and pink Arcadian tiles. The off-white tub, capacious enough for four, and raised a foot from the stone floor on moulded ball-flower feet, was water-ridged at a metre and rust-stained from the plug outlet to an overflow, fashioned as the mouth of a caboshed deer. Above the taps was a fin-de-siècle gas-geyser, its ventilator as imposing as the firestack on a Grasshopper locomotive. In this tub, the Wadias had once floated reflectively, above the sheltering geckos, cockchafers, silver-fish and spiders. Large mirrors, chromium shelves, a rack of hot towels and jars of perfumed salts and oils made it a not unpleasant refuge from the morning's troubles. The boom of the cistern and the humming transit of water through pipes echoed in the cavernous room, masking most of the sounds from outside, although Rosie detected Fram's voice talking to someone. Distant doors opened and closed and when she had been in the tub some time, having twice replenished the bath with steaming water, she was surprised by a knock on the door.

'Rosie?'

It was Fram.

'Yes, Frammy?'

'Are you all right?'

'I'm fine.'

'You've been in there for nearly two hours.'

There was an irritated whine to the concern he expressed. She responded cheerfully.

'I'm relaxing,' she called.

But matters were more complicated than that. Quite simply, Rosie had spent her time in the bathroom considering whether she should consummate her marriage or not. The chilling realisation that the middle-aged husband who was waiting outside was probably not the man she imagined came to her with the dramatic discovery of Soli and Kety in bed. Nor was Peccavi the house she hoped it would be. It was puzzling how a lover who had excited her only hours before during the night drive from 'Cheelchinar' had been transformed before her eyes into a grey, elderly man. It was a terrible thought, in view of what was now expected of her.

She had of course been warned. 'Do you really care for the old lad?' her father had demanded.

'I'm think I'm excited by him,' she admitted.

'Well, I'm sure your mother was never excited by me, so that's a good sign,' Bert Sweetwater decided. Her father paused then added, 'Shush fancies you something rotten you know.'

'He's married,' she sighed.

'You, er, haven't with him, have you?'

'No,' Rosie replied flatly.

Bert Sweetwater smiled.

'He's had your mates, you know. Heloise and little Mother-bunch.'

'I know,' she said in a matter-of-fact voice.

She suspected that the money had meant more to both of them than they would concede to one another.

'Money isn't everything,' her father had reminded her.

'No,' she agreed.

And things had seemed so dreamy at Singleton's Hotel. While the Shalimars played in a shimmering blue light, Fram danced with his dusky harlot, looking as seductive as any man she'd ever seen. Sheeny, raven hair, white teeth and John Barrymore moustache. But the hot, bitch-like itch she'd experienced when they kissed and she felt his hardness against her had inexplicably evaporated. The thought that she could run away from him came to her like a warming inspiration. Not immediately, perhaps. That might be too crass. But at eighteen, there was plenty of time for her to change direction. Towelling her body, she was elevated by these audacities. She cupped her breasts before the mirror and smoothed the satin convexity of her belly appreciatively. Rosie smiled. This is what Chutrivala was paying for. The privilege of getting between her legs; of fucking her. It would be prudent, she decided, to privately regard herself as a whore: a more stimulating proposition than the prospect of being his wife and a less exacting level of emotional commitment.

Peccavi, she reflected, was a mess. The place needed a builder to attend to the hideous cracks and crumbling plaster. Perhaps two additional servants might have to be engaged to clean the house to her satisfaction. And something would have to be done about Theresa, who chewed her fingernails down to unseemly pulp and whose hair looked coarse and unwashed. She would insist on the girl bathing and shampooing under her supervision, dusting herself with scented powder and changing into a freshly

116

laundered uniform every day. It was the very least she would expect.

'Rosie?'

It was Fram again.

'I'm coming,' she promised.

Rosie unlocked the door and went into the bedroom. She resolved to encourage him to suck her off. It was the sort of thing old guys liked doing to young girls, Heloise had told her. And she was quite prepared for unnatural practices as long as there was no pain or disgusting demands. Rosie had often dreamed of guys going down on her while she was asleep. A long procession of figures in the dark shuffling up to her bed. It didn't matter how ugly or old they were for one never saw their faces when they were slurping away. As long as they didn't do anything dreadful with their teeth. Rosie shivered.

But the marriage starts, Heloise warned her, at the moment of penetration. She would only really become Mrs Chutrivala at the moment his organ slid into hers. The sacramental significance of that thought made her shudder.

Rosie was naked below her Japanese willow-pattern dressing-gown. She allowed him to catch a glimpse of her white body in the mirror, while he reclined in an armchair, sipping his whisky.

'I'm thinking of taking up smoking,' she chattered. 'Small, sweet, scented cigarettes that don't make me cough too much.'

Fram glanced at his watch.

'It's twelve thirty,' he announced. 'Shall we have lunch before we retire?'

'I'd better slip on a dress,' she said.

'We're very informal at Peccavi,' he replied as she stepped out of her dressing-gown and walked unclothed past his chair.

He watched her wriggle into a pair of pink French knickers and put on a lace brassiere, holding his breath at the sinuous shimmy of her hips as she then put on a blue silk dress.

'Dilduktha should be here in the morning,' Fram said over a slice of papaya. 'I've arranged for him to take Kety back to Kapoli for a long rest.'

'She's still screaming,' Rosie observed with a frown.

'He'll sedate her if she's too noisy.'

'Have you spoken to Kety?' Rosie asked anxiously.

'Of course.'

She noticed Fram's twitch for the first time. He only did it when extremely tired, having learned that controlled breathing and muscle relaxation avoided the more dramatic spasms.

It had started to drizzle by the time they returned to the bedroom, lightly at first, then quite forcefully, spraying onto the terrazzo floor through the open terrace shutters. The shouts of workmen caught in the rain and the nervous barks of the banjaras drifted across the compound.

'Shall we close the shutters?' she asked, standing by the door to watch the flooded terrace.

'Nobody can see us here,' he replied, divesting himself of his shirt and releasing his trouser belt.

Rosie slipped out of her dress and undid her brassiere, coming to him in her pink knickers, which she invited him to take down. He knelt before her in his nakedness, thinner and narrower than she imagined he would be, burying his face in her straw-coloured pubes, holding her firm, rotund arse in his palms as he lapped the chubby crest of her opening. Heloise was right, she reflected. She lifted a thigh to afford him greater scope. The transaction was awkward and she nearly overbalanced. The rain slanted against the shutters and the wind gusted a spray over the giant conches by the door.

Ignoring the rain, he impatiently drew her down onto the bed. He was, she thought, lithe and boyish in his movements, wriggling quickly between her raised thighs, his mouth smacking the peach-pink folds with noisy kisses, probing her opening with a crazed tongue and sucking her warmth with ardour. She jumped at the unexpected encompassing of her scut, reaching down to restrain his head. Eventually, he mounted her, slithering before he entered her quite easily. He said afterwards that he was pleased that his ingress had not provoked discomfort, swearing that she would be the last virgin he'd ever enjoy. She fretted a little when he repeatedly slipped out but, remembering Heloise's advice, encouraged him with a modest lament at her violation, whimpering persuasively as he quickened his stroke. She deduced an ejaculation when his teeth relinquished her nipple and he shuddered to trembling repose against her shoulder. She sat up and put a towel between her thighs before hobbling to the bathroom.

'What's the matter?' he enquired.

'I think I'm bleeding,' she called, conscious that she was now probably Mrs Chutrivala.

Fram waited in bed as she washed herself, pouring himself a scotch. She did not return for some time. He felt the misty rain over his face. One side of the bed was damp. He sipped his drink and thought of his new wife, planning many departures from the old life.

Rosie came in naked from the bathroom, sliding on the wet floor around the bed and squealing as it splashed her bottom.

'You're mad,' she laughed, 'lying in the rain.'

'I'm celebrating the happiest day in my life,' he said, pulling her onto the bed. She fell along the leeward side of him, reaching out to hold his pensile cock and seeing it closely for the first time.

'It looks as though it's broken,' she concluded critically.

'That's the way mine is,' Fram murmured, putting his arm around her and kissing her tenderly on the cheek.

'Did you bleed much?' he asked solicitously.

She stared at him thoughtfully and shook her head.

'Just a symbolic smear,' she reflected.

Chapter 14

Bert Sweetwater had decided to use his twenty-five thousand rupees to return to his native Liverpool. He told Rosie that he had long been excited by the idea of starting a fish and chip business. In the meantime, he spent his days knocking around with Shushtary and other friends, shooting, attending race-meetings and playing poker until the small hours.

Shushtary and he called at Peccavi whenever they needed to use the ice-factory freezer for a large carcass, required a spare gun, felt like a drinking-session or wanted to see Rosie. Fram deplored the laconic Iranian's tactility with his wife, unpersuaded by his claims of avuncular dispensations. When at Peccavi, he hardly took his eyes or hands off the girl and, despite the disclosure that he'd produced all her publicity stills for the Shalimars free of charge, Fram had serious reservations about the man's decent intentions. Besides, he could never efface the memory of his wife pissing in the red Duesenberg with Shushtary, still at the wheel, listening inevitably to the shameful plash of her water above what had been widely advertised as an extremely quiet engine. And although Bert Sweetwater thought the story highly diverting, Fram was humiliated by its tiresome telling. Particularly the dubious rider that the Iranian would never replace the carpet as Rosie's uric stain was, for him, a sentimental souvenir.

'But it's not true, Frammy,' Rosie protested. 'Shush took me to a friend's house.'

'Then why does your father insult us with that vulgar story?'

'It's a sort of joke,' she explained.

'How can any father joke about his daughter passing water in a stranger's car? Is nothing sacred?'

Rosie shrugged.

'Not where Daddy is concerned.'

'Has that bastard ever photographed you in the nude?' Fram demanded.

'A couple of times,' Rosie admitted. 'Once, when I was thirteen. But it was terribly discreet. You know, all Chinese lanterns, coolie hats and shadows. Daddy was present. Shush won an international contest with his study of me as a Manchu concubine.'

'And the other time?' Fram asked in a stifled voice.

She told him that Shush had taken a set for Amazing Films just before her marriage. The prints were, she assured Fram, for Jimmy's eyes only. This was little comfort to Fram, for he distrusted the Raja of Pinjrapore as much as he did Shushtary.

'Why do you allow him to maul you?' Fram enquired.

'He's an old man,' she laughed. 'Almost fifty.'

'I'm nearly that,' Fram shouted.

'If you're going to behave in that ridiculous manner, I'm not going to tell you my news.'

Fram sulked for twenty minutes or so before he approached Rosie again, asking her what she had meant to tell him.

'Jimmy has offered me a dancing part in *Pylee Pyari*.'

'Are you mad?' he screamed. 'You're my wife. The film business is out of bounds for respectable, married women.'

Rosie gave him an owlish look, advising him that she hadn't made up her mind, as the standard of dancing expected might be beyond her, but Friski felt that with additional lessons she might be ready for the auditions in six months.

'Why should you take lessons when I don't intend to allow you to audition for that shit Pinjrapore?'

Rosie smiled at his rage. She reminded herself cheerfully that she was nothing more than his whore. The thought gave her strength.

'What's so funny?' he asked irritably.

'I see no harm in taking dancing lessons, whatever you may think,' she declared without rancour.

She left him alone in the drawing room. Her unconcern disturbed him. Even Banoo had never been so detached on issues that were pivotal to their harmony. He wished that she was less even-tempered. Nothing alarmed him more than serenity at the wrong time. Fram started to tremble. He had a premonition that something terrible was about to damage his new-found happiness. Then, suddenly, he started at an unexpected sound. Rosie was playing 'Am I Blue?' on her trumpet. And however much he tried, he could not restrain his foolish tears.

Kety had returned to Peccavi. Although she'd been away for only two months, her hair was much greyer and her cataracts had now so impaired her vision that she was apprehensive about crossing the compound to feed the buffaloes without Theresa. And although Soli hadn't been near the house since the row with Fram, she never mentioned his name. The screaming spirit that had her consigned to Dilduktha's clinic had been exorcised.

Bert Sweetwater, determined to bag a big tiger before he left the country, had organised a final shoot with eight guns. He told Rosie and Fram that they needed another car.

'Take the Chrysler,' urged Fram.

And brushing aside expressions of Sweetwater's gratitude, he insisted on providing Jockey as well. Two express rifles and a Purdey from Byramji's collection were borrowed, and Fram lent Sweetwater a pair of binoculars and a rope ladder for the machan. Shushtary photographed Fram arm-in-arm with Rosie, proceeding to take several dozen of Rosie by herself.

'She's a wonderful model, Mr Chutrivala,' Shushtary declared, circling around her as he clicked.

Fram beamed. Things were at last working out. The homecoming of his sister had made him happier than he imagined it would. His lovemaking with Rosie had so improved that they thought little of doing it two or three times a night and at least once in the afternoon after lunch. What is more, she appeared to enjoy his attentions. Even the imminence of Bert Sweetwater's departure for England gave him pleasure, for it was Sweetwater who brought along his Iranian friend to haunt him. An agreement had been reached whereby Rosie was allowed dancing lessons with Friski on the solemn undertaking that any decision about working in films would rest with Fram. However, Rosie, who had put on weight since her marriage, found the dance training extremely difficult. When she collapsed during the third session, a local doctor was summoned.

'I'm pleased to inform you, Mr Chutrivala,' he said, 'that your wife is pregnant.'

*

It was, Fram felt, as though God had intervened on his behalf. He could not stop laughing with crazy joy, writing immediately to Meroo in Lahore and Soli in Gowalia Tank with the wonderful news.

'I have forgiven Soli,' Fram shouted, pouring himself a twenty-five-year-old fine champagne.

'You're not going to allow them to live together at Peccavi, are you?' Rosie asked.

'Separate rooms of course,' Fram said, lifting his glass. 'Life is too short for unhappiness.'

He embraced her in his free arm, drawing her to him and smothering her face with kisses. But Rosie escaped to another room. Fram cornered her as she leaned against a window. He approached her noisily.

'Perhaps,' he said, 'we have made a son.'

'Oh Frammy,' she sobbed, holding her face in her hands, 'I'm so frightened.'

Bhonsle's statue of Byramji was a disappointment. Although he had resculpted the upper body, Fram felt it looked like the effigy of a deformed man.

'He looks like a hunchback,' Rosie decided, walking around Bhonsle's studio at Dhobi Talao.

'How can you make such a magnificent specimen of a human being look so grotesque?' Fram demanded angrily.

Bhonsle showed him the original photographs and his detailed measurements, arguing that there was a problem with the photographs.

'That lump on his back is the effect of his coat,' Fram said.

'I'm not clairvoyant to know these things,' Bhonsle replied wearily.

They compromised on a bust and a reshaping of the back to eliminate the unwanted protrusion. Fram considered that Byramji's bust mounted on a pedestal could be located in his office at the ice factory.

'It almost looks like him,' he assured Rosie as they took a taxi to Singleton's Hotel, where they had planned to lunch.

They were surprised to see Sweetwater and Shushtary in the

bar. The look on Sweetwater's face informed Fram that something unfortunate had occurred.

'It's the chauffeur,' he said to Fram quietly.

'Jockey?' Fram asked. 'My Jockey?'

Sweetwater explained that Jockey had been sent to Yeotmal for food and was returning through the jungle with a tiffin-carrier when the tigress got him.

'But he was a chauffeur, not a food-carrier,' Fram cried in outrage. 'An old man and a family friend.'

'It was a bloody accident, old son,' Sweetwater declared sourly.

Fram told Rosie that he didn't feel like lunch. He was returning to Peccavi to make arrangements for Jockey's funeral.

'Hey, just a minute, mate,' said Sweetwater. 'We've done the decent thing, burying the bits and bobs of him we could find.'

'He has to be cremated,' Fram insisted. 'Disinterred, brought to Bombay and cremated.'

'There's no need to get sodding regimental about it,' Sweetwater protested. 'The poor bugger's dead and no amount of frigging around is going to have him back on muster, mate.'

But Fram nodded to Rosie and indicated that he was ready to leave. She looked at her father, shrugged, then followed her husband through the door.

Five months after Jockey had been seen off by a tigress near Yeotmal and Fram had arranged the transfer of his remains for an appropriate Hindu cremation in Bombay, Shushtary turned up at Peccavi with a black envelope. It contained twenty exposures of Jockey's remains, taken as he was found near a thorn bush in a dry nullah.

'I know you have a taste for my more macabre work,' he warned Rosie grimly, 'but give yourself at least a year before you even look at these.'

Fram supported the accursed Shushtary's plea.

'Remember your condition,' he said. 'We can do without shocks in the sixth month. Another few days and you will be carrying a child capable of survival. Don't take risks, my dove.'

But Rosie unsealed the envelope and examined the photographs immediately. She looked up at the tall Iranian in horror.

'He's been eaten,' she declared, demonstrating her disgust with a shudder.

'Partly,' Shushtary mumbled with a mixture of compassion and drollery. 'Jockey was her ninth victim. There was nothing we could do.'

To Fram's annoyance, Shushtary slipped a comforting arm around Rosie's well-padded shoulder, shocking him with the familiarity of his supportive squeeze. Her eyes filled with tears as she turned over the prints again and again. When she started on the process for the tenth time, Shushtary placed his hand over hers.

'No more,' he insisted, kissing her lightly on the right temple.

Rosie looked at Fram uncertainly, then, shaking herself free, moved a pace away from Shushtary who remained uneasily where she had left him, scratching an eyebrow self-consciously with a little finger and watching her tenderly.

'Allow my wife to weep in peace,' Fram declared, imagining a bulge above Shushtary's crotch.

Fram blamed the Leica definition, reflecting that it would have been aesthetically more appropriate if Shushtary had contrived a fuzzier treatment for such a terrible subject.

'You can't help being a gifted photographer, Shush,' Rosie sniffed, going through them once again.

'Why,' shouted Fram at Shushtary, 'did you provide my wife with the means after you'd expressed such hypocritical reservations about the ends? Pick up your gruesome photos and buzz off.'

'Oh Frammy,' Rosie protested. 'Shush is a good friend.'

Shushtary gazed through Fram ruminatively as though he were no more significant than a lace curtain. Rosie's eyes narrowed in curiosity as she turned to the photographer.

'Exactly how much of Jockey did this tigress consume?' she asked.

Shushtary took out a silver cigarette case and, taking one, lit it with an extravagant flare.

'His left hand, part of the same forearm, most of his stomach, buttocks and . . .'

He paused and Rosie regarded him with raised eyebrows.

'And?'

'You know,' he murmured in a hushed voice.

The next day Shushtary phoned Rosie and expressed his love for her. His admission was not unexpected but she pointed out that an affair would at present be clumsily inconvenient, for not only were they both married but she was grotesque with child.

The ancient Persian sages, he assured, had recommended at least nine positions to deal with a swollen belly. 'Besides, it is inconceivable that you love Chutrivala.'

She confessed that what had started as a financial arrangement had prospered somewhat and she had, by submitting herself to her husband three times a day, begun to take more seriously the possibility of comparative fidelity.

'You must not be trapped in a monogamous cul-de-sac before you try my cock,' he pleaded, sounding, she thought, sadly sincere.

Although she felt there was a grandeur and moral dimension to her orgasms, Rosie said that she was unconvinced about her need for extra marital assistance.

'I love you,' he groaned.

'It seems,' she sighed, 'that all you want to do is to make use of my sweet young pussy.'

'Don't make fun of me, you mad bitch,' he cursed.

Rosie tittered and confided that she was taking instruction from Father Garibaldi from St Mary's, a learned but cheerful member of the Society of Jesus who was an acknowledged expert on the mystery of the spurt, a metaphor for the spiritual leap in the dark that led to life and truth.

After he'd rung off, she phoned Heloise to whom she confided Shushtary's profession of love.

'It's the wrong time for an affair,' Heloise advised. 'Pregnancy imposes severe limitations on the female body.'

'Life is too horrible for words,' Rosie sighed.

'Do you love Fram?' Heloise enquired.

'I think I almost do,' Rosie admitted, adding, 'He's so wonderfully dependable. Like an old dog.' The thought made her inexplicably tearful.

'How absolutely shitty,' Heloise reflected. 'There's nothing more depressing than virtue in a man.'

The following day, Shushtary rang again, inviting her to lunch at the Taj, pointing out that he retained a suite in the hotel where they could eat without being seen.

'I'll have to ask Fram,' she decided.

'Your husband hates me,' Shushtary complained. 'I suspect he's jealous of me. Smallcocks usually are.'

There was a pause as Rosie considered Shushtary's accusation.

'He's not small enough for slanders of that sort, Shush,' she purred.

'OK, come on. How big? How big? I've got ten inches here that says he's nothing.'

'He's not a horse either, Shush,' Rosie murmured defensively.

'Let's have lunch together tomorrow, please,' Shushtary pleaded.

'I don't think I could be duplicitous right now,' she decided.

Fram had made known his views on Shushtary in unusually forceful terms after his call with the photographs of Jockey's mutilation.

'I care little for that bastard's artistic ability,' he informed Rosie. 'Take it from me, he only has one objective.'

She gave her husband a bored look, as she poised an unpeeled plantain before her mouth.

'You know so much about everything, don't you?' she sneered.

Fram twitched. Even during their happiest spells, they had always disagreed about Shushtary.

'About this guy,' he said, wagging a finger, 'I know everything.'

She bit into the plantain, staring owlishly. Fram laughed bitterly.

'It's simple. He wants to get between your thighs.'

Rosie screwed up her face in disgust, mocking him with ostentatious mastication. It was how she used to confront her father's reproofs when a little girl.

'I hate him,' Fram assured her.

After a miserable silence, he enquired whether the baby had kicked much that day.

'Not much,' she muttered. 'He appears to be a lazy little bugger.'

When Shushtary phoned again at his usual time, she advised him that it would be imprudent for their friendship to continue unless he accepted its platonic basis. He informed her very emotionally that she was the most important person in the world for him and he would prefer to die than not share a private lunch with her at the Taj. The remark made her laugh. Shushtary, encouraged by her response, whispered once again that he loved her.

'What about your wife?' Rosie asked, 'and your six children?'

'My family,' Shushtary reminded her, 'are in Kerman and there is little prospect that I will ever see my wife again.'

'But she's still your wife, Shush.'

'In recent years,' he complained, 'she's become withered and skinny. Her teeth are black stumps, breasts hardly more substantial than bootlaces, and, in bed, she feels as coarse as a pouch of dried tobacco. My marriage, alas, is at an end.'

The prospect of being unloved in old age had always filled Rosie with horror. Now, the thought of an atrophied Mrs Shushtary made her shiver. Charitably, she planned an anonymous gift parcel of fattening halvas, perfumes, dentifrice, a bust-pump, body-rubs, unguents, oils and vaginal grease-cartridges. She made Shushtary promise to provide her with his wife's address in Iran, assuring him that his wife would imagine that he was the sender. The request perplexed him.

'Why,' he asked anxiously, 'do you want to involve yourself with that crow?'

'Because all women are sisters,' Rosie declared, 'and one day I too might be discarded because some perfidious man considers that I'm insufficiently juicy for his depraved needs.'

'I don't care whether you're juicy or not,' he said.

'Serves you right if you discover that I'm just rusty razor blades.'

'I'lll take a chance,' he laughed.

At that moment, she was surprised by Fram's entry into the room. He hovered around, pretending to search for something in the bureau.

'Call me some other time, Heloise,' Rosie dissembled, glaring at Fram.

'I love you,' Shushtary reminded her before replacing the receiver.

'That was Heloise,' Rosie explained, passing blithely through the door.

During the same afternoon, Shushtary called again. 'This is Heloise,' he joked, adding tenderly, 'You lied for me.'

'I lied for both of us.'

'Lunch tomorrow,' he declared.

'Not tomorrow,' she replied.

'The day after,' he urged.

'Impossible,' she sighed.

'The day after that,' he insisted.

'That's Wednesday,' she reflected, doodling skittishly in her diary.

'It's settled then,' he hissed.

'Wednesday?'

'Why not?' he demanded in a voice that asked and answered many questions.

For two nights Rosie's sleep was disturbed by strange dreams. She imagined that she was being taken like a beast by a partner whom she knew by the movement of his hairy, lean body over her back. The abnormal flooding these reveries induced alarmed her. It was as though a stream had been unblocked somewhere in her core. She rose, fearful for the child within her, washed, and returned shivering to bed. But no sooner had she dozed off than the secretions started again. She roused Fram, drawing him towards her.

'What's the matter?' he gasped, taking her.

'I don't know,' she panted.

After they had done it, he confided that Banoo was particularly lascivious near her time.

'Who?' she mumbled sleepily.

'My first wife,' he said.

Rosie was pleasantly resolute with Shushtary when they went up in the lift. She reminded him that her presence was largely in recognition of their long-standing friendship and patted her belly to emphasise her commitment to the family ideal. Comforted by his assurance that her visit would involve nothing more profound than light-hearted chatter, lunch and a few photographs, she rewarded him with the offer of her cheek, which he furnished with a modest brush of his lips.

His suite overlooked the Arabian Sea. The room was filled with flowers and the overpowering fragrace of jasmine. A table had already been laid for lunch. A three-funelled white liner steamed across the almost motionless green water, past the Gateway of India on the left, towards Ballard Pier. Shushtary handed her a pair of binoculars, which she trained on the passing ship.

'It's a Lloyd Triestino,' he said. '*La Simpatica.*'

'I can see faces quite clearly,' Rosie said. 'Moustaches, spectacles, even smiles.' She paused. 'Why do the passage of great liners make me restless?'

'Perhaps they represent the wish to escape from your life,' he suggested.

'I always imagine them to be filled with happy people.'

'I hope they're as happy as I am,' he breathed, stepping back to click several times.

'I'd like to do a profile,' he suggested, 'against the window. Down to your waist.'

'What waist?' she pouted. 'And my breasts are obscenities. Too ugly for words.'

'Nonsense,' he protested, stepping forward and kissing her cleavage before she could move.

'Shush,' she cried, waving him away, 'you promised.'

He suggested that they would have to consider the progress of her career after the baby. Jimmy was interested in a few private exposures. He talked as he focussed, changed lenses and moved around her. She was surprised to hear that Amazing Films might consider using her in a non-dancing part. He informed her that the series he'd taken of her in the nude had persuaded Jimmy of her general potential.

'Doesn't she know I'm pregnant?' she asked.

Shushtary nodded.

'Pregnancy had its own beauty, of course,' he said, capturing her surprise as she half-turned towards him.

'I'm not happy,' she said, frowning.

'Upper body only, if that's the way you feel,' he smiled.

'I'll think about it,' she promised.

Lunch was a simple affair of gazpacho, a crumbed black pomfret with orange Curaçao sauce, sautéed potatoes and spinach. It was followed by a Neapolitan ice cream on Danish pastry.

She was impressed by the elegance of the room, with its Rajput murals and onyx ornaments. He informed her that it was rented by the Raja of Pinjrapore who allowed him to use it for international clients and joint ventures.

'Does he know you're entertaining me?' Rosie asked.

'Of course,' Shushtary smiled. 'Jimmy is well informed about most things.'

She prepared herself in the bathroom, removing her blouse and brassiere before sitting on the bed. He came in and regarded her for a while without speaking, then adjusted a light and posed her arms lightly with his fingers.

'You're very tense,' he murmured, advising her to take her shoes off.

She looked down at her swollen belly unhappily.

'Its a mistake,' she decided, partly occulting herself with a cushion.

Shushtary opened a case and took out a glass ampoule that he snapped and poured on a handkerchief.

'What's that?' she asked, catching a whiff of its acrid smell.

'Something harmless to relax you,' he soothed, passing it over her face.

She sensed that she was falling through space, open-eyed yet not really apprehending his movements around her. It was not unpleasant, the imagined touching and turning, her levitations and slow descents. And when she drifted back through a dark tunnel, she was surprised by the brightness of the room but comforted by the familiar sounds of the Leica.

Shushtary gave her a glass of cold water.

'You can dress now,' he said quietly.

The suspicion that she'd been violated in some way began to distress her. She asked him what had occurred as they walked back towards the lift.

'I took a few photographs,' he said, stroking her arm lightly.

She felt oppressed by the shame of having been used and her inability to define the nature of the offence against her.

'I don't want any explanations, Shush,' she said sadly, shaking her head.

He shrugged and assured her that she would think differently in a little while.

'You're a very coiled up piece of business,' he sighed.

Declining his offer of a lift, she left him in the hotel foyer and made her way into the bright sunlight, taking a taxi back to Peccavi.

'Where have you been?' Fram asked, when he saw her. 'You look so white.'

131

'I went to lunch with Heloise,' she replied, rushing past him to the bathroom. Although nauseous, she found it difficult to get sick.

Thereafter, she never answered the phone. When Kety lifted the receiver instead, she grew accustomed to the silence at the other end and subsequent disconnection. Rosie did, however, hear from Heloise who told her how unhappy she'd made Shush, reminding her of his importance if she ever intended a film career.

'He's very close to the Raja of Pinjrapore. What more could a girl want?'

Rosie found herself crying.

'I'm fatally pregnant,' she sobbed. 'I really don't want to discuss Shush or my career until I've liberated myself of this lump.'

Chapter 15

When Rosie Chutrivala first examined her crinkled and crooked Minocher Byramji, later more familiarly known as Minoo, also derisively referred to as Turtleback, Snailpot, Drumbo and Oont, she screamed. Her distress could be heared as far as Opera House to the east and Chowpatty Beach to the west of Silla Batliboi's Maternity Home on French Bridge. Judging by the notices posted throughout the clinic like 'Loud Noises Forbidden', 'Whisperers Tolerated', 'Subdued Voices Much Appreciated' and 'Absolute Silence Is Our Ideal', commotions of any sort were clearly unpopular with the management. Certainly, Dr Batliboi, disturbed as she supervised the snipping of an extremely important umbilical cord (a niece of the Fakir of Ipi no less), was inclined to be irritated by histrionic displays of temperament. Acknowledged to be a gynaecological genius, Silla Batliboi, a lady familiar with the orifices of the wealthiest and most celebrated women in the sub-continent, expected mothers from the more fortunate classes to behave themselves. Indeed, at the time of Minoo's arrival, Bombay's sweetheart of the silver screen, Leela Kotnis (remember *Theri Ma ki Chabook, Shurum* and *Bookh*?), was spreadeagled in the grunting process of delivery; Shanti, the wife of the cotton croreputty, Tulsi Tatjee, was fretting in the Labour Room, while Sarojini Biswas, a best-selling novelist, had just produced her first-born, a jumbo-sized fourteen-pound girl, a birth that had involved blood transfusions, intravenous drips, abdominal compression, thirty-seven stitches and the threat of an action for negligence. It had been an unusually stressful day. So the waddling transit through the wards of a scowling Silla Batliboi in her surgical cap and gown in the direction of Mrs Chutrivala's excessive noise was not surprising. And if the drawing back of the counterpane to deliver a resonant thwack across the right cheek of her hysterical patient's peach-coloured arse shocked Fram as much as it did his wife, it almost did the trick. The crazy screeching subsided into shuddering sighs that were barely audible.

'There was no need to strike her,' protested Fram quietly.

He wiped the snot from Rosie's upper lip with his maroon silk handkerchief.

'It's the accepted therapy,' boomed Dr Batliboi, wagging a menacing hand before her.

Fram frowned at the doctor. He had been warned against excitement by Dilduktha, who hinted that he was the sort of man who could expect a cardiac arrest. He had hoped that the birth of a son in his forty-fifth year would be an occasion for joy. Instead, it had been an afternoon of misery. A disappointed Rosie. And now violence. He took a deep breath, staying Silla Batliboi's fleshy arm with his trembling palm. It was a modest restraint for he suspected that Rosie had not been entirely blameless. He explained that his wife, being a musician, had an artistic temperament.

'Have you heard of the Shalimar Swing Sextet?'

Silla Batliboi shook her head.

'They have helped to raise money,' Fram said, 'for a range of disaster charities. Famines, earthquakes, floods and communal violence. Even smallpox epidemics. Mrs Chutrivala used to play the trumpet with them before her marriage. She was a Rosie Sweetwater in those days.'

Fram was inclined to boast about Rosie's musical past. He informed Dr Batliboi that the Shalimars had made a record on which his wife played two solos, 'Marcheta' with a mute on one side and 'Yes, We Have No Bananas', without one, on the other. Dr Batliboi gave him a glazed look. It was clear that she was not musical.

'Furthermore,' Fram said, 'she's still in a state of shock. Our little Minoo was hardly at his best when presented to her, being slippery, rather gamey and flecked with the detritus of parturition. But mark my words, all will be sunshine, once he has been washed, powdered, dressed in his blue nightshirt and returned to his mama's nipple.'

Dr Batliboi warned them that she had other patients to consider and requested Rosie to dispense with puerile displays of self-indulgence. She told then that she tended to believe in the law of compensation.

'Who knows? The slight infirmity of the child's body could be balanced by intellectual prodigy.'

'He has a very large head,' Fram conceded gloomily.

Dr Batliboi nodded her approval.

'We may have another Thomas Edison on our hands,' she said, 'or even a Jamsetjee Jeejeebhoy. Physically speaking, the lad's about ninety per cent there. Fourteen annas in the rupee isn't a disaster, you know.'

Rosie sniffed unhappily.

'If he's only fourteen annas in the rupee,' she brooded, 'it means that we've been short-changed.'

It was the complaint of a young woman who expected perfection. Fram squeezed her hand.

'Ninety per cent,' he declared brightly, 'is far better than fourteen annas in the rupee. It's very nearly fourteen annas, five pies.' He'd always been good at instant decimal conversion.

'That's the spirit. Think positively,' urged Silla Batliboi, wagging an admonitory finger. 'Remember, small fish are often sweet.'

Fram puzzled for a moment on the physician's piscatorial metaphor, but Rosie looked troubled.

'Why is she talking about fish?' she asked.

'It's a saying,' Fram murmured uncertainly. 'I suspect it's Parsee, our community being great fish-eaters.'

He attempted to cheer Rosie with a jaunty smile but, despite his advertised optimism, the advent of Minocher Byramji was not regarded as an auspicious event by his young mother. Soli and Kety arrived with flowers and fruit, Soli barefoot with a shaven head and Kety, in dark glasses, tapping an ashplant before her. She told them that, although she was not yet blind, it was as well to prepare for the inevitable, devoting two hours a day to the practice of Braille.

'You have cataracts,' Fram declared impatiently, 'a twenty-minute job, once they're ripe.'

She gave him a sceptical look and predicted the worst with a tired smile.

'I'll require a large, trained dog, when I lose my sight,' she reflected.

Soli, who had brought his nephew a silver hammer and sickle pendant on a necklace, pointed to the infant's concert-pianist fingers, classical nose, sensitive lips, curly black hair, soot-black eyes and plump genitals. But all Rosie could settle her restless mind upon was his curved spine.

Fram had ordered a tray of cream-cakes and Viennese pastries from Felice Carnaglia, four dozen red roses, a presentation bottle of Huschkey's Eau de Cologne, a pack of Macropolo's 'Mignon', the tiny Turkish cigarettes Rosie had taken to smoking, and a magnum of Pol Roger (1924). They lay unconsidered on the table beside her. And after Soli had led Kety away, but not before Fram had reproached him for wandering about without his shoes, Rosie allowed herself to weep again. She stared at the white ceiling fan, subdued by the electric humming of its electric motor, and asked him once more whether he was certain their infant hadn't been appropriated and replaced by an unwanted hunchback. She had heard that such things were not uncommon in the more expensive nursing homes. He smoothed her sheets solicitously, conscious that she had been bruised by recent events. The Chutrivalas, he reflected, unlike the Sweetwaters, had a tradition of tribulation.

'I was present when he slid out,' he confirmed quietly, bending over to peck her damp forehead.

Rosie bit her lip in anguish, and stared hopelessly at her husband. He reminded her that she had given him what he had always wanted, lightly caressing her hair. She asked him for a cigarette. He tapped out a Mignon and lit it for her. Rosie struggled a handsbreadth higher against the pillow, looking glumly through the green venetian shutters at the shiny Delahayes in Jammy Jasdan's Auto Bazaar, pouting a plume of smoke through the broom of dehydrated marigolds fanning out of the tall Moradabad brass vase on her bedside trolley.

I have been punished for my sins, she ruminated miserably, remembering a conversation with Father Garibaldi. She meditated on the shameful exposure of her body to Shushtary and the years of masturbation that had started at boarding-school, continuing until just before her marriage. Garibaldi had assured her that although the amount and the regularity of the self-abuse was excessive, it was a lesser offence than fornication; but she neglected to confess what had finally happened to the bananas.

136

'It is clear,' Heloise contended, 'that there was an element of charity in employing the fruit debased by your vagina for the Holy Mother's and Sisters' fritters.'

'But you must recall,' Rosie reminded her, 'that my puerile intention was malicious, anti-clerical and an intended blasphemy.'

'Yet the Holy Mother and Holy Sisters were not damaged by the act,' Heloise observed. 'Indeed, their ignorance as to how the bananas were employed preserved them from the humiliation of your overt contempt.'

'It is my sin,' Rosie admitted to her friend.

'Confess it,' urged Heloise.

'I can't,' said Rosie, 'and that is the greater impiety.'

'Why don't you take a lover, like any other self-respecting convent girl?' Heloise had asked her.

But Rosie had always been terrified of springing seed, remembering how their friend Motherbunch had fallen at the first fence. Her penetrator was a soldier in the 1st Somersets, a clever inside forward called Curly Arthur. They had done it at twilight under the grandstand at the Cooperage while Rosie kept cave. It was all over in three minutes, the incautious Motherbunch lifting her skirt and arching herself over a metal stanchion as Curly Arthur invaded her through the side of her knickers. After she had fallen Curly Arthur gave her a wide berth, claiming piously that as Motherbunch hadn't been a virgin, there was no certainty that he was the guilty ejaculator.

'Why didn't you tell him that you'd trained on cucumbers?' Rosie asked.

Motherbunch shook her head. 'It's not the sort of admission a girl can make to a man. Blood and cries of anguish are all the buggers want.'

Curly Arthur compounded his villainy with unchivalrous conduct, spreading the slander throughout the battalion that Motherbunch was as slack as a nigger-minstrel's mouth. Heloise arranged for Shush to pay for the termination.

'In general,' Shush warned the girls, 'Tommies can never be trusted.'

It was Friski's opinion that girls who had lost their virginity should first marry rich, old guys who were infinitely more grateful for the benediction of nubile bodies than picky young batchelors. For, once married, it was far easier to find eligible

137

lovers. Nobody expected to deflower a married woman, widow or divorcee.

'But who wants shitty old guys?' Rosie had complained to Heloise not long before Fram gawped at her as she played 'Am I Blue?'. It all seemed a million years ago.

The next day cards arrived from Friski Dalal, Dilduktha, Jerry Patcheco, the Sergeant's Mess of the King's Regiment stationed at Jubbalpore, Heloise and the Raja of Pinjrapore. Then, at nine in the morning, long before visiting hours, she saw Shushtary's red Duesenberg parked on French Bridge. He came through the door with a bouquet of carnations and a box of Turkish Delight.

'Where's the little lad?' he demanded, ordering a nurse to bring Minoo in, explaining that Silla Batliboi was an old friend of his.

'Have you heard about my son?' Rosie asked, moist-eyed.

Shushtary shook his head before bending over her to kiss her lightly on the mouth. When the nurse returned and laid Minoo on the cot beside Rosie, he greeted the infant with a gentle prod of his forefinger.

'What beautiful eyes,' he exulted.

'But his back,' Rosie said, 'look at his back.'

'It's a photographer's back,' Shushtary declared brightly. 'In his last incarnation he probably spent too long in the darkroom stooping over the pyrogallol.'

He resolved to give the boy a Leica on his first birthday and start him off in life with a fully equipped studio.

'Why can't you be serious?' Rosie demanded.

'May I kiss you again?' he asked.

'No,' she snapped, averting her face.

It was at that moment that Fram came in with more flowers. Fram regarded Shushtary with a frown. Shushtary smiled.

'Hello, Chutrivala,' he said. 'I've just promised Rosie that I'll train little Minoo to be a photographer.'

Fram nodded courteously.

'I had in mind more serious pursuits for my boy,' he said stiffly. 'Like medicine or the law.'

'There's nothing like vaunting ambition,' Shushtary observed cheerfully, taking Rosie's hand to shake formally before he departed.

'What was that bastard doing here?' fretted Fram.

'He means well,' she sighed, hoping that the Raja of Pinjrapore might drop in.

But a day before she was discharged, a card arrived from Amazing Films with a scribbled message that, had he not been in Bahrain, he would have called in to see her. It was signed 'Jimmy'. Rosie tucked it in her handbag, taking it out to read several times. It was something she kept to herself. Not even Heloise was told, although she did ask her friend whether she'd ever gone with Jimmy.

'I don't really think he's all that interested in girls, darling,' Heloise murmured, tickling Minoo.

Nothing more was said, but Rosie knew in her bones that Heloise was being slightly malicious.

Chapter 16

When Rosie returned to Peccavi with Minoo, an ayah was engaged to take care of the child. She had agreed with Fram that a Catholic girl would be preferable, they being easier to discipline than Hindus. 'Speaking as somebody who was educated in that faith,' Rosie said, 'there is nothing like the concept of eternal damnation to concentrate a timorous girl's mind.'

Fram agreed. 'Look at our Theresa and Cessara,' he said. 'The prospect of regular confession and the fear of hellfire has terrorised them into a state of nervous obedience. What more can one desire in a domestic servant?'

Rosie called on Father Garibaldi and informed him of their need. The swarthy Italian, a short, powerful man with blue jowls, bushy eyebrows, black curly hair and fingers like sausages, was delighted to be of assistance, shaking Rosie's hand and inviting her to settle her bottom upon his most comfortable chair. He rarely stopped smiling. It was as though, being close to the heavenly corridors of power, he was in on the big joke. Garibaldi had been diligently engaged in trying to restore Rosie to the faith of her father, viewing her lapse as a pleasant, vocational challenge. He had felt particularly privileged at having been able to debate masturbation with such a beautiful young woman and enlightened by her disclosure that there was more to bananas than he once foolishly imagined. Indeed, he had used the information in the confessional, nudging his more reticent female communicants with enquiries on whether they had ever entertained themselves with the more obviously phallic vegetables. Garibaldi was diverted with replies that admitted defilement with objects that ranged from muddy rugby boots to the Book of Common Prayer.

'What we require, Father, is a virtuous person, not dramatically prepossessing or sensual in demeanour. Humility, obedience, cleanliness and industry is the least we would expect at Peccavi.'

He rested a palm on Rosie's shoulder and pointed through the window to a girl in blue by the steps.

'Her name is Angelica,' he said. 'She could be just the sort of person you need.'

Rosie was impressed by the girl's snub nose, closely set eyes and protruding teeth but had some reservations about her pointed breasts and long, well-shaped legs. Father Garibaldi read her thoughts instantly.

'Don't worry about her, my dear,' he declared. 'She's as pure as my own daughter.' He grinned at Rosie's consternation.

'It's a joke,' he assured her with a giggle.

And so Angelica was called into Father Garibaldi's office, introduced to Rosie Chutrivala and whisked up the road to Peccavi in the Chrysler, seated beside Chakramkhan the new chauffeur. The priest handed Rosie a number of pamphlets, gifting her a cheap, black rosary and providing a tin crucifix for Minoo.

'May I call on you during the next month or so?' he murmured, reaching through the rear window for Rosie's hand, which he held and shook for some time. She received the ardour he expressed in this prolonged farewell with gratitude. It seemed so vibrantly chaste. Garibaldi's subtle pressures were more impulses then squeezes, a providence she hoped might shepherd her through the darkness of her present unhappiness.

Minoo was a quick and precocious child, delighting his father and Aunt Kety, even if his progress did not appear to enthuse Rosie overmuch. Garibaldi arrived on his bicycle once a week, engaging in general conversation for half an hour or so before leaving. He devoted these visits to talking to Fram about the ice business and to Rosie about jazz. He induced her to blow a few rasps on her trumpet and borrowed her Jelly Roll Morton records. He gave advice about the restoration of the Peccavi murals, the control of rodents, the elimination of mosquitoes and recipes for pork marinades and vindaloos. Occasionally, he sold them raffle tickets, asked them to sponsor a leper in a project he directed and tinkled with the Chrysler if there was a mechanical problem. Religion was never discussed. Minoo was thrown in the air, Angelica patted on the head and Rosie shown how to dance the fandango. He listened with wide-eyed interest at Rosie's ambition to become a film star and bought Fram Cuban cigars for New Year. The smiling Garibaldi became, for both of them, a much valued friend.

Shushtary also called regularly to see Rosie and Minoo, his two Leicas dangling from his neck, bearing flowers, halva, bolts of silk and silver jewellery. Although he was at the time keeping Motherbunch, having set her up in a flat in Apollo Bunder, his pursuit of Rosie was tediously obvious to Fram. He missed, of course, the knowing winks and Shushtary's whispered protestations of love but he smelled the Iranian's lust in the air, despite Rosie's reminders that Motherbunch was the girl with whom Shush was living. But the fact that Motherbunch, under the name Bhabee, had made her first movie for Amazing Films depressed her as much as the dismal realisation that she had been sidelined in Shush's affections by her friend.

'How's Motherbunch?' she'd sneer whenever he arrived.

Shushtary would laugh and quietly remind her that it could have been her.

'Motherbunch and I aren't in love,' he'd assure her. 'We only sleep together. Say the word and I'll fix you and Minoo up in our own place at once.'

His joyless reminder that Minoo was now a part of her life brought tears to her eyes as she sat with Fram in the drawing room later that evening.

'What's the matter?' he asked, guessing the worst. 'Are you jealous of that whore with whom Shushtary is sleeping?'

She advised him of another matter Shushtary had raised during his visit.

'He's offered me a half share in an Arab three-year-old that he feels could win the Bombay Arab Derby.'

'So this makes you cry?' Fram shouted in disbelief. 'A man offers you a half share in a horse and you cry? Do you think I'm mad?'

Rosie got up and left the room. When she had composed herself she rang Heloise.

In the two years after Minoo's birth, business, already poor, got even worse. Two smaller ice factories cut their prices and it became clear to Fram that the level of profits that Byramji had enjoyed had gone for ever. Instead of purchasing a half share in the Arab three-year-old Shushtary had offered her, Rosie lent Fram fifty thousand to cover his overdraft at Grindlay's Bank, and he gave Friski first refusal on a substantial proportion of his Singleton's Hotel stock. A five per cent stake was all he intended to retain.

'For old times' sake,' Fram pleaded.

'How much do you want?' Friski asked. 'Times are bad.'

His suggestion of sixty thousand was met with a derisive laugh. The following day Patcheco phoned and offered him twenty. Fram suspected that he was acting as Friski's agent. He confessed to Rosie that all was not well.

'We could sell Peccavi to a developer,' she said, 'and live more comfortably elsewhere. Colaba perhaps.'

'I'll never sell Peccavi,' he replied, humming tunelessly over her voice when she declared that the roof would not stand another monsoon.

'It's leaking in seventeen places,' she complained.

He went out onto the terrace, just in time to notice the red Duesenberg nosing up the drive. The thought of having to receive Shushtary with civility was unendurable. Fram made his own way down the stairs and escaped through the side door, before his unwelcome visitor rang the bell. He waited until the Iranian entered the house before instructing Chakramkhan to drive him to the Meredith Club on Lamington Road. It was his first visit since his marriage. He had to wait an hour at the bar for Xenia who was with a Tommy but he waved to her as she came in painting her lips and squinting into a vanity mirror.

'Hello,' she smiled, as though she was genuinely pleased to see him.

They scraped through a slow fox-trot which she thought was 'The Forks That Live On The Hill'.

'It's Folks,' he said.

She giggled self-consciously.

'I could never understand that title,' she reflected.

Xenia charged him thirty rupees but let him fuck her twice as he ejaculated prematurely the first time. The room smelled of over-ripe fruit and jasmine and it looked dirtier and smaller than his memory of it.

'Do you get a lot of Tommies now?' he asked as they dressed.

'Too many,' Xenia laughed, crossing herself. 'They all have tattoos, ginger jacks and want to lick my cunt. Rule Britannia.' She seemed to possess an assurance that she never had before.

'God bless you,' Fram murmured, kissing her on the mouth.

'Come again,' she called. 'Afternoons are best.'

Chapter 17

Rosie first met Stollmeyer when he called to see Fram at the ice factory. He was hardly her sort. An ugly man. Thinning strands of platinum across a pink, freckled skull, a beaky nose and a pursed dog's arse of a mouth. And so frightfully thin. He had, she conceded, dreamy, blue eyes, deep-set and hypnotic, yet he was undeniably ugly.

But she was flattered by his attention and intrigued by his apparent knowledge of jazz. His approach was much more scholarly and serious than hers. Rosie either liked numbers or she didn't. Stollmeyer on the other hand, knew the name and history of every player on the most obscure labels. He impressed her with his vast technical knowledge and anecdotes about the principal characters on the jazz scene, referring to them by their first names and nicknames as though they were members of his extended family. She had never realised that there was so much to the jazz business. Then when he offered to lend her his collection of Bix Beiderbecke records, she perceived his intentions, not instantly, but by and by as he endured Fram's banal chatter.

When Fram advertised and exaggerated her musical skills, Stollmeyer, admitting to a modest facility on drums, would not be deflected until she had returned to the house for her trumpet, fitted the mute and squeezed out a few plaintive bars of 'Marcheta'.

'That's unbelievably brilliant, Mrs Chutrivala,' he enthused. 'Such poignancy.' If he lied, it was with gentle conviction.

Fram was all smiles, calling for 'Carolina Moon', and 'Ramona', demands that Rosie resisted, catching an amused look in Stollmeyer's eyes.

'I'll only frighten the pigeons,' she laughed.

But she blushed when she noticed Stollmeyer watching her intently as Fram chattered on about her concentration and how, when he fell in love with her, she had her eyes screwed shut and her cheeks distended like balloons. Fram, she thought, was behaving like an idiot.

'It was at Singleton's Hotel,' he informed Stollmeyer. 'Rosie was playing "The Japanese Sandman".'

'I thought it was "Am I Blue?",' she countered.

Fram reached across the desk and patted her hand.

'That was later,' he reflected. 'My moment of truth arrived during the last few bars of "The Japanese Sandman".'

Stollmeyer's attentive stare burned right through her and she was conscious of a restless excitement she had not experienced since she had watched the progress of the Lloyd Triestino liner from Shush's window at the Taj. She wondered for a moment whether she really liked this man, suspecting the answer as the question formed in her mind, puzzled how such an ugly man had stirred her. She found it difficult eventually to meet his gaze, certain that the brain behind the blue eyes was seething with impure thoughts. Although aware of Fram's voice and occasional laughter, she was unable to listen to what he was saying. How she wished he would shut up.

Then suddenly, as Stollmeyer rose to take her hand before leaving, she felt feverishly receptive and a little afraid.

'What a strange man,' she murmured to Fram after the Swiss had left.

Fram told her that Stollmeyer worked for Volkart Brothers and was hiring space in the refrigerated room for the testing of scientific instruments. He was optimistic about his unforeseen extension to the business and talked about building a refrigerated laboratory with Stollmeyer's help.

Stollmeyer had disclosed that he drank at Singleton's Shikari Bar on Saturday mornings, a fact Rosie mentioned to Heloise on the phone.

'We must meet there so you can point him out to me,' decided Heloise.

'I'll die if he sees me,' replied Rosie.

'Wear dark glasses and a big hat,' her friend suggested.

They both giggled at the thought and planned to sit in a corner behind some palms where they would be unobserved from the bar. But although Heloise's estimation was not unexpected, Rosie was subdued by her confirmation of Stollmeyer's lack of beauty.

'He's an ugly bugger,' Heloise said dismissively, peering at the Swiss through a leafy fringe. Stollmeyer was alone, drinking German beer. A morose and solitary man. But Heloise warned her about his eyes.

'They're rotter's eyes, darling.'

What an unpredictable complication. A Swiss. Back home, Rosie searched an atlas for several minutes to locate Switzerland, the name having been obliterated by a staple between two pages. She had never been much good at geography. The country was hardly more than a smudge, easily hidden by a little finger. Kety, who appeared to know everything about matters of that sort, informed her that Switzerland, also known as Helvetia, although smaller than the Bombay Presidency, made the finest timepieces and the most succulent liqueur chocolates in the world. But when Kety retrieved a slightly mildewed *Blackie's Family Encyclopaedia* from a tea-chest in Soli's room and turned to the section on Switzerland, the smell of the rusted pages instantly evoked the tedium of Rosie's schooldays. She recoiled at the pictures of skiers on snowy pistes, lugubrious St Bernards and wooden chalets beside neat piles of logs. It seemed, she thought, a cold and boring sort of place.

That night she dreamed that Stollmeyer kissed her breasts and slipped his fore and middle fingers into her wet vagina. She awoke breathless, her nose pressed into the pillow, palpitant and trickling sweat between her thighs. And in the light of morning, the thought of Stollmeyer touching her there made her tremble with mad fear. It passed. Later, when she undressed for her shower, she was vexed by her fleshiness, grabbing rolls of body fat in disgust. Bearing Minoo had destroyed her figure. Who would have imagined that such an undersized brat, hardly bigger than a squirrel, would have so seriously impaired her appearance?

When she phoned Heloise before lunch, she mentioned Stollmeyer only in passing. However, the following afternoon, she bumped into the Swiss at Phipson's, the wine merchants.

'Woza coicidence,' he called loudly.

She blushed when everyone in the shop turned around. He shook her hand, and asked her to lunch. She declined, having just eaten. Stollmeyer gave her his card, inviting her to call in on her way home to see his record collection. She looked at the card and noticed that he lived on Wodehouse Road.

'We used to live on Wodehouse Road,' she exclaimed.

'Anozer coincidence,' he laughed.

She thanked him with as little fuss as possible, vastly relieved when he left the shop. When she got back to the car, now a white Terraplane convertible that Chakramkhan disliked, she instructed him to drive to Stollmeyer's address. She sent Chakramkhan to the house for the records but he returned a few minutes later empty-handed. There was a twist to the message that he brought back that was unexpected.

'Stollmeyer Sahib presents his compliments and would be honoured if Madam would accept the hospitality of his wife and him for a short time.'

'His wife?'

Chakramkhan smiled slyly.

'Stollmeyer Memsahib was in the next room when I called.'

Rosie puffed out her cheeks wearily. Chakramkhan shrugged. There was more than a hint of scepticism in the lift of his shoulders. Bending lower in the car to protect her ribboned boater from the hot, gusting wind, she snapped open her vanity mirror and, peering unhappily at her shiny nose, dusted it with petulance, uncertain whether she was to meet Mrs Stollmeyer or not.

Raising her head, she was horrified to see a red Duesenberg pass and draw alongside the kerb, a few yards ahead of the Terraplane. Shushtary loped back to her with a broad smile.

'And what clandestine enterprise is my lovely Rosie engaged upon?' he asked, leaning into the car and taking her hand.

'I'm taking afternoon tea with a friend,' she murmured, glancing away from him towards the house.

Chakramkhan walked discreetly away towards the Duesenberg. He had previously worked for an elderly doctor, whose young wife had many admirers. He had been trained not to eavesdrop on conversations that might only confuse his allegiance.

'I love you,' the grey-haired Iranian whispered.

'Don't be bloody ridiculous,' Rosie snapped. 'What about Motherbunch?' Shushtary looked hurt.

'Motherbunch is fine. I've provided her with an apartment in

147

Lenton Court, a Wolseley for a runaround, two servants, including a black maid from Dar-es-Salaam who is a trained masseuse, and a season ticket to the Member's stand on the Cooperage. Besides, she's being dated by the Raja of Pinjrapore himself so there's no room in her life for me.'

Rosie's heart sank. Heloise had hinted that Motherbunch's film career was taking off. Shushtary wiggled her little finger.

'And so,' he said wistfully, 'Shush is waiting for Rosie.'

She gave him a look of contempt, keeping an eye on Stollmeyer's house, hoping he wouldn't join them at the car.

'There is,' she reminded Shushtary bitterly, 'the small matter of your wife and six children in Kerman.'

He looked solemn.

'They're dead,' he informed her miserably. 'In the Khorram Shahr earthquake.'

Rosie was unsure whether Shushtary was lying or not. He looked unhappy enough but one could never be certain with the Iranian.

'I'm deeply sorry, if it's true,' she said.

He took her hand in his again. 'Let me ring you tomorrow,' he pleaded.

She looked at him anxiously. 'Why do you complicate my life?' she complained.

'After ten,' he proposed, giving her hand a squeeze before striding back to his car, rewarding Chakramkhan with a rupee coin and acknowledging the young Pathan's grateful salute with an affable nod.

Stollmeyer had been waiting for her, opening the door the instant she reached it.

'Zez no need for a hat in my house,' he said, as he led her into a partly shuttered lounge at the back that led onto a balcony overlooking a walled garden. 'I insist on seeing your beautiful hair.'

The room was furnished with racks of books, records and several abstract paintings and lithographs. Stollmeyer pointed with pride to an original Klimt. Rosie placed her hat on a table and settled her untidy hair with her fingers.

'Ze artist was a friend of my brozer-in-law,' he remarked, going to a cocktail cabinet constructed of tubular chrome and mirror shelves.

'Where's Mrs Stollmeyer?' she enquired, smiling at him.

He grinned. It looked painful in a face that rarely expressed joy.

'It wouldn't do for your man to suzpect we're alone,' he explained.

Stollmeyer informed her that he was going to provide her with his speciality, a chilled orange Curaçao and lemonade. She declined, informing him that it was not usual for her to take alcohol, but he insisted on her making an exception of this special occasion.

'Special?' she murmured.

'Iz not spezial?' he enquired with a hurt, wide-eyed expression that amused her.

He clicked on the radio-gramophone and, bringing a tall, frosted glass to her, offered her a cigarette.

She was still awkward with cigarettes, not holding them properly between her lips as she feared tearing her skin.

'I mustn't be late,' she announced, sipping her Curaçao and looking around at the carved walnut furniture and screens. In particular, she was taken by a mahogany elephant with a howdah. It was the size of a large pig. The pyramidical howdah was the glass shade of a rotating light that cast a kaleidoscope of colour on the ceiling.

'Do you wanzit?' he asked, moving up close behind her.

Rosie turned sharply, surprised by the nearness of his voice. She remembered that the music was 'Blue Heaven' as he took her drink and set it down. He kicked the silken rugs away, making a space on the bullseye floor for them to dance. They started a little stiffly, Rosie's left hand raised, still holding the cigarette and dancing almost sideways on in an arc around the room. Then Stollmeyer took the cigarette from her hand and dropped it on the floor, extinguishing it with a deft step as he drew her closer to him. She was taken by the seductive way he danced, his fresh peppermint breath and strong, sensual hands. She was trembling when the record ended and reflected on the friction of their heated bodies when her belly rubbed against his stiffness. Retrieving her glass, she refreshed herself, watching him warily as he attended to the gramophone, uncertain whether she wanted the afternoon to proceed to its inevitable conclusion.

'I really can't stay,' she said, a note of sudden desperation edging into her voice when she realised that she would.

'Let's sit down and lizen to zum Bixie,' he suggested, taking her to a cushioned divan in green silk. It was below a figurative painting of a bare-breasted Naga girl with a turquoise headdress and a luminous smile. She knew, of course, as they made their way around a black, upright Broadwood to the divan, that it was not their primary intention to listen to Mr Beiderbecke upon that broad silken bed but to couple there. Her apprehension was not sustained beyond the first kiss. It would be better, he suggested, after his hands had encompassed her body and she had rubbed her lips and cheek against his neck, if they undressed. She did so without equivocation, settling herself on the divan with lubricious assurance. He knelt between her parted thighs and she reached out a cupped palm to weigh the velvet substance of his hairy red scrotum. He asked her whether she would like to slip a rubber over his curved white cock, but she shook her head and smiled, taken by its elevation and ivory elegance.

'No, you do it,' she murmured sweetly.

Stollmeyer engaged her with ferocious authority, sucking her nipples, then using her mouth, as she heaved below him, before panting to a flooded resolution when he could give and she receive no more.

She lay beside him watching the coruscating light on the spinning ceiling fan and listening to the hissing of the needle trapped in the record's silent groove. He informed her that she had an extremely large clitoris, a discovery that did not surprise him as women with thick and stubby thumbs like her always did. Rosie examined her pollex with interest. Stollmeyer said that he had noticed her thumbs when he first met her in the ice factory, this fact alone determining his resolute pursuit and guaranteeing his early success.

'My thumbs?' she asked in dismay. 'I'm no more than a pair of abnormal thumbs to you?'

'Zay are important,' he assured her. 'Like nize eyes, breasts or hairs.'

He leaned over and kissed her on the nose.

'I have always been a tumz man,' he reflected. 'Tumz are also an indication of hyperactive Bartholin's glanz, which is why you are so slippery.'

Stollmeyer sat up and, looking down intently, slowly furled his rubber off. Then, knotting the end, tossed the used sheath onto the carpet.

'See how I look afzer my gelz,' he boasted lightly.

Rosie noticed that he was erect again. He fished around in his trouser pocket for another contraceptive, handing it solemnly to her.

'Pliz?' he whispered.

She sat up and fussed the sheath over him, rolling it down his thick stem, before straddling him and capturing his nozzle in her warm mush.

Rosie stayed with Stollmeyer an hour before she washed, dressed, collected her case of records and adjusted her straw boater.

'Tomorrow?' he asked hopefully.

'I can't,' she said, offering him her mouth and giving his bulge a valedictory rub.

'You liked it?' he enquired, running his hand up her dress and indulgently over her arse.

She nodded and looked up at him with big, anxious eyes.

'And you?'

He gave a knowing shrug.

'Wiz dose tumz of yours we couzent miz,' he declared genially.

They walked arm in arm to the door.

'What's your Christian name?' she asked before leaving.

'Tony,' he said, surprising her with a protracted Frenchy and a painful pinch on the bottom before allowing her to escape.

Chapter 18

Stollmeyer began to place a great deal of business with the ice factory. He introduced several other companies to Fram and soon the laboratory testing facilities were extended to include two more temperature-regulated ice-chambers.

'Tony has offered to teach me German,' Rosie told Fram. 'Maybe it's a good idea. We've already got three German-speaking clients.'

'Everybody is supposed to speak English in the British Empire,' Fram replied.

'Tony thinks that the days of the Empire could be numbered. There's this fellow Hitler. I understand that he's a very clever man.'

'To hell with clever men. Look at Gandhi. In and out of prison. Not to speak of our Soli. Where has cleverness got my brother?'

Soli, who had just been released from Yeravda Jail after serving part of a fourteen-month sentence for throwing a brick at a British soldier cycling past the Victoria Gardens, was in the isolation hospital recovering from small-pox. He alleged that he had been injected with the disease in prison, once they knew that he'd been paroled.

'Smallpox, cholera, plague and typhoid,' he told Kety, 'are merely instruments of colonial policy. If those monkey-faced white bastards had really wanted to, they could have eradicated these diseases from the sub-continent. Instead, they secretly spread them, using prisons, army hospitals and mission schools.'

'You must not speak like that in front of Rosie,' warned Kety. 'She's almost white; well, white enough to swim at Breach Candy anyway.'

'I have nothing against white people generally,' Soli sighed. 'Only the fucking imperialists and their lackeys.'

He held his sister's hand.

'Do you know why I hit that Tommy with a brick?' he asked.

'You offered no defence,' Kety said.

'It was because,' Soli said, 'the bastard ran over the foot of a beggar child. If I'd have mentioned that in court, who knows what reprisals they might have carried out on that luckless brat? I kept silent. And now, I shall carry my pock marks with pride; wounds received in action against the accursed enemy. They even look like the blast of a shot gun.'

'My poor darling,' Kety sighed, touching his scabs.

All this she had told Fram when she returned from the isolation hospital. Fram, carefully using those parts that wouldn't cause Rosie offence, reported Soli's accusations.

'So you see,' Fram concluded. 'Cleverness does not get one very far. A man doesn't have to be clever to give it, or a woman clever to take it.'

This she knew was one of his Koli fishermen's sayings, that she deprecated. They seemed pointless and in poor taste; like the one about it being safer for a woman to open her legs than open a book, or that there was nothing more ignorant or useful than a standing cock. Her impatience with Fram was compounded when, later, in bed, he was afflicted with premature spurts. They had become quite usual with him recently.

'Oh my beloved pumkin,' he'd groan apologetically after a few feverish strokes. His contrition, after a seemingly endless number of failures, was hardly bearable. Fortunately, there was Tony Stollmeyer.

'Well,' she sulked, taking advantage of his abjection, 'have you any objection to Tony teaching me German?'

'Not on principle,' he said.

He enquired how often and where the lessons would take place.

'Perhaps twice a week at Tony's place,' she suggested.

Fram did not seem entirely comfortable with the suggestion.

'Alone? Without a chaperone? I hardly think.'

She reminded him that Mrs Stollmeyer would be present.

'I had no idea there was a Mrs Stollmeyer,' he said. 'Maybe we should invite them to dinner.'

And that is how a dinner was arranged at Peccavi, when Mr and Mrs Stollmeyer took meat with the Chutrivalas. 'Mrs Stollmeyer' was a Calcutta prostitute called Brenda Bright, a handsome lady, unknown in the western province, who contracted to play Tony's wife at two hundred rupees an appearance. Not only did she captivate Fram with her genteel charm but assured him that she would always be present on the Wednesday and Friday afternoons Rosie was scheduled to call.

'Rosie is much too pretty for comfort, Fram,' she joked. 'I have my own interests to protect as well.'

Stollmeyer and his wife squeezed hands affectionately throughout the evening and Fram was not only convinced by the duplicity but earnestly considered that no man was likely to cheat on a woman of Brenda's quality. He wondered over cigars how she would look unclothed, impressed by the proportions of her breasts and the auburn tinge in her hair. How, he puzzled miserably, did uglies like Stollmeyer find females of this quality? He put the question to Brenda discreetly.

'Where did Tony and you meet?'

She gave him a frank and disarming look.

'In Montevideo.'

'Montevideo?'

'Uruguay, darling.'

'Are you from that side?' he asked in a subdued voice.

'Daddy had a ranch there.'

Fram was confused by very distant countries. And South America for him seemed only to exist to provide titles for dance numbers and locations for movies about bloody revolutions. It was he imagined, a tuneful if extremely violent place. Brenda had already turned to discuss something with Rosie before he could articulate the next question. He waited for his second opportunity, which came when she glanced momentarily in his direction.

'Do you speak Spanish?' he asked brightly.

'Pardon?'

'Spanish?'

'Oh no, darling. I'm a frightful duffer.'

In a curious way, the admission of lingual deficiency convinced him of her authenticity. He spoke of her to Rosie after the Stollmeyers had departed.

'I like Brenda,' he admitted as they undressed.

Rosie looked thoughtful.

'They're terribly in love,' she mused.

He nodded but did not reply. The depth of the Stollmeyer's affection for one another had made him see Tony in a new light.

Rosie's affair with Stollmeyer lasted four years. During that period, Shushtary remained a regular caller, giving little Minoo his first camera, a Compur Leica with shutter speeds from one fifth to one five hundredth of a second and constructing a dark room in the attic at Peccavi. Before Minoo went to kindergarten, he had taken several hundred photographs and, under Shushtary's supervision, began to develop his own prints.

'Are you sure the little man will be safe using all those chemicals?' Kety enquired.

'Let's hope he's not a genius,' Fram frowned, grateful for Shushtary's attention but apprehensive about the curse of intelligence. Fram's attitude towards the Iranian had mellowed, for it seemed inconceivable that anyone could spend so many hours instructing his Minoo without being basically decent. And there was the matter of the loan. Shushtary had offered him an interest-free lakh for a year.

'I suspect you're under-capitalised,' he said.

'I am, I am,' Fram agreed.

'It is my opinion,' declared Shushtary, 'that the scientific side of the business will do very well.'

'What can I do for you?' Fram asked.

'Allow me to be little Minoo's uncle,' Shushtary said simply.

Fram realised that he'd been particularly fortunate in his friends since his marriage to Rosie. First Stollmeyer, who had provided a new impetus to the ice factory and now Shushtary, a man he'd never liked in the past. It is not every day that one comes by interest-free lakhs. And the touching and hand-pressing of Rosie had all but ceased. Although Fram watched them carefully, he could detect no indication of an improper interest on Shushtary's part. Indeed, Shushtary generally called at Peccavi to see Minoo when Rosie was studying German with Stollmeyer.

'You know, Shushtary,' Fram confessed over a scotch and a Sumatra, 'I've really misjudged you.'

'I know what you mean,' Shushtary smiled. 'You were jealous of Rosie, were you not?'

'A little.'

'I've always regarded her as my daughter,' the Iranian assured him. 'After all, I'm nearly fifty.'

'Only a year older than me,' Fram said.

Shushtary, however, never failed to supplement his visits to see Minoo with regular phone calls to Rosie.

'It's Stollmeyer, isn't it?' he asked.

'That's none of your business, Shush.'

'I love you,' he insisted.

In the third year of her German lessons with Stollmeyer, Shushtary told Rosie about his intention to provide an interest-free lakh for improvements to the ice factory.

'What are you after?' she muttered irritably.

'Don't you think your husband knows about you and Stollmeyer?' Shushtary asked.

'There's nothing to know,' Rosie replied.

Shushtary suggested that Fram turned a blind eye to her affair with the Swiss as Stollmeyer was an important source of business.

'I really am studying German,' Rosie exclaimed.

Shushtary proposed that he'd call at Peccavi when Angelica took Minoo out in the Terraplane with Chakramkhan. As Minoo's favourite haunt was Chowpatty Beach, they rarely returned for two hours. He suggested that they meet in the dark room.

'But what about Kety?'

'She'll never open her mouth even if she sees something. A penurious female relative is hardly likely to upset the apple-cart.'

'And Fram?' she asked, dazed by his audacity. 'How can you explain your presence with me when Minoo isn't here? He's a profoundly suspicious man.'

'I'm paying for his trust, darling.'

'I feel like a whore,' she sighed miserably.

Minoo had been recommended to St Mary's by Father Garibaldi, Fram being reluctant to allow him to attend St Monica's in view of Soli's allegations about Mother Marie-Thérèse. Before his sixth birthday, he'd learned to count up to a hundred, memorised the letters of the alphabet and worked his way through the fourth reading-primer.

But even more astonishing, Shushtary had shown him how to

use a light-meter, assess shutter speeds, operate an enlarger and print negatives. Minoo snapped animals, birds, flowers and the little beggar girls he induced into the compound with a copper coin. Most of all, he liked photographing little girls. It was Father Garibaldi who conveyed a message from Sister Veronica D'Abreo that Minoo was too advanced for his age.

'His brain,' he explained to Fram, 'has developed too fast for his strength and size.'

For Fram, this was depressing news, remembering Soli and Meroo.

'There's nothing you can do about his cleverness,' Kety told Fram.

'But have you seen those terrible pictures he takes? Blind and mutilated children, lepers, amputees. It's hardly what one would expect from a five-year-old.'

Rosie laughed at Fram's concern.

'He's strongly influenced by Shush's work,' she said. 'He sees beauty in the most unlikely places.'

When Soli saw Minoo's photographs he considered that his nephew showed great social awareness.

'We could have a political reformer on our hands.'

'God forbid,' said Fram, who thought that politicians were insincere loudmouths.

The idea that his son might be another Soli disturbed Fram. But other developments had also begun to concern him. Like the fact that Stollmeyer was not using the ice factory as much as he had been.

'How are you getting on with your German?' he enquired, as little had been said recently of Rosie's visits to the Swiss engineer's house. And it seemed that now she'd acquired a Riley two-seater for herself she was rarely to be found at home.

'I haven't much of a head for languages,' she admitted. 'I suspect that Tony has despaired of me.'

The truth was, that for several months now, the time Fram imagined his wife was spending with Stollmeyer was being devoted to Shushtary. They met at the Raja of Pinjrapore's suite at the Taj. Also, she now had a member's ticket for the Cooperage and went to football matches most evenings. It was a game Fram couldn't endure. On the way back from the matches, she invariably called in at the Taj to see the Iranian.

She had begun to find it quite unendurable for a day to pass without having made love with Shush. They fought occasionally over Motherbunch.

'Why do you still keep her?' Rosie asked bitterly.

Shushtary shrugged.

'She has other lovers,' he said. 'I only pay the rent. Like an elder brother.'

'When did you last do it with her?' Rosie demanded.

'What?'

'You know.'

'But you're still with Fram,' Shushtary observed with a smile. 'Who are you to tell me what I should do?'

'You know it's finished between Fram and me,' Rosie fretted. 'Why can't we live together?'

'I would not want the woman I loved to be despised as a concubine,' he said.

'What about Motherbunch?'

Shushtary kissed her gently. 'But that proves I don't love her, my dear.' He paused and drew her to him. 'There is also the matter of my wife and children in Kerman.'

Rosie shouted that he was a liar, reminding him that he'd sworn that his family had been killed in the Khorram Shahr earthquake.

'They were dug out and taken to a hospital in a different province,' he asserted. 'I did not hear of their survival for several months.'

When they quarrelled like this, Rosie would storm out, often calling at Singleton's to have a coffee with Heloise and sometimes make a phone call to Stollmeyer.

'I haven't seen you for weeks,' he'd complain.

'Tomorrow perhaps?'

'My place?'

'I'll try to make it for one.'

But she rarely went, making some excuse for not keeping the appointment.

It was Heloise who told Rosie that Shushtary had got Motherbunch a leading part in one of the Raja of Pinjrapore's productions. Amazing Films were making a costume drama about Hanuman the monkey-god. It had action, music and lots of dancing. The thought of Motherbunch doing well revived Rosie's interest. She asked Heloise if Jimmy was around at Singleton's.

'Not for a year,' Heloise said. 'He's sold out his Singleton stock to Friski, who is helping with the film choreography.'

The news depressed Rosie. She motored back to Peccavi with dark thoughts in her head.

'Who won the match?' Fram enquired over a drink.

'The East Yorks,' Rosie said. 'They beat Bombay City Police four nil.'

'Tommies are far too rough,' Fram observed.

'The police are not exactly fairies,' she replied.

After dinner, she rang Friski Dalal about the possibility of a dancing part. Friski burst out laughing.

'I saw you at Singleton's about a month ago. You looked extremely well padded.'

'What do you mean?'

'How much do you weigh, darling?'

Rosie was silent. She had been acquiring a pound every six months for several years.

'Nine stone or thereabouts.'

'Nearer ten,' Friski retorted, 'but come and see me anyway.'

Fram having overheard Friski's name, approached her after she'd concluded the conversation. He warned her that the police had interviewed him about the use to which Singleton's was being put. Apparently, Patcheco was providing girls and accommodation for British Army officers and they felt that Dalal was aware of the practice. Rosie declared that the police would be more gainfully employed chasing real criminals.

'But this is criminal,' Fram reminded her.

'I'm thinking of taking dancing lessons again,' she said, popping a grape into her mouth and watching him carefully.

Fram came to her and kissed her on the cheek. She looked unhappy. Maybe she was bored, he thought. And he was suddenly struck by her youth and beauty. Perhaps he'd been taking her for granted.

'And what about your German?' he reproved gently.

She gave him a sly smile. Did he really know, as Shushtary suggested, that his wonderful Stollmeyer had been fucking her?

'I'm seeing Tony tomorrow,' she murmured.

'And how's Brenda?' he enquired.

'She's just missed her second period,' Rosie confided.

'My word,' Fram exclaimed. 'I must congratulate Tony. A little gift perhaps.'

'I wouldn't mention it,' Rosie warned. 'It's all rather tenuous. She has miscarried several times.'

His face clouded.

'I'm sorry to hear that. I often wondered why they didn't have a family.'

Fram appeared to be delighted that she would be seeing Stollmeyer the following day, as the contract for instrument testing was due to be signed and he feared he would be underbid by a competitor.

'Tony seems so remote these days,' he brooded.

'I'll tell him how much the contract means to us,' she promised.

Fram reached out and held her hand as she tried to leave the room. He told her that Kety was seeing Gidney in the morning about her cataracts.

'Gidney is a wizard,' Fram declared. And before she disappeared, he asked her quietly whether she would spend the night with him.

She shook her head, apologising that it was the wrong time of the month and, anyway, suspected that one of her black headaches was coming on.

Chapter 19

Stollmeyer seemed a little cynical when she called, enquiring whether Fram had asked her to plead for the new contract.

' 'E 'azn't stopped phoning me all week.'

She told him that her husband hadn't mentioned it to her but that any business would be welcome as Fram desperately needed to pay off loans and overdrafts.

He unbuttoned the front of her dress and slid his hands arrogantly over her breasts, moving his head down to nibble her gently on the neck. She had long realised that she disliked this thin, supercilious Swiss who appeared to enjoy her humiliation. She now found his kisses cold and contrived and the prospect of his curved white cock violating her body was not a welcome one. She stepped away from his groping hands and, taking a deep breath, gave him a not unfriendly smile.

'I'd like a large sidecar to start with,' she said.

Stollmeyer smiled.

'I've taught you very bed habits,' he said, going to the cocktail cabinet. She watched him fill the shaker with crushed ice before he added the Courvoisier and Cointreau. He squeezed in the juice of half a lemon before he whisked it. Stollmeyer was expertly quick when it came to mixing drinks. He poured out the two sidecars and brought one to her.

'Fram asked about Brenda,' she said, sipping her drink.

He joined her with an amused grin.

'Ah yez, Brenda.'

'I told him she was pregnant.'

This information amused him greatly. He poured her a second drink.

'You wanz to get drunk before we make love?' he asked as

161

she gulped half the second sidecar down.

She did not respond to his reproof. Instead, she walked across to a portrait of a man with a toothbrush moustache in a brown shirt. She had begun to see the face in many places and knew who it was. The face in the picture was meditative, prescient and resolute. It was the face of a shaman.

'Ze moz important man in ze world,' he remarked, joining her.

'He seems very unhappy,' Rosie said, draining her glass and setting it down.

Stollmeyer's grin as he undid the epaulette buttons of her dress was almost unbearable. She drew it over her head, unfastened her brassiere and took off her knickers. He kept his eyes on her as he undressed.

'I had almoze forgotten how zexy you are,' he said, leading her to the divan. She noticed that he was losing his hair and the nostrils of his beaked nose were even narrower than she had thought. Taken by dizziness, the moment she lay back she closed her eyes, preferring not to regard his pinched face or curved white prick. He took her twice. It was more difficult, she reflected, to endure his probing tongue in her mouth than his penis in her vagina, as no sexual conjunction is more intimate than a kiss. For while she could generally conceal her indifference during the penetration of her body, she found it significantly more tedious to tolerate unwanted osculation.

She used the shower room, drenching herself for ten minutes in cold water. He kissed her fingers with slightly contemptuous elegance before she left.

'You haff earned everyzing you came for,' he mocked at the door.

'Thank you, Tony,' she replied simply, her mind having already vacated the experience. And, after over-choking the Riley twice, she scraped her mudguard against a parked lorry before zipping erratically home.

Shushtary was at Peccavi with Minoo. He seemed to sense that she'd spent the afternoon with another man and drew her away to a corner of the room to question her.

'You're stinking of alcohol,' he reproved. 'Whom have you been with? Stollmeyer?'

'Don't be stupid,' she snapped, trying to evade his eyes.

But it was Fram who let the cat out of the bag when he came in.

'Rosie has been for her German lesson, Shush,' he informed the Iranian amiably.

Shushtary directed an accusatory glance at Rosie, who puffed out her cheeks, a customary response when embarrassed. He announced that he was backing a movie planned by Amazing Films on the life of Hanuman the monkey-god and would be going to Pinjrapore in a few days to arrange the contractual details. Rosie commented sourly that she'd heard that Mother-bunch had been given a role. Shushtary nodded, then surprised her with an invitation.

'If Fram has no objections, perhaps you'd care to accompany me,' he suggested to Rosie. 'We could drive down to Pinjrapore in my car and I'll arrange with Jimmy for you to stay at the palace.'

Fram looked doubtful. He had never approved of Pinjrapore or the film business. The prospect of his wife cavorting on the screen for the entertainment of village half-wits distressed him. He pointed out that, although the prevalent view in India that all girls who appeared in films were of easy virtue was facile and naive, it was not a risk he'd care to take with Rosie's reputation. Shushtary replied that it was premature even to consider Rosie getting a part, but it was a good opportunity for her to watch a few days' shooting and appreciate the sacrifices a career in the business would involve. Rosie did not betray any enthusiasm for Shushtary's proposal. She pursed her lips and looked thoughtful. Shushtary then disclosed that Jimmy had engaged the Shalimars to play at the palace for a week or so during the evenings to wind up each day's activities.

'What activities?' asked Fram.

'Camel races, mock battles, polo, wrestling, weight-lifting, singing, nautches, kabadi, toxophily, pig-sticking and elephant obedience trials.'

'How wonderful,' Rosie exclaimed.

'Will Rosie be invited to play the trumpet?' Fram enquired.

Rosie shook her head and declared that she hadn't the lips or the wind any more. Fram was less pessimistic.

'Rosie blew a serious trumpet for years,' he said, looking anxiously at his wife.

Shushtary pointed out that Rosie's place in the Shalimars had been taken by Zubie Chinoy but that maybe they would use her in occasional numbers.

'Nobody can play "Am I Blue?" with a mute better than my Rosie,' Fram claimed. He paused before adding. 'There are, of course, other considerations. A chaperone will be necessary, given that I'm tied to the ice factory here. Kety, I'm afraid, is not well enough to travel.'

Shushtary and Fram both looked at Rosie.

'She doesn't seem very keen,' the Iranian observed.

'How long will it be for?' she asked solemnly.

'A week, ten days. No more,' announced Shushtary.

She turned to Fram.

'Would you consider Heloise a suitable chaperone?'

Fram shook his head and frowned.

'What about Grace Mumford, you know, Motherbunch.'

Fram had heard that Shushtary was associated with this girl.

'She's a friend of mine,' Shushtary admitted. 'We have what you would call a "live-in" arrangement. A local bunderbusth, my wife and family being in Kerman.'

'Very modern indeed,' Fram laughed. He looked at Rosie, owl-eyed.

'She was in school with me, Frammy,' Rosie reminded him. 'The girl who plays drums for the Shalimars.'

'I know, I know,' he said. 'I remember her well.'

Fram expressed the view that as the Raja of Pinjrapore was a dangerous womaniser, Shush would have to bear the responsibility for Rosie's well-being.

'I would rather,' he reflected, 'she did not stay at the palace. These rajas are adept at drugging and violating young women.'

'Oh Frammy,' Rosie laughed.

'I suppose,' Fram said, 'that you need a holiday. And it's against my nature to chain you up in this place. It's not up-to-date, is it?'

He looked at Shushtary plaintively for support. The Iranian nodded.

'I think you're extremely up-to-date in your outlook, Fram,' he said.

The following day, to prove his goodwill and up-to-date thinking, Fram bought Rosie half a dozen dress saris, three Punjabi salwar kamize with pants and some new gold bangles for the trip. She told him that she would probably wear dresses, which concerned him as all her skirts appeared to be Bombay lengths, that being hardly long enough below the knee. He felt that in up-country and jungli places like Pinjrapore, bared, female legs gave the natives obscene ideas. Rosie reminded Fram that Jimmy was an England-returned and progressive in his outlook.

'That won't stop the bastard keeping a dozen concubines under lock and key,' he remarked angrily.

Rosie put her arm around him. 'You hardly know the man,' she said. Fram did not reply. He left the room, conscious of a pain in his chest. When he was alone, he unscrewed a glass phial and, tapping a pill onto his palm, placed it carefully under his tongue. He walked across to the window overlooking the goldfish pond and the statue of Sir Maneckji Wadia. He gave a little start when he noticed that the hairline crack in the pediment had widened and Sir Maneckji's left hand had been severed at the wrist. The discovery so distressed him that he went down into the compound as quickly as he could to examine the damage.

Kety, having had her cataracts successfully removed by Henry Gidney, stared down at her brother prodding about around the pond with his cane. She opened an upper window and called to Fram.

'It's in the water,' she called, 'the hand is in the water.'

She informed him that the boys from St Mary's often climbed over the wall during the lunch hour to play in the pond and that she had meant to mention it to him before but her personal worries had made her forget.

Fram waded into the water up to his knees and found the missing object. Climbing back onto the bank, he tried to fit the severed limb back in place, but noticed that there were several fragments of marble missing. As it was growing dark, he decided to investigate the matter further in the morning and lodge a complaint with Father Garibaldi.

Kety, excited by the vexatious happening, came down to possess Rosie of the facts, but found her on the phone, laughing and talking with animation to Heloise, a woman she had seen at Peccavi on several occasions but had never met. Rosie's friendship with this woman, whom she knew Fram disliked, alarmed and depressed her. Kety suspected that this liaison, like Rosie's association with Shushtary, was against the interest of the family and, in particular, Fram. Rosie, sensing Kety behind her, stopped and placed her hand over the receiver to question the interruption with a weary smile and raised eyebrows.

'Fram has been wading in the pond searching for Sir Maneckji's hand,' Kety exclaimed. 'The one holding the reins of his horse.' Her concern did not appear to communicate itself to Rosie, who looked blankly at her sister-in-law.

'That was done days ago,' she declared, turning her back on Kety to resume her conversation. She was still talking to Heloise when Fram, soaked to his thighs, returned with the black hand of Sir Maneckji. He placed the marble on the table and called peremptorily to Rosie.

'I must phone Father Garibaldi before he retires for the night,' he declared.

'What now?' Rosie asked, irritated at being disturbed.

'Yes, now,' Fram insisted in an obdurate voice.

Kety reappeared, apprehensive, standing by the door to witness her brother's assertiveness with his wife. Rosie shrugged, excused herself to Heloise and, although visibly angry, did not defy her husband.

'Those young bastards from Father Garibaldi's school have been trespassing on our property,' he shouted.

'What property?' Rosie mocked, swinging out past Kety. 'It's only a matter of time before everything falls apart.'

Fram spoke to Garibaldi in forceful terms, demanding that the culprits be found and their parents held responsible for the damage. The priest asked his friend when the incident had occurred.

'Who knows?' Fram sobbed, suddenly and inexplicably breaking down in tears, to Kety's dismay. He left the receiver on the table and went to the window again to look at the mutilated statue in the dusk. Kety picked up the receiver and informed Garibaldi that her brother was extremely distressed. She replaced the instrument on its rest and came to Fram.

'You must change your clothes immediately,' she urged.

Fram rubbed away his tears with the palm of a trembling hand. He made his way to the bedroom where he found Rosie packing a travelling case.

'You're going tonight?' he enquired, taking his trousers off.

She shook her head slowly. Fram put on his dressing-gown and went into the bathroom. When he returned, he found Rosie had left the half-filled case on the bed to resume her telephone conversation in the drawing room. Minoo had appeared and was seated like an old gnome on the dressing-room stool, waiting for his father.

'What happened, Papa?' the boy asked, noticing the wet trousers.

'I fell in the pond,' Fram said ruefully.

Minoo looked at him with concern.

'There's nothing to worry about,' Fram assured him, smoothing an affectionate palm over his hump.

He told his son that he intended to transfer him to another school.

It was Rosie's intention that Minoo should complete his education at St Mary's, which was where Father Garibaldi taught.

'You are going to Christ Church,' Fram announced, 'and in the meanwhile, I'm arranging for private tuition in the sciences. Science is the future of our world.'

Minoo looked at his father, wide-eyed.

'But I want to be a photographer,' the boy asserted.

'There is nothing wrong with photography,' Fram agreed. 'It is, after all, a branch of science.'

'A branch?' Minoo asked. 'Like a tree?'

'Like a tree,' Fram said, hoisting Minoo onto his shoulders to return to the drawing room.

'Papa is sending me to Christ Church,' Minoo announced to his mother who was on the point of terminating her telephone conversation.

She did not choose to question the decision at the time but mentioned it later that evening when Minoo had retired.

'I thought Minoo was going to stay at St Mary's,' she said over a drink.

'The Catholics have done enough harm in my life,' he declared, lighting a cigar. 'First Meroo, now this vandalism and, of course, Angelica.'

'What about Angelica?' Rosie asked.

Fram considered his wife in the lamplight. She looked, he decided, more beautiful than she had ever done. More than ever she reminded him of the luminous Vanessa Beauchamp, long since retired to Redhill with her Bulldog.

Fram told her that Angelica had confessed to a relationship with a senior boy at the school.

'Confessed to you?' Rosie asked.

'No, Garibaldi. It was in the box.'

'But he's not supposed to divulge the secrets of confession.'

'It was in the girl's interests. I warned her that if her association with this boy went any further, she would lose her job.'

'What form did this affair take?' Rosie asked.

'It went no further than touching.'

'Touching?'

'Yes,' Fram said, 'he touched her there and she held his thing.'

'You mean his cock?'

'If you choose to be coarse, yes.'

She gave him a pained look. 'In other words, there was some genital play?'

'Yes, yes,' he muttered, adding, 'Garibaldi expelled the boy, of course.'

Rosie frowned. 'St Mary's would have been so convenient for Minoo. Besides, Garibaldi would have kept an eye on him.'

'St Peter's is not too far,' she suggested.

'You mean that place managed by that one-eyed pederast who runs behind the boys, whipping them along the streets? The pupils look like beggars and are unbelievably barbarous. I understand the little shits pull the heads off pigeons to drink their blood.'

Rosie perceived that, on the issue of Minoo's education, Fram appeared to be unusually resolute.

Rosie asked Fram if he was aware that a large section of plaster had fallen in the sewing room. He nodded glumly, his eyes taken with the wear in the Ladik prayer-rug below Rosie's slippers.

'Did you hear that Stollmeyer has gone back?' he asked quietly.

'Really? Will it affect us?'

Fram shrugged and bent down to examine the threadbare patch on the blue and red floral rug. It was, he remembered, one that Zarina had kept by her bed. He kneeled before her to inspect it more closely.

'What's the matter?' Rosie asked, moving her legs.

He caught the scent of mimosa wafting down from between her thighs. He had forgotten how pleasant Rosie always smelled there. Crawling to her, he lifted her skirt and buried his head against her knickers.

'Are you mad?' she protested, pushing his head away. 'Kety or Minoo could come in at any moment.' He reminded her that they hadn't made love for many months.

'I didn't think it mattered,' she said, drawing her skirts down but sensing that it was a night when it might be difficult to deny him. She hoped that he would be content with a quick lick and suck.

In the bedroom that night, while Rosie brushed her hair, he sorted idly though the underwear she had packed in her travelling case, chancing on three pairs of black knickers with button-flaps along the crotch.

'They're convenient when one is taken short,' she laughed.

He undid and buttoned one of the flaps several times before holding the perfumed silk against his cheek.

'How accessible for a lover,' he mused, poking his middle finger in and out of the opening in the garment. 'All the better-class whores wear them.'

She eyed him wearily.

'What are you trying to say, Frammy?'

He stared at her with a dull sensuality she recognised. Drawing her shift over her head, she settled on the bed, enticing him by cupping her breasts and raising her parted legs in the submissive posture that she knew he desired when they played their private game.

'Are you a whore?' he asked softly, gazing at her disa uniflora.

'Of course,' she murmured, framing her orchid with two fingers.

'Do you go with many men?' he demanded, moving his head between her thighs.

'Dozens,' she whispered, as he began to eat her with noisy fervour.

When he did eventually penetrate her, it did not take long. He muttered his usual apology and padded into the bathroom, already setting their brief transaction behind him.

As he streamed into the pot he thought of Soli's prediction that war was imminent. His brother had changed his views about the Raj, although he assured Fram that it was a matter of political expediency. Soli considered that it was important that the forces of Fascism were crushed and resolved that he would serve in the future war as a non-combatant.

'You're too bloody old,' Fram laughed.

'One is never too old to tie a bandage or staunch a haemorrhage, comrade.'

He was still thinking of his brother as he fell asleep, awakening with a start when Rosie returned to his side. He noticed that it was two o'clock and asked her sleepily what she'd been doing.

'Washing my diaphragm,' she whispered, snuggling against his shoulder.

PART THREE

Minoo

Chapter 20

Wesley Pithers was a rather down-at-heel Anglo-Indian. He had a large, Darwinian head and a pugnacious cast to his features, softened by a puckish upturn of the mouth. His slim, sinewy body, well exercised and modestly nourished, moved with a nervy quickness, and his staring, dark eyes appeared to see more than they did. For Pithers dwelt largely within himself, given to the problems he teased at inside his balding skull. At forty-five, he was still a batchelor, a Master of Science from Madras University and a teacher of Physics, Chemistry and General Mathematics. These skills earned him the nickname of Pythagoras among schoolchildren, a soubriquet that would have bewildered and saddened him, for Pythagoras evoked for this atheist the transcendental resonances Jesus Christ did for believers.

His shirts and frayed cotton coats were always worn a day or two longer than they should have been and his shoes were shamefully down-at-heel and unpolished. He only had, apart from his absent-mindedness, one serious vice. Pythagoras was an inveterate gambler, spending every Saturday at Mahaluxmi racecourse and every night playing cotton figures. An orphan, raised in charity boarding-schools, the young Pythagoras had acquired a university education through scholarships which he won quite effortlessly. He had always been slightly bemused why others couldn't manage what he considered to be his standard of mediocrity.

'But you're brilliant, Wesley,' his peers grumbled when he produced Firsts in every paper he wrote. These accusations of abnormal ability invariably provoked a mad stare and a self-deprecatory response.

'Brilliant? Me? Don't be a bloody arse.'

He lived in a single room near the school where he taught, beset by moneylenders to whom he was always seriously in debt and subsisted in general, on Irani-shop fare, a salted biscuit and tea in the morning, several cups of tea during the day and a bowl of kheema with a moghul-roti at night. He drank, on average, forty cups of tea a day, recognising instantly, after a sip, the tea-house where the cup was brewed.

Sex for Pythagoras was no more than an inconvenience, disturbing the fine balance between tea-drinking and gambling. Because he was so desperately impoverished, he was reluctant to purchase it and found a compliant Goanese lady who made herself available once or twice a week to service his needs. As Mrs Fernandes, the lady in question, was married, he was unwilling to compromise either her reputation or his professional status by using his own room. Being rather old-fashioned about appearances, Pythagoras was never seen publicly with her. They had evolved an elaborate convention of signals that enabled them to communicate at a distance, their progress to a rendezvous usually involving his hawkishly vigilant figure striding fifty paces ahead of hers. They made love in the family room of the Evergreen Café, having come to an arrangement with Sohrab the proprietor, who allowed him half an hour behind a latched door of opaque glass and flimsy, plyboard partitions. Here, he enjoyed Josephine Fernandes on the marble table after the bar-wallahs had cleared away the empty kheema plates and tea cups. She was a slight, avian creature, apprehensive, as he was, during their moments of coupling. She came knickerless to their encounters, perching at the edge of the table while Pythagoras invested her.

In time, despite their circumspection, the knowledge of their love-making became the property of the older, more bog-minded boys from the school. Pythagoras and his paramour were followed at a distance and eventually spied on through holes bored in the partition with compass points. Occasionally, the risibility of the schoolboys alerted the lovers and Pythagoras would rush wildly out of the cubicle, buttoning his flies and searching for the voyeurs. Sometimes, they would be caught. To his credit, he did little more than cuff their ears.

It was Pythagoras who answered Fram's advertisement for a tutor, arriving on a borrowed bicycle within twenty minutes of a preliminary phone-call. And although Fram was not instantly encouraged by the teacher's appearance, Minoo and Pythagoras took to each other at first sight. He was engaged to teach Minoo general mathematics and sciences, twice a week for fifteen rupees a one-hour session.

It was only when Fram was walking with hi... to where he'd left his bicycle that he discovered what an extraordinary fellow Pythagoras was. 'Of course, my son, being a hunchback, has special emotional needs,' Fram observed.

Pythagoras looked shocked.

'Hunchback? Hunchback? What on earth are you talking about?'

The teacher, who had joked and talked to Minoo for half an hour, had failed to notice his deformity. This deficient perception alarmed Rosie who considered he looked like a dangerous adventurer.

'How can a man be a scientist, who can't see what's before his nose?' she demanded.

'Because what's in his mind is probably much more beautiful,' Fram suggested.

The trip to Pinjrapore lasted ten days. Shushtary reserved adjoining suites at the Vishvanath Hydro, procuring from Mr Chemburkar, the under-manager, a key for the connecting door. It cost him a modest hundred rupees. It was an arrangement with which Chemburkar was familiar, being used by the film people who visited Pinjrapore. Certain very important people, Shushtary disclosed, booked as many as six interconnecting suites, occupying one themselves, leaving four vacant and locating the lady star in which they had an interest in the farthest one. The four vacant suites were registered in the names of junior technicians who were accommodated in less expensive rooms elsewhere. In these circumstances, keys were purchased for five connecting doors at five hundred rupees a key and the meals not consumed by the absentee residents were charged to the studio account.

He told Rosie that particular care had to be taken in cases where a Brahmin girl was associating with a man of lower caste. There was once, he informed her, a certain Rani, also a Brahmin, who was having a love affair with her privy-cleaner, an Untouchable. The man used to pass himself off as a Christian, arriving for their assignations in a limousine with shuttered windows and registering himself under the name of Dr Vasco DeGama. Two entire floors were reserved, the Rani occupying the suite farthest from Dr DeGama on the opposite wing of the lower floor. Sixty-five keys had to be purchased and upwards of two hundred non-existent meals a day charged to the palace account so that the Rani could meet her lover.

'It is beyond dispute,' Shushtary said, 'that the present Raja is the son of that privy-cleaner, for not only has he demonstrated an acuity and intelligence that had been wholly absent in the royal house for generations, but he has quite ostentatiously incorporated a thunderbox into his insignia. Uncorrupted by an English public-school and university education, he is an overt supporter of the Independence Movement and a tireless writer of subversive letters to the *Manchester Guardian*.'

'Jimmy?' Rosie gasped.

Shushtary nodded. 'You see,' he said, 'the previous Raja was a hermaphrodite and so not seriously capable of continuing the line, a secret that was immediately evident to his privy-cleaner, for as you know, a hermaphrodite's turd replicates a coiled serpent when deposited, often attaining lengths of six feet or more, although rarely thicker than a skipping-rope.'

Rosie looked incredulous. 'You're pulling my leg, Shush,' she declared.

'Fifty per cent of the story is probably true,' he said.

'You bastard,' she laughed.

They showered, made love and showered again before they dressed for dinner at the palace.

'I'd rather stay here, Shush,' she pouted.

'The Raja of Pinjrapore is expecting us,' he said, pointing out of the window to the courtyard. 'Two caparisoned elephants and an escort of lancers are waiting restlessly downstairs.'

Jimmy looked more dashing than ever in his turban and ceremonial robes. He wore a jewelled talwar, golden slippers and a chain of rubies around his neck.

'Mrs Chutrivala,' he beamed, coming quickly to her and taking her hand between his. 'I remember your dear husband well. And, of course, you too for your trumpet-playing days at Singleton's,' he said, adding softly, 'I insist you call me Jimmy.'

'I always have,' she replied impishly.

'That's the ticket, darling. That's the ticket.'

He informed her that the Shalimars were scheduled to play for three nights and he expected them to arrive with Jerry Patcheco the following day.

'Cheek to cheek dancing in the Shivaji Ballroom,' he winked.

Rosie smiled.

'Perhaps,' he asked, miming a trumpet player with his fingers and bloated cheeks, 'we may hear you tootle as well?'

She told him that she hadn't played a trumpet in a professional group for eight or nine years. He held her hand once more and warned her that, being an incorrigible flirt, he had arranged for her to sit on his right hand at dinner, Shushtary being relegated to another table with less amusing guests. Then, moving his face close to hers, he whispered that a suite was being prepared for her at the palace, overlooking an enclosed court with peacocks, dancing fantails, parakeets and spotted deer. Also a ten-spouted fountain and a pavilion of musicians.

'We have a blind tabla player,' he boasted, 'who is the envy of the world. He has been known to raise body temperatures by two degrees Fahrenheit.'

The Raja refused to allow her to stay at the Vishvanath Hydro. It was, he sneered, fit only for British civil servants with prickly heat and swollen ankles who subsisted on pink gin, and their freckled memsahibs who talked incessantly of 'home' in tones that sounded as though they were being slowly garrotted.

'I understand that you were at Oxford yourself, Jimmy,' she mocked.

'Oxford? Oh God protect me,' he sighed. 'The only decent thing Oxford has ever produced was the 1917 Morris Cowley two-seater.'

Over dinner he told her that she would have to dye her hair black for a screen-test and work through a few simple dance routines with Dr Dalal whom he expected that night.

'If it comes to the worst,' he said, 'we can use her feet and your upper half. I'm sure your breasts will be extremely photogenic.'

When Rosie had an opportunity to escape from the Raja, she spoke to Shushtary.

'Jimmy wants me to move into the palace tomorrow,' she mooned.

'We have tonight,' Shushtary replied.

'What does this all mean, Shush?' she asked anxiously.

Shushtary shrugged philosophically.

'You know film business, darling.'

Chapter 21

Apart from mathematics and general science, Pythagoras taught Minoo to ride a bicycle and play split-tops, taking a spinner with a Cupalari spike on his palm, over his wrist and along his arm. He also instructed the boy in the arcane principles of kite-fighting.

'It's basic science, Minoo,' Pythagoras said. 'A kinetic activity that investigates the resistance ratios between the opposing sharp strings or manjas. A kite fight,' he reflected, 'takes place in two places. In one's mind and in the sky. These events are generally almost simultaneous, synchronisation being an experience too exquisite to bear. When the fight in one's mind is a psychic moment ahead of the fight in the sky, it is a portent of victory; when behind, an omen of defeat.'

Minoo loved the way Pythagoras's tenacious face was lit by passion when speaking of matters dear to his heart.

'But first,' Pythagoras said, 'I'll teach you how to make manja.'

The master arrived on a Saturday morning with a firkee of white, glazed twine (Hanuman Chap No. 6), and tied several lengths between two posts fifty yards apart. Then, using a steel pestle and mortar, he broke and pulverised a sodawater bottle into fine dust. Next, he broke an egg into a bowl of boiled rice, adding a salmon-pink powdered dye, this being Minoo's preferred colour, to the mix. It was massaged into a sticky, pink dough.

'Spit on it,' Pythagoras ordered Minoo.

'Spit?'

'For luck,' Pythagoras grinned. 'For luck is first cousin to the principle of chance.'

After Minoo had spat, the glass-dust was incorporated into the dough and carefully kneaded in. Finally, the glass-impregnated ball was rubbed gently over the taut strands of twine, until they were covered with the abrasive substance. It was left to dry in the sun. The twine had been converted into manja. Minoo found the sight of these lengths of pink twine, stretched across the ice-factory compound, strangely compelling.

'The rice,' Pythagoras declared, as he reeled the manja onto the firkee, 'symbolises Life, the broken glass Death, and the egg is the mystery of Immanence.'

'Immanence?' asked Minoo.

'A convenient term to describe the presence of a creative logic in the world,' Pythagoras said.

'God, Sir?'

Pythagoras laughed.

'I prefer to call it the Uncertainty Principle, for it is out of uncertainty that wisdom comes. But first, we must welcome your manja to the world. Can you crow like a cock?'

Minoo tried. Then Pythagoras threw back his head and crowed so realistically that the shrill sound seemed to pierce the heart of the resident rooster and set all the hens clucking in expectation.

'What's the matter?' Fram asked, poking his head through the office window.

'We are welcoming the manja,' Minoo explained, crowing proudly at his father who appeared to be perplexed by the commotion.

'What, Sir,' asked Minoo as they reeled the finished manja onto the firkee, 'is the most important ingredient?'

Pythagoras had no hesitation in providing an answer.

'Spit,' he replied, 'because it is part of the maker and serves notice on all who come to fight that the manja is spiced with Minoo's luck, a factor that can snatch victory from defeat.'

'Please, Sir,' Minoo said, 'will you allow me to photograph you holding the firkee of manja?'

'On condition you memorise Euclid's Parallel Axiom, reciting it tonight like a mantra and remembering it holds more meaning than any run-of-the-mill prayers.'

Minoo promised that he would do so and went up to his room, returning with the Leica Shushtary had given him for his eighth birthday. He took three pictures of Pythagoras: the first, smiling in an unreal manner at something far beyond the camera, the firkee sloped casually on his shoulder; the second, an expression of sadness with the firkee held between his extended hands like a dead child; and the third, advancing, eyes manically ablaze, the firkee raised over his head like a club. In the next few weeks, Minoo's lessons on kite-fighting were dovetailed with observations on Newtonian laws, speculations on the magic of number nine, Russian methods of computation and stories about the supremacy of Arabic symbols.

The Shalimars' engagement at the Pinjrapore Palace was their last as a professional sextet. Motherbunch, now Bhabee, the emerging star of Amazing Films, used the occasion to announce her retirement as a drummer. Heloise had decided to leave for England before the war broke out, having been offered a solo engagement in a Wardour Street club that belonged to a Greek called Harry Petros. They had met at Singleton's and slept together while he was in town.

'Harry was almost a boy friend,' Heloise murmured.

'He had a big hooter and gold teeth,' Motherbunch sneered.

'I like gold teeth in the right sort of man,' Rosie observed. 'You know, hairy guys who wear silk shirts and smell of money.'

'I'll have you know,' Heloise boasted, 'that I'm one of the few singing female bass players in the business.'

Motherbunch made a face. 'Now if you tap-danced as well, that might be something.'

'That's a Sunday extra, in between juggling, selling cigarettes, doing tremblers in the alley, and waiting on table,' Heloise retorted.

Zubie Chinoy, the girl who'd replaced Rosie, was also leaving. She was three months pregnant and had agreed to be the Bombay mistress of the father, an elderly silversmith from Aden.

'If it's a boy, I could become his fourth wife,' she said hopefully.

'I could never be a fourth anything,' Motherbunch grunted.

'We're looking for replacements, of course,' Jerry Patcheco said glumly, conceding that it would be difficult to replace three key performers and that it was only fair to change the name.

'Perhaps a quartet of piano, drums, guitar and bass.'

'No trumpet or sax?' Rosie asked.

'A more intimate sound,' he explained.

The ten days provided an opportunity for Rosie and

Motherbunch to build bridges. The drummer explained that Shush had never been in the frame for her and that although he'd paid for her three abortions he wasn't the father of any of them.

'I have no scruples,' Motherbunch said 'about using rich bastards like Shush to pick up the bills. A girl should always have one or two around to take care of emergencies.'

'I think I love him,' Rosie confessed, 'and have done since I was fifteen.'

Motherbunch stared at her for a moment, then offered her a ganja cigarette. She smoothed one for herself and lit them both.

'You wouldn't let him in those days, would you?' she said.

Rosie shook her head. 'Nope.'

Heloise helped herself to one of Motherbunch's loosely packed tubes, poking the green leaves in with a long nail before she sucked it into life from Rosie's offered light.

'Shush was almost my first,' she admitted. 'A corporal from the Black Watch who I don't remember got there a week or so earlier at a party I shouldn't have attended.'

'Almost everybody I know has had Shush,' Motherbunch brooded.

She turned to Rosie with an enquiring look. 'Do you mind?'

Rosie shook her head sadly. 'You can't undo that sort of stuff. It was my fault really. I wouldn't because everybody had.'

She confessed that her own marriage was unsatisfactory. The girls nodded. It was no secret. Friski Dalal never stopped gossiping about the Chutrivalas, claiming that they were all crazy.

'I hear your boy is physically handicapped,' Motherbunch said.

'He's a hunchback,' Rosie replied starkly, giving them an owlish look of despair. 'The terrible thing is,' she continued, 'I don't really care for him.'

They smoked quietly for a little while, each trying in their own way to get back to the girlish fun they had always had together. Rosie was not surprised by Motherbunch's hint that Jimmy had his eye on her, the attention she had received during the three days she'd spent at the palace being ostentatiously ardent.

'I've never had him myself,' Motherbunch confessed with a laugh.

'Nor me,' said Heloise.

'I thought,' Rosie said to Motherbunch, 'that's how you made the big time in Amazing Films?'

'Cheeky bitch,' Motherbunch said. She gave Rosie a sardonic grin.

'I suspect,' Rosie confided, 'he's almost at the point of asking.'

'You will, of course,' Heloise said.

'I don't know,' Rosie replied flatly.

'Jesus Christ,' shouted Heloise.

Rosie now felt a little light-headed. She turned to Motherbunch.

'So what's your secret?' she asked, leaning towards her.

Motherbunch shot her a slit-eyed and playful look.

'Urinary diversions with Mohandas the director, darling. See, I've provided you with information that could change your life. Don't ever say Motherbunch doesn't help her mates. Of course, talent played a part as well.'

'Mohandas directed two of Leela Kotnis's pictures,' Heloise mused. Motherbunch shrugged.

'I can't speak for the glorious Leela,' she said, 'but with me, he progressed from listening to the sound of me tinkling in a bucket to observing the function and finally submitting himself to be my urinoir.'

Rosie looked dreamy. She was not excessively surprised, having heard about similar aberrations when she was with the Shalimars.

'When I was sixteen,' she confessed, 'I was offered two hundred rupees to so use a major in the Somerset Light Infantry.'

'Munro,' Motherbunch shouted instantly. 'I remember him well. A tall, ginger-haired man with a feathery moustache. What did you say to him?'

'I told him,' Rosie recalled, 'to piss off.'

Heloise disclosed that Munro had asked everybody in the band including poor Wendy Rodriguez, offering her an extra fifty if she would play 'Prince Albert', the regimental quick march, on the piano, while she peed over him. Motherbunch lit another ganja cigarette. She observed that her compact with Mohandas, a great director by any standards, obviated the tedium of having to sleep with the male star, the producer being safely homosexual.

'Well,' she reflected, 'irrigating the face of a famous director is a small price to pay for success.'

The three of them were now quite high. But Rosie suddenly felt despondent as she remembered the conversations with

Shushtary that she had tried to forget. He had told her that he intended to return to Iran before war broke out, advising her that he had important business arrangements to conclude before hostilities began. She had turned on him tearfully.

'But what has the coming war to do with Iran?' she demanded bitterly, recalling his earlier deception about the earthquake in Khorram Shahr and the deaths of his family.

'Oil,' Shushtary declared, 'will shortly be an even more valuable commodity than it is now. The Germans have their eyes on Iranian oil.'

'Take me with you,' she said in a bleak and unhappy tremor.

Shushtary told her that it could be all over in a few months.

'I'll kill myself,' she sobbed suddenly.

He placed his hand on her shoulder.

'Don't be unhappy, little dove,' he soothed. 'The time will soon pass.'

'Take me back to Bombay,' she demanded.

He declared that their early departure would probably rule her out of Jimmy's consideration for the new film and prejudice her career. He had heard from Friski Dalal that Rosie's dancing was less than adequate, weight and a lack of Oriental facility being the main problems.

'She moves like a Jumbo,' Friski reported gloomily.

Shushtary suspected that Jimmy wouldn't be outfaced by Friski's complaints about Rosie's incompetence. He had even instructed the director that Rosie had star-quality, dancing breasts.

'But Your Highness,' the man had pointed out, 'dancing is at least a fifty-per-cent-below-the-navel activity.'

'And what about face and breasts?' Jimmy scoffed. 'That, my dear Mohandas, is what the Indian public pay for.'

So Shushtary, who unknown to Rosie was aware of the politics of her presence in the film, advised her that if she ever wanted to become a dancing star Jimmy was her only chance. But only one issue now concerned her.

'What will happen to me when you disappear to Iran?' she asked.

Shushtary gave her the key to his flat in Lenton Court, a place to which she could escape if Peccavi became unendurable. It would also be a convenient address for him to write to her.

'I see you've made up your mind,' she accused.

From the Shivaji Ballroom came the sounds of Zubie Chinoy's trumpet playing 'Margie', rather quicker than the arrangement Rosie remembered. She rummaged about in her handbag for one of the three ganja cigarettes she had been given and, lighting up, drew strongly on it.

'What are you smoking that shit for?' Shushtary demanded with a frown.

Rosie rose a little unsteadily. She looked back at him with a smile as she walked away.

'Rosie?'

'Don't worry about me, Shush,' she sniffed, giving him a friendly wave as she made her way back to her private suite. After the second door closed behind her the sounds of the Shalimars could no longer be heard. A different sort of music drifted up from the courtyard. Kicking off her shoes, she settled on her bed, listening to the hypnotic pulses of the tabla player. Soft, then almost imperceptible at times, the hand-drummer's subdued insistence, like the heartbeat of an animal caught in a trap, drew her through whorls of intermittent silences, challenging her acuity. She drifted, smoking the ganja, looking across at the copper tray beside her on which lay three spiced paans, a carafe of sherbet and a black velvet box. She opened it. Inside was a shining diamond-and-emerald bracelet and an ambiguous message scrawled across one of Jimmy's visiting cards. It read, 'I trust you will permit me to ask you a simple question.'

What? she wondered, as the tabla quickened as though it were answering her. And when?

Kety's continuing eye problems had now been diagnosed as iritis and glaucoma. Overcome by persistent pain, she was admitted to the Eye Hospital for observation the day Rosie was expected back from Pinjrapore. Soli, miserably conscious of his small-pox scars, fed the bullocks and, twice a day, scattered grain for the chickens and pigeons. He had confided to Kety that he could get no relief from the sounds of a baby crying until he had performed these simple acts of charity. Sometimes he would rise in the middle of the night, to scatter grain from his balcony across the compound.

'Eat, enjoy, my children,' he'd shout, disturbing the household.

Minoo was enthralled by Soli and took several flashlight photos of his grey-bearded uncle offering food to the sleeping birds.

'Did you hear the baby crying, little Minocher?' Soli would ask when he caught sight of his hunchbacked nephew watching him from the door.

'Yes, Uncle Soli. It always cries loudest during the full moon.'

But Fram was less sanguine.

'Why make such a fuss about a ghost?' he'd demand. 'You're only encouraging the bloody thing.'

He spoke to Dilduktha about his brother but Soli was not prepared to go to Kapoli, as he did not believe in tinkering with the human mind.

'If I ever become mad,' he told Fram, 'I want to be confined in a proper madhouse like the one in Thana. Until then, allow me these simple expressions of love.'

Sometimes the uttering of the word 'love' set Soli off. 'Love,' he'd shout, laughing joyously at its sound. 'Love', he'd shout once more, his face upturned to the night sky.

Then, one day, after Chakramkhan reported seeing him in the bazaar, his eyes bandaged like Kety's, walking precariously as he tapped a stick before him, Fram gave him an ultimatum. Either he behaved himself or arrangements would be made to certify him. Soli looked at his brother with scorn before going out into the compound to shout to the skies, 'Mother, Father, I am the lost child.'

'Why don't you,' Fram suggested gently to Soli, 'give me a hand in the ice factory?'

Soli replied that he was considering doing something for the Civil Defence of Bombay.

'I understand that they're advertising for trainee firemen,' he said.

'But you're over fifty and look ten years older,' Fram snapped. 'Nobody will give a fellow with a long, grey beard and hair to his shoulders an interview. But even if you do tidy up your hair, your tight trousers will disqualify you. They're quite disgraceful. Rosie has grumbled about them on several occasions.'

'Since when has it been against the law to wear fitting clothes?' Soli demanded.

'It looks as though you've got a couple of footballs and a police truncheon in your pants,' complained Fram.

'I've always had large genitals,' Soli retorted. 'Why bitch now?'

Fram pointed out that his brother had grown fatter with age.

'You think like a Fascist,' Soli cursed. 'Anyway, Kety loves me in tight trousers.'

On her return to Peccavi, Rosie was surprised to see Soli sitting on the steps. The grey and melancholic figure ignored her as she hurried past. The smell of decay that she had almost forgotten in the ten days at Pinjrapore overwhelmed her on her passage through the house. Looking out of the drawing-room window, she saw that the head was missing from Sir Maneckji's statue. Theresa informed her that it had been sawn through during the night but that the master had recovered it from the pond.

'Have the police been informed?' Rosie asked, unclipping her earrings and making for the bedroom.

Theresa reported that she had seen an inspector sahib talking to the master.

'What happened to Byramji's head?' she asked, taking her dress off as Fram entered the room. He looked pained at her reference to Sir Maneckji as Byramji.

'It's Sir Maneckji,' he corrected, sitting on the bed.

It was not a subject he wanted to discuss, aware that there was little he could do to protect the great Wadia, short of a permanent chowkidar. Convinced that it was Garibaldi's schoolboys again, he had written to the headmaster, Father Pirelli, in forceful terms and had seen Mr Fazal about initiating a damages suit against the school. Mr Fazal had not been helpful.

'The place smells of rotten fish,' Rosie complained.

'It's not the Pinjrapore Palace,' Fram conceded.

Rosie took all her clothes off and sat, legs crossed, in the armchair before him, lighting up and puffing at a ganja cigarette. She gave him a brazen look, amused by his horny interest in her flaxen pubes.

'They only dyed the hair on my head,' she smiled.

Fram looked at her with despair.

'How did things go?' he asked.

She told him that she would be called Dinky and was scheduled for a five-minute dance slot as a courtesan. He indicated surprise.

'A dancing part?' he murmured doubtfully.

'Only the top half,' she explained. 'Friski is doing the feet movement. Jimmy thinks I've got star-quality breasts.'

Fram mentioned her hair, reminding her how proud he'd been of her fair curls.

'I know,' she said. 'Like Vanessa Beauchamp's.'

'She was auburn,' he murmured. The name of Vanessa Beauchamp was like a dagger in his heart. The bitter notion that it was a defilement on her lips was too depressing to endure. He sensed that Rosie had passed beyond his influence.

'Why are you smoking ganja?' he asked, sniffing the air.

'It settles my nerves,' she said, frowning.

He glimpsed the moist sheen of her fossa navicularis as she adjusted her legs before covering her lap with a cushion, suddenly uneasy at his hungry stares.

'What's the matter with Soli?' she asked.

'A sort of depression,' he replied, 'but he's going to help me in the ice factory.'

'I was thinking about that funny man,' she said. 'The one they call Pythagoras. I feel Minoo would be better off with a woman.'

'Why?'

'He needs a mother substitute,' she said.

'What about a mother?' Fram asked.

Rosie gave her cigarette a final draw before killing it and rising to her feet. He followed her into the bathroom, watching her as she soaped herself under the shower.

'He's in Skinner House.'

'Who?' she asked.

'Our Minoo.'

Fram came to her, holding her wet buttocks and running his fingers along her slippery slit. He was drenched by the spray.

'Easy,' she cautioned, as he groped her, laying his head against her soapy breasts.

'I want you,' he murmured.

She stepped out from the shower and dried herself, eyeing his dripping figure warily.

'Please,' he whispered, coming to her.

She raised a restraining hand. 'No, Fram,' she sighed, 'no.'

He watched her from the door as she got dressed, speaking to him quite affably about her prospects in the movie business before announcing that she was going downstairs to write some letters.

Chapter 22

When Minoo started at Christ Church, he was judged to be a year ahead of his age and put into Standard Three, where his form mistress was a Miss Olive Southey, an obese, bespectacled lady in her thirties. The red-faced Miss Southey was quite unlike Pythagoras. She shouted a great deal and threatened to whack anyone who made a mistake or was guilty of the most minor infringement. A boy was slapped for wearing open-toed sandals and a girl shaken for stinking of perfumed talc. Miss Southey boasted that she was capable of stunning a man weighing one hundred and fifty pounds with the palm of her hand and took delight in telling the class of petrified nine- and ten-year-olds how she had once done just that to a servant who showed her extreme discourtesy by wearing woollen socks in the house.

'I broke his jaw,' she exulted, before side-stepping the lesson on long division to recount to her class how Joe Louis had unscrambled Max Schmeling's brains in the first round.

'When you punch,' Miss Southey advised, 'always aim for a spot six inches beyond the target. You should wham through your opponent with a clenched fist, delivering the blow with the force of your shoulder, remaining properly anchored at the time of delivery with both feet firmly planted on the ground.'

'Please Miss did Max Schmeling die?' enquired an anxious boy who'd raised his hand.

Miss Southey glared at the little figure.

'I'll slap your chops,' she thundered. 'What we are discussing in this room is how many times three hundred and sixty-five will go into one.'

A solemn, undernourished girl with a shingled head that seemed too heavy for her neck raised her hand.

188

'No times, Miss.'

Miss Southey looked disappointed.

'Do not be surprised, Eva Rebello,' she boomed, 'if I shake you until your rotten little teeth drop out. Remember what I told you about divisions of ten.'

'Decimals, Miss?' Minoo asked nervously.

Miss Southey beamed. 'We have one attentive pupil in the class.'

She peered at Minoo.

'Announce your name to the class, attentive boy.'

Minoo got up and, looking around apprehensively, whispered, 'My name is Minoo Chutrivala.'

'Where do you live, Minoo Chutrivala?'

'At the ice factory, Miss.'

There was a long silence as the other pupils regarded their hunchbacked colleague. Living in an ice factory had an exotic charm they all seemed to envy.

'Ice,' Miss Southey declared, 'is what boxing seconds compress on fighters' faces to reduce swellings. Now, Master Chutrivala, where shall I stick the decimal point?'

'After the one, Miss,' Minoo replied.

Miss Southey busied herself on the board, preparing the division of 365 into 1,00000. She half turned for a moment towards her class.

'What sports are compulsory at Christ Church?' she demanded.

Several hands shot up. She pointed to a thuggy, dark boy with slanted eyes and an inbuilt belligerence in his scowl.

'Boxing and swimming, Miss.'

She looked at Minoo over her glasses.

'Can you box, Chutrivala?' she asked the little hunchback.

He stood up and shook his head. She glared at him for some time.

'You don't want to be a slop, do you, Chutrivala?' she demanded.

'No, Miss.'

'Then take care to glove up and have a go at the next gym.'

It was at gym, taken by Mr George Kismet, a short, muscular man with a dark-chocolate complexion, that Minoo discovered that he would have to play a part in a Pageant of Patriotism. He was to be a hunchbacked Beefeater and would stand motionless for three hours, shit-flies and red ants notwithstanding, at the entrance of the hall, a plyboard halberd in one hand and a collection-box around his neck. The proceeds were to be divided equally between the Empire Fund for Service Orphans and the Saraswati Leprosy Foundation. Duplicated song-sheets were passed around the gymnasts with the words of 'Land of Hope and Glory'.

Mrs Gomes, the wrinkled, hoar-headed music teacher whose grandfather had been in the Siege of Lucknow, struck out a few resonant chords on the upright below the boxing ring, to lead them into the hubristic lyrics. The singleted boys managed to sing in relative unison at the third attempt but were threatened with further rehearsals before the day of performance.

'Like crows,' Mrs Gomes pronounced unhappily, as she collected the song-sheets. 'Like crows squabbling over stinking entrails.'

When Mrs Gomes left the gymnasium, the gloves, suspended like brown and red bloaters on a pole, were raced in on the shoulders of two prefects.

'Glove up,' barked Mr Kismet, 'glove up.'

Minoo was provided with a pair of sixteen-ounce cushions that laced up to his elbows. The smell of the sweat-soaked leather made him nauseous and he was troubled by an irresistible desire to urinate, only the obvious inconvenience of having to pass water with boxing gloves on deterred him.

It all happened very quickly. He was assisted up the steps to face a rat-faced, blond lad with a tiny head and large ears.

'Box on,' were the last instructions he heard, recovering consciousness as he lay on his side upon a wooden form with Mr Kismet applying a cold sponge to his neck. He discovered to his relief that the only damage he'd sustained was a slightly swollen lip and was able, after a few minutes, to hobble unaided to the dressing room.

The humiliation came later when he was reported to the gym master for having pissed himself. Mr Kismet did not appear to be pleased at his lack of bladder control.

'That was a slop thing to do, Chutrivala,' he said grimly. 'To what house do you belong?'

'Skinner House, Sir.'

'I'll have to send you up to Mr Pithers,' Mr Kismet decided.

The thought of Pythagoras hearing of his disgrace depressed him. But he had no need for concern. Pythagoras, finishing a cup of tea in his cramped study, grinned at the little hunchback.

'When I played rugby,' Pythagoras reflected, 'I often pissed myself. I mean, one just didn't have time to leave the field.'

And having cheered Minoo with this confession of his own lapses, Pythagoras talked at length about the reflex nature of the bladder mechanism.

'Urination,' he declared brightly, 'is one of the signs of life in an animal. Once one ceases to expel the unwanted toxins from the body, life ceases. Think of it as a sort of celebration.'

He observed that the reservations society had about wetting one's pants were cultural and had little to do with the basic rhythms of life. He expressed the view that dogs were probably more fortunate insomuch as they could piss where they liked.

'And, of course,' he added, 'they have no pants.'

But just as Minoo had been persuaded of the advantage of being a dog, Pythagoras reminded him that dogs were almost certainly ignorant of mathematics.

'The poor creatures have probably never heard of Euclid,' he brooded, sipping his tea and looking suddenly glum.

By the time Minoo had left his house master, he was convinced that it was, on balance, preferable to be human, wear dry pants and understand Euclid.

'But,' Pythagoras reminded him, 'the balance in favour of humanity is finer than we suspect.'

If Fram was unhappy about Rosie's jet-black hair, movie name of Dinky and work as a minor actress for Amazing Films, he realised that there was little he could do to change the course of events. She now spent much of her time in Pinjrapore, appearing without warning at Peccavi in one of Jimmy's Rollers, wearing beautiful saris and bedecked with jewels. She sent Fram what money she could spare and regretted that she could not do more to help with the household expenses.

Her needless affirmation to Fram that she had not been unfaithful with the Raja of Pinjrapore was, for a considerable time, technically true. Kety, however, felt the issue was academic for everybody in the movie business believed the contrary. Furthermore, Rosie's long absences, at times six months or more, meant that the marriage, for practical purposes, had ended and Fram's interest might, as Kety expressed it, be better served by divorce. Fram thought otherwise, and preferred to consider his marriage suspended, hopeful that Rosie would return when Pinjrapore and the film industry tired of her meagre abilities. Friski encouraged his guarded optimism by the disclosure that Patcheco had approached Rosie to join the Melodics, the name of the quartet that had replaced the Shalimars at Singleton's. A return to the band, Fram felt, would at least keep her in Bombay. But in this matter Kety was nearer the truth, having long ascertained that Rosie would never be happy at Peccavi.

Fram's health had deteriorated to a point, where he could not walk a dozen paces without discomfort and he had to exercise the greatest circumspection about any form of sexual excess.

'Do you consider,' he asked his doctor, thinking of Rosie and the possible restitution of his marriage, 'that it would be prudent for me to attempt coitus twice a week?'

The doctor pursed his lips and tapped a pencil on his desk.

'We could, of course,' he remarked evasively, 'prescribe medication to suppress your wife's sexual desires.'

He waited for Fram's reply before adding quietly that it would not be necessary to advertise the matter indicating with a smile that a drop or two in the morning tea would probably be sufficient to blunt her libido.

'Is that strictly Hippocratic?' Fram asked.

The doctor tugged at his ear.

'I was approaching the problem from the *de facto* status of women in our society. As a wife is her husband's chattel, it follows that the desires of that chattel are also his exclusive property within the union. And a temporary suppressant hardly preempts her future rights should the union end.'

It was a point of view Fram was resolved to debate with his friend, Dilip Dilduktha.

Rosie's time was consumed in a whirl of parties, travelling to film locations around Pinjrapore, reading trashy magazines and American comics, gossiping with Motherbunch, resisting randy playboys, listening to dance music on the collection of records Jimmy bought her and being instructed by the great Mohandas on how to wiggle her arse and shake her head in a flirtacious manner.

She was introduced to international cricketers, taken on tiger hunts, photographed for screen magazines and given voice lessons by the great Popatbai, an ancient chanteuse whose vocal resonance was achieved by the ingenious use of thoracic phlegm.

'Spit will not do,' she warned, as she demonstrated her legendary gurgle.

Motherbunch told Rosie that, although Popatbai was over eighty, young men queued at her door, captivated by the sensual power of her voice. Rosie's deficiency in phlegm restricted her progress as a singer, but Jimmy was more than satisfied by her modest efforts. She was even complimented by Casamali the celebrated sarod-player, who appeared with her in *Toofan ki Bibi*, an escapist movie about a girl who was abandoned in the jungle, raised by wolves, and who fell in love with the sunyasi who found her. It was Rosie's most successful movie with Friski Dalal's feet and Popatbai's phlegmy vocals supporting her voluptuous eye movements and wobbling breasts. Casamali drove her back to the palace after the final day's shooting, surprising her when he exposed his cock as they rolled into Pinjrapore City.

'It is nothing less than you deserve,' he whispered, placing her fingers over his purple plenum.

'Please, Casamali,' she pleaded, drawing her hand away politely.

'Don't be fright,' he said, 'accept it as a token of my humble esteem.'

She escaped at the traffic lights and hailed a cycle-rickshaw, directing him through the crowded bazaar to evade Casamali's pink De Soto. The cycle-rickshaw driver trembled with awe when she alighted at the palace gates, declining her ten rupee note, but reaching for her painted toenails. Rosie kicked him in the shins. The man smiled gratefully and begged to be allowed to touch her feet. Rosie kicked him again and, dropping the note, ran into the palace yard. She turned and saw the ragged driver watching her hungrily through the iron bars of the railings. It was the terrible price she had to pay for being a recognised movie-actress.

'You should have scratched Casamali's face and whacked the other bastard with your slipper,' Motherbunch advised. Rosie shuddered.

'Draw blood,' her friend insisted. 'India is filled with demented cunt-chasers.' Motherbunch paused and looked at Rosie thoughtfully. 'Unless of course, you want to do it.'

'My God,' Rosie protested, shaking her head. She was, of course, thinking of Jimmy. But there were other films to be made and pursuits to be evaded before the Raja of Pinjrapore showed his hand. During the making of *Diwana*, Casamali exposed himself again and she caught Mohandas coming out of the cubicle next to the one she was occupying in the ladies' toilet. He smiled at her as they walked back to the set.

'You have,' he confided, 'an extremely powerful stream.'

She stared at him blankly and asked him about a dance movement that was proving difficult. The sudden appearance of Friski Dalal was a welcome diversion.

Minoo wrote to her every week. He usually enclosed a photograph he'd taken of local grotesques. Fram was rarely mentioned. She was bored by her son's reports of Christ Church, which she suspected was an unpleasant place. Even Minoo's snapshots made her yawn. The subjects were invariably diseased or old. Mohandas was alarmed when she asked the great director his opinion of her son's work.

'Confidentially,' he declared, 'the boy is mentally unbalanced. These pictures of mutilated beggars horrify me. When I was a youth, I was only interested in healthy female bodies. Breasts, until I was fifteen or so. And then the other part.' He smiled. 'That other part has been my life. It inspired me to become an international film director.'

Rosie took up bridge and mah-jong. Generally, Jimmy and she played with Peter and Michaela de Roosbroeck, a pair of jolly Belgian anthropologists. Michaela's book, *The Whistling Chirriyasi of Pinjrapore* (Thacker & Co., 1935), was the definitive work on the small tribe of tree-dwelling aborigines, who built nests like birds, spoke a chirrupy-sounding language and subsisted on a diet of worms, small rodents and rotting fruit. Peter was a giant of a man, six foot six or more with bushy black hair and an untidy beard. Michaela was toothy, blonde, diminutive and intense. Motherbunch hinted that she was having an affair with Jimmy but there seemed little evidence of this, apart from some occasional hand-holding when they walked in the palace gardens. The de Roosbroecks were friendly if rather tactile people. Peter often kissed her when they met and was not above a happy squeeze or two on parting. He delighted in taking her through the bazaar, where she was recognized as Dinky.

'Look how famous you are,' the big Belgian exulted, waving happily to the excited crowds. He introduced her to a group of wrestlers who practised in a large cage with a sawdust floor. The bull-like power of these oily men fascinated him. He told her that he had once stripped down to his underpants and tried to grapple himself, only to be thrown within seconds. The wrestlers worked in a narrow alley where charas, bhang and apheen were sold over the counter, between a tea-house and a black magician's consulting rooms. Here, were to be found the kite-shops, sugarcane stalls, sari emporia, jewellers, bunias selling foodstuff, street barbers, brassware merchants, leathergoods vendors and a snake-oil retailer. Peter pointed out a crumbling yellow building where he said, young boys and girls could be buggered for a few annas. But Jimmy warned them that he was apprehensive about these visits to the city shops.

'Its all very well for crazy anthropologists,' he complained to Peter, 'but the sight of Dinky walking in the bazaar could cause civil unrest.' However, Rosie recognised several men from the Amazing Films Publicity Department inciting the crowd, something that escaped Peter's notice.

On 23 May, 1940, she noted in her diary that she had not had sex for fifteen months. Not since Shushtary had left for Tehran. She confessed this to Motherbunch, who gazed at her with horror.

'You'll grow cancerous down below,' she warned. 'Why don't you return to your husband for a month or so?'

It was then that she realised that the resumption of married life with Fram was quite impossible for her. The thought of spending time at Peccavi made her ill. When she drove down to Bombay, she usually stayed with Motherbunch or at the apartment Shush had provided for her. In the meanwhile, Rosie waited.

Jimmy was not a precipitate lover and his pursuit of Rosie was leisurely. He indulged her with gifts: an elephant, a grey Arab stallion called 'Am I Blue?', a dancing lemur, white cockatoos, a pair of borzois and trays of jewellery. And he encouraged her to share his bhang-laced hookah and titillated her with a variety of hallucinatory paans. The expensive gifts were unfortunately unconvertible for they were kept at the palace where Jimmy took childlike delight in inspecting them when she visited him.

'Show me your bracelets,' he'd plead, examining and counting them carefully. 'And your nose-studs, and your belly chains, and your pubic pendants,' he'd demand, not content until the glittering collection had been displayed upon her bed.

The sale of 'Am I Blue?' alone would have provided sufficient capital to have completely restored Peccavi and modernised the ice factory. But Jimmy had hinted that the disposal of gifts was an insult a great prince could not endure. And most of her salary, for complex tax reasons, was taken in stock options in Amazing Films. By 1942, Amazing Films had released four movies in which she had supporting roles as Dinky. And although she never received the frenzied adulation enjoyed by Bhabee, for whom young men dived before express trains and slashed themselves in ecstasy, the thrill of being mobbed whenever she alighted from a white Rolls Royce, wearing her golden sari, sapphire ear-drops, glass sandals and green polaroids, was an experience of which she never tired. The knowledge that the demonstrations were managed by Amazing Film's Publicity Department, did little to diminish her joy as the crowd of star-worshippers struggled like beasts to touch the hem of her sari.

On the other hand, her friend Motherbunch, now Bhabee, had acquired the prestige of a goddess. She lived in a pink, air-conditioned villa overlooking Bombay's Juhu Beach, protected by half a dozen alsatians, attended by a dozen servants and lusted after by an equal number of big-shot suitors. Her contracts were settled in Swiss dollars and a biographer reinvented her past, passing her off as the daughter of a Maharashtrian school-teacher. Her repeated declaration that it was her ambition to marry a simple man and have many children, brought dozens of proposals each week, while the assertion that she was a non-smoker, teetotaller, vegetarian and spinner of khadder, made her the inspiration of thousands of Hindu households throughout the land. But she confided to Rosie, that the guy who had the inside track was a six foot four, American master-sergeant called Leonard Rosenthal from San Francisco, with whom she shared a unpublicised appetite for bourbon on the rocks, rare T-bone steaks toasted tobacco and fucking.

'After this goddam war is over,' she grunted, 'I want nothing more than to traipse in the Californian sun with Lenny, eating trashy food, listening to trashy music, and breeding freckled and snub-nosed brats.'

Rosie, however, had dreams that could not be reduced to the happy simplicity of Motherbunch's domestic ambitions. Even after three years, she still yearned for Shushtary, expecting his return on good days and despairing of ever seeing him again on bad ones. He rarely wrote and did not appear to be receiving many of her discursive and sensual reflections. She planned to visit Tehran after the war but remembered, glumly, Shushtary's warnings that it was not a place where they could live comfortably together.

One night, after a session of filming at Pinjrapore, Rosie was asked to report to the Pinjrapore Clinic, where she was advised by a young physician that she had been selected for a routine medical examination. Amazing Films, the physician explained had a duty to protect the health of their dancers both from the perspective of responsible employers and as prudent risk-takers.

'Our insurers are much happier with a planned programme of screening that identifies, and a course of treatment that ameliorates, the more usual infections to which young people are subject.' The tests took an hour. She had a phone-call shortly after her return to her suite at the palace. It was Jimmy. He sounded cheerful.

'You've passed your medical,' he announced. She admitted that not only had she not expected to receive the result so soon but had hardly imagined that the Raja of Pinjrapore would be the messenger.

'There's a reason,' he giggled. 'I want you to sleep with me.'

'Sleep?'

She was depressed by the duplicity. Jimmy enthused that he had wonderful plans for her which would necessitate her immediate retirement from Amazing Films. He also warned that sleeping with him would preclude her association with other men.

'As a ruler I dare not contaminate my line,' he said. 'Cleanliness is a divine responsibility. The Pinjrapore dynasty has been chancre-free for generations.'

Rosie found it difficult to respond to his arrogant assumptions. And exchanging her minor celebrity as an actress for what she suspected was the doubtful status of confinement in luxury as Jimmy's concubine did not exalt her. Taking up permanent residence at Pinjrapore without the alibi of film-making would, she suspected, sever links with her family. Although that prospect was not wholly unacceptable, she felt that theoretically a sacrifice of that degree had a price.

'Just how much am I worth, Jimmy?' she asked thoughtfully.

'As an option-holder in unissued Amazing Films stock?' he enquired.

'Uh huh.'

'About fifty lakhs,' he mused, 'give or take a thou.'

The magnitude of the sum mentioned astonished her.

'I would like, say, five on account if that's possible,' she said.

'Sure,' he laughed. 'We can talk about it in bed.'

He was knocking at the door before she'd had time to change into something more comfortable. After they had enjoyed a pipe of apheen Rosie seemed to float above the bed. The sound of the tabla outside throbbed down her spine into her wet cloven flesh. In the velvet darkness, Jimmy mounted her. She gasped at the prodigy of his performance as he took her again and again, careful to stop when she begged him to and start again when that was her need. He confessed that he had always been in love with her and she sobbingly expressed the realisation that, until then, total fulfilment had eluded her.

At first light, she reached down for his cock, gripping it as he turned sleepily away. She sat up, blinking in horror at the huge rubber dildo that came away in her hand. Jimmy opened a playful eye.

'I had it made,' he informed her, 'for the Pinjrapore Stud. Something to titillate the mares before the stallion climbed on her.'

'It was so good,' she said in wonder, circling its girth with her fingers.

'You must give me some credit,' he pouted, 'Many of my girl friends have never guessed the truth. The apheen helps, of course.'

She leaned over and kissed him on the lips.

'Thank you,' she whispered.

He drew her hand down under the sheet, surprising her with

the modesty of the authentic specimen. Jimmy did not appear abashed by the comparison.

'Now it's my turn,' he reminded her, moving beween her dutifully parted thighs.

They settled down together afterwards, Rosie with her head on the Raja's shoulder, holding his limp cock affectionately as they dozed.

'It's not that small,' she mused. 'I mean it works all right.'

Jimmy smiled.

'I'm pleased you didn't get picky about it because there's something rather special I want to ask you.'

She looked sideways at him, warmed by his beauty. He tugged rather shyly at a free nipple as he asked her if she would consent to becoming the Rani of Pinjrapore.

'But what about my husband?'

It was then that she learned that he had for three days withheld the news that Fram had succumbed to a heart attack and that death was instantaneous. She stared at him wide-eyed. He placed a hand over her mouth.

'The answer to that unasked question need not be articulated,' he observed.

Then, as the tabla started again, they took each other's mouths with ferocious certainty.

Chapter 23

The problem of Fram's intestacy was addressed a few hours after his body was taken to the morgue. Kety and Soli, having agreed that Rosie should not inherit any part of the estate, typed a will on a sheet of back-dated contract paper Soli procured from a solicitor friend of his and, having arranged two witnesses, handed the document to Mr Fazal, who was not even slightly convinced by its authenticity.

'This,' he said to Soli, 'is a forgery.'

'What do you mean by that?' asked Soli.

Mr Fazal pointed out that Palkiwala and Cama, the two witnesses, had twice been convicted of perjury and the Probate Court would view with grave suspicion any deposition in which their names appeared. Mr Fazal thumbed quickly through his diary, then rang for Mr Dossa. He asked him to check the date on the contract paper, before advising Soli that it would be prudent to leave the larger portion of the estate to Fram's son, with an interest for his daughter, Meroo.

'He hadn't seen Meroo for nearly twenty years,' Soli remarked.

Mr Fazal smiled.

'When one is forging a will, a certain amount of creative imagination is important.'

'The truth is, Mr Fazal,' Soli said, 'without the ice factory and the house my sister will be destitute. It is important we don't end up on the pavements of Bombay. My poor Kety is almost blind.'

'The law, my dear Chutrivala, is no different for unsighted criminals.'

Mr Dossa came into the room and showed Mr Fazal a note which he read before addressing Soli again.

'On the date Palkiwala was supposed to have witnessed this

will, he was serving a six-month gaol sentence. If you and your sister filed this will, both of you could be behind bars yourselves.'

'What will we do?' asked Soli plaintively.

Mr Fazal suggested that they leave the matter to him. He undertook to produce a more plausible document witnessed by credible witnesses. But before Soli left he warned him that the widow would probably contest any will that excluded her.

'She's the Raja of Pinjrapore's whore,' Soli declared.

'So I hear, so I hear,' Mr Fazal said, 'but fornication *per se* does not extinguish a person's rights of inheritance.' The fat barrister showed Soli to the door. He suggested that in his opinion, their only hope of winning Mrs Chutrivala's acceptance of exclusion was to make her son the major legatee.

'He's a hunchback, I believe.'

Soli nodded. He did not look happy.

'We could appoint you a joint trustee of the estate, with Meroo Chutrivala, until the boy's majority. Since, from what I understand, Meroo is unlikely to participate in any administration, you will be whole and sole.'

'But why Meroo?' Soli asked.

'Because it's nice and messy. Just the sort of nonsense Fram Chutrivala would inflict on his heirs.'

'Poor Fram had good intentions,' Soli remarked sadly.

'He was brimming with them,' Mr Fazal agreed. 'Quite honestly, the poor bugger would have been vastly improved by a little malice.'

Rosie paid a brief visit to Peccavi to ascertain what arrangements had been made for Minoo. Soli assured her that Kety and he would care for the boy, retaining Angelica as his personal servant.

'How is little Minoo?' Rosie asked, looking around Fram's old office.

Soli assured her that he was in good health and happy at school.

'And Kety?' she asked, rising to leave.

She was informed that Kety was in the house and would no doubt be pleased to see her. Rosie glanced at her watch with a frown.

'Another time perhaps,' she suggested, the chauffeur having already opened the door of her white Rolls Royce.

Minoo, on his way home from school, watched her departure

from behind a coconut tree, careful not to be seen by her. Most of his memories of his mother were of her in a rush to be somewhere else. It was plain to see that this would have been another such occasion. It was only when the Rolls Royce had swept through the gates and disappeared from view that he made his way happily towards the ice factory.

Minoo spent most of his evenings and weekends helping Soli. Although he had not given up his ambition of being a photographer, the fact that the business had been bequeathed to him made him conscious of the responsibility with which he had been entrusted by his father. Soli, who had started bringing out *Red Tiger* again, warned him that he would be expected to run the ice factory once he'd matriculated.

'But I want to be a photographer,' the boy brooded.

'Do both,' Soli urged.

Minoo suggested that the storeroom where they kept the sacks of paddy husks used for insulating the ice tank could be converted into a much larger darkroom, as the attic in Peccavi leaked. The paddy husks, he felt, could be stored in the stables. Soli agreed. It was Minoo's second idea that caused some concern.

'I would like to convert part of the space into a studio,' he said, 'a place I could use for indoor photography and perhaps even sleep in.'

'Sleep? In the ice factory?' asked Soli, adding with a shiver, 'It's haunted.'

'You mean the baby?'

'It's a ghost,' Soli declared, 'and ghosts can drive a person crazy.'

'Whose baby was it?' asked Minoo.

'It happened a long time ago,' Soli told the boy, 'in Byramji's time.'

Later, at the evening meal, Soli told Kety that Minoo wanted to sleep in the ice factory.

'Oh my God,' she cried in horror.

But the darkroom and the studio were built and furnished before Minoo's sixteenth birthday. And when he started to sleep in his studio, neither his uncle nor his aunt raised too much fuss. They had moved into Fram's bedroom, sharing quite openly the great, Wadia bed. Soli used to peer across at the light in Minoo's studio, wondering why the boy found such contentment in solitude. Soli needed the warmth of Kety's body and the comfort of her flesh. The opportunity of living together again at Peccavi had given them great happiness in their middle age. They made love every night. It was as enjoyable as a drink of warm milk and relaxed them in the same agreeable way. One night, as they prepared to enjoy each other, Kety was suddenly aware that something Soli confessed confirmed for her that the relationship some imagined a curse was, in fact, a glorious benediction.

'You have saved me from madness,' he whispered, licking her stricken eyes with passion as he slid into her.

It had been Minoo's impression that Christ Church, although uncouth and at times violent, was a fairly friendly place. The hunchbacked boy from the ice factory was soon assimilated into the robust ways and manners of the school. Even his nicknames, Oont, Turtleback and Snailpot, eventually lost the sting their puerile perpetrators had intended, for he confronted the insults and exorcised them with dismissive scorn.

'It would be rather pleasant being a snail or a turtle,' he'd sneer when abused in these terms, 'for it would enable me to slip back into my shell and not have to endure your moronic faces.' Or, 'If I was an Oont, I'd take great pleasure in gobbing evil-smelling thack in your eye.'

In time, Minoo Chutrivala's hump had become an unexceptional and familiar object. Touched and stroked during gym and swimming, it lost the resonances of evil with which humps are invested by writers of melodramatic fiction. Indeed, Pythagoras, in a geometry lesson, had Minoo's hump projected and traced onto a screen, proceeding stealthily from that asymmetrical image to the properties of curves and the use of the boy's curvature as a protractor which, although imperfect, was far better than any competing projections. And if Pythagoras's droll celebrations of the kyphosis were a factor in its unsentimental acceptance by the hunchback's peers, Minoo's cheerfulness and intelligent scepticism gained him the respect of even the more doltish members of staff.

Kismet, the gym master, who also took the sixth standard, trusted Chutrivala sufficiently to entrust him with the purchase of cigarettes, gin and then delivery of confidential notes to married women. He was the first adult to enquire genially after Minoo's sexual progess.

'Do you masturbate, Chutrivala?' he enquired as he walked to class with his pupil.

'Occasionally, Sir,' Minoo admitted solemnly.

'I'm very pleased to hear it,' Kismet replied genially. 'Self-love is the safest form of sex for a boy growing up in pox-infested Bombay. We do not want our pupils wandering around Kamatipura, hazarding their young manhood in the two-rupee cages. Love yourself to distraction, my boy.'

Kismet himself had long since advanced beyond self-love. His use of servant girls and banana women during the tiffin intervals, when his wife was at work, had been observed by most of the residents of Piccadilly Mansion, the crumbling tenement block where he lived. And the thirteen-year-old girls in his class were conditioned to the movement of his hand up their skirts as he corrected their work at his desk. To the other young observers, the location of George Kismet's fingers was a subject of lively speculation. The girls who were subjected to the deeper explorations never complained. Uncompliant pupils with narrow concepts of propriety rarely felt George's hand more than an inch or two above the knee; many were not averse to an excursion along the outside of their thighs and a few did not protest at the fondling of their pubescent rumps. But there were two or three, whose innocent smiles could not be erased by any audacity and who tolerated the enterprises of his fingers making barely palpable excursions along their wispy down.

In time, Mr Kismet fell, losing his right index finger in Miriam McClusky's mush. She was a small, frisky looking English girl with ginger hair, freckles and a gap between her incisors. Particularly proficient at netball and athletics, the trim and wiry Miss McClusky was the daughter of a mill manager.

Success went to his head. He repeated the act daily, achieving penetrations of an inch or so, for almost a minute at a time. Miriam came first in geography, the only subject he marked, and received a special tribute in her term report for good behaviour and ésprit de corps. Appointed class monitor, Miss McClusky was asked to stay behind most evenings to organise the filling of inkwells and cutting of blotting paper. A little on from the two-finger stage, Mr Kismet locked the doors and kissed her on the mouth, provoking screams he did not anticipate. It transpired that while the obtuse Miss McClusky believed that Kismet's groping was unconscious, no more than the absent-minded fingerwork of an intellect with more cerebral preoccupations, the unsolicited meeting of lips had unacceptable sexual implications.

Kismet was suspended for a fortnight, investigated and finally restored to duty because of a lack of evidence. None of the other pupils talked and the girl, far from being pitied as the victim of assault, became the object of obloquy. An informer was never admired at Christ Church.

Chapter 24

Apart from Pythagoras, the master who played the most formative part in Minoo's education was Barton Fry, a tall and flabby teacher of English. Fry, an Anglo-Indian homosexual, was a stern but fair-minded man. There was no evidence that his proclivities ever involved the male pupils. His reputed lover was the local archdeacon, Cecil DeLisle, an affable but slightly mannered cleric, who, apart from his ecclesiastical duties, taught Divinity and Greek. It was Fry who introduced Minoo to Gibbon, Macaulay and Carlyle, encouraged him to read Stendhal and was dismissive about Forster's stab at an Indian novel.

'It's a predictable product,' Fry said, 'of the Oxbridge–Bloomsbury triangle, an incestuous gang of intellectual thugs who take in each other's washing. Nobody can succeed without their approval. They are distinguished by their insularity, envy and unrealistic estimation of their own talents.'

Fry often made these ferocious judgements in class. Pythagoras attributed his bitterness to the fact that Fry was a failed novelist himself, having tried without success to get published three novels he had written about the Raj.

'The humanity of the Raj,' Fry observed, 'is a figment of the British imagination. Our high-minded rulers have always patronised, despised and discriminated against us. No Indian who is not naive beyond imagination should take at face value the moral weight of the white man's burden. For while it is not unreasonable for conquerors to exact tribute, only *la perfide Albion* insists on sentimentalising her rapacity. The rewriting of history is a British obsession, central to the myth of their notion of being uniquely civilised.'

'But what about the Germans, Sir?' Minoo asked, having been lectured by Soli on the evils of Nazism.

Fry gazed at the hunchback sadly.

'I'm afraid, Chutrivala' he agreed sadly, 'those blighters are behaving rather monstrously as well.'

When Minoo reached Pythagoras's class, he was already sixteen and permitted long trousers. It was the year in which he achieved minor celebrity. With the Head's permission, Minoo photographed every pupil and teacher in the school. The three hundred rupees netted from this photography were donated to the Bijapur Famine Relief Fund. Minoo's smiling face appeared in the *Jam-e-Jamshed* and Charles Smallbush, the Head, awarded him his colours for Social Conscience, the first time such an award had been made at Christ Church. Generally, only distinction in sport and academic attainment was recognised and the Colours Committee agonised over a departure from accepted practice. Although Archdeacon DeLisle was in favour of introducing a moral dimension to the awards, Miss Flinto, the Headmistress of the Lower School, felt that colours for Social Conscience could favour the richer pupils like Chutrivala, who could always afford to donate significantly larger amounts than the poorer children who represented the majority in the school. Kismet nodded his agreement.

Pythagoras supported DeLisle in principle but felt that Christ Church should support Chutrivala's gesture in a more positive way. In his view, the Relief Fund was just a sanitised way of demonstrating altruism and suggested that a child victim of the famine should be given a scholarship to the school, providing the pupils with a tangible example of what the proposed colours for Social Conscience really meant.

'There would be,' Miss Flinto protested nervously, 'grotesque lingual problems.'

'And what precisely is the purpose of a school but to surmount educational deprivation of the sort described?' demanded the Archdeacon.

Mr Kismet pointed out that a child enfeebled by famine and disease would hardly be up to gloving up and swimming the mandatory fifty yards in the first term.

'Surely we could defer the fisticuffs and American Crawl until the lad was strong enough,' suggested Fry with concern.

'It could be a girl,' argued Miss Flinto, 'in which case we are talking about the Long Jump and twenty-five yards Breast.'

'Christ Church is about standards or nothing,' Kismet observed grimly. 'I certainly wouldn't want a boy here who couldn't glove up or swim.'

The Head pointed out that they had departed from the agenda, responding like lemmings to Mr Pithers's diversion about awarding a place to a starving peasant. Pythagoras smiled. But it gave him particular satisfaction when Miss Flinto, still shaken at the prospect of a famine victim in the Lower School, moved the motion of approval and Kismet seconded. It went through nem. con.

Later, the Archdeacon asked Pythagoras whether he'd been trained by Jesuits. The science master shook his head but admitted that he had two aunts who cheated at mah-jong.

The marriage of Mrs Rosie Chutrivala to the Raja of Pinjrapore was reported in most of the Indian papers and a few foreign ones, like the *Daily Telegraph*, *The Times* and the *New York Herald Tribune*. Five hundred guests attended but, although Minoo was invited, the invitation arrived three days after the wedding. Minoo asked Pythagoras's advice.

'Decline the invitation in the politest term without disclosing that it arrived late,' he counselled. 'That could be construed by your mother as a reproof. Invent a plausible excuse like influenza, a broken leg or even paratyphoid, taking care to stress that there is no need for concern as the worst is over.'

Minoo nodded.

'And send a present as quickly as possible,' the teacher instructed.

'A present?'

Pythagoras looked thoughtful.

'What better present could a mother receive than a picture of her son?' he asked. 'Send her an enlarged copy of that self-portrait you took recently, the one with the John Barrymore moustache, suitably framed and signed with an expression of affection.'

Tears came into Minoo's eyes.

Pythagoras frowned. 'What's the matter?'

'She wouldn't like that, Sir,' he murmured.

Pythagoras declared that the best presents were those that had an emotional charge. They were certainly far superior to objects whose worth resided in their market value.

'You must not allow your mother to escape from her obligation to love you,' he reminded Minoo. 'That would be uncharitable.'

And so Minoo took several more self-portraits to be on the safe side. The one he finally selected was a frontal pose in a white suit, wearing a dark bow-tie and a matching handkerchief in his jacket pocket. He felt that his eyes were too dark, big and lustrous so that even when he smiled, showing the sheen of his full lips and the whiteness of his flawless teeth, the face looked sad.

'I have the eyes of an animal,' he complained to his aunt, as he thumbed through the prints.

She peered at the photographs through a magnifying glass.

'You look a bit like your father,' she said, 'but more handsome.'

Minoo laughed in disbelief.

'But Papa looked like John Barrymore,' he said.

'So who says Minoo Chutrivala hasn't got the edge on that American show-off?'

But although he sometimes forgot his crookedness, he could never forget the laughter and derisive shouts from a group of drunken Tommies as he passed them on the Causeway.

'Get your small pack off, you silly little bastid.'

'What do you mean?'

'Your fucking small pack.'

He only realised what they meant when they pointed to his hump with coarse and high-spirited incivility.

Theresa, Chakramkhan and Angelica all modelled for Minoo. Many of the photographs were taken by flashlight in the ice factory. Much of his juvenilia consisted of poses in the large freezer rooms, among pendant sides of beef, mutton and pork, or in the poultry area, below the carcasses of geese, turkeys, chicken and pheasants. He induced Angelica to be photographed bare-breasted before the frozen meat and even took a nude study of her back, mirrored in a block of ice. Although intensely shy with him, she was his first nude, understanding almost intuitively the magic of his imagery and fantasies. He'd ask her to wear strange hats, shawls, strings of beads and feathers and allow her body to be painted. And although he was aroused at times by the sight of her rump or parted legs, he took care never to show his excitement, but to relieve himself discreetly after she had left him.

It was while he was examining a negative of Angelica in the freezer room that he noticed a reflection in a corner of the exposure that puzzled him. When he developed the negative, he saw it more clearly. Going into the room where the photograph had been taken, he found that below some damaged plaster in the corner was a metal strip. Minoo scratched away and discovered what was obviously the side of a small tin. Chipping away at the cement, he removed first one brick and then another. Finally, he had before him what was a miniature ice-box.

He knew when he saw the way the refrigeration pipes coiled over the tin that great care had been taken not only in concealing the box but also in preserving its contents. He removed the box from the wall and took it from the refrigerated room to his studio, placing it on the table. After he'd set up the lights and loaded his cameras, he took the first few shots of his discovery, recognising, despite defacement of the artwork, that it had originally contained Sharp's Toffees, but that it had, he suspected, long since been appropriated to another use.

As he ran his fingers around the lid, he noticed, for the first time, italic writing scratched on the top below the glacial shield. He scraped the melting ice quickly away and examined the looped script. It read, '*Ardeshir Maneckji Wadia, son of Byramji Wadia and Freni Kapadia. 11.9.1895.*' Knowing and yet not knowing what to expect, he temporised for a few minutes, debating whether the creature that had lain inside its icy sarcophagus for nearly half a century should be disturbed. Deciding to open the tin, he forced the lid with a knife and it fell away with a clatter. There before him was a tiny, perfectly preserved infant, hardly bigger than a newborn piglet, fish-lipped and open mouthed as though astonished by death. The corpse of Ardeshir had thick black hair and a beaked nose with nostrils of decorous sensitivity. He prised apart waxy, worm-like fingers and, lifting the stiff, white gown, found the crinkled mauve evidence of its maleness. How, he wondered, had this forgotten son of Byramji died? He twisted the head to investigate what he at first suspected was the shadowy mark of a ligature around the throat but discovered that the curious effect was no more than the refracted light from a beard of ice crystals projecting a purple penumbra around the baby's goose-thin neck.

Minoo photographed his discovery many times, posing the body in Byzantine configurations. He ran his finger wistfully along the spine of the middle-aged homunculus, tracing faint branches on its palms, and marvelling at the capillaries and tassels blueprinting a future that was not to be. He watched water drip from puttied flesh, sensing that he was releasing the icy spirit that had profaned little Ardeshir with the immortality of a maquette. Then, before dawn, having restored the inexorable progress of decay, he replaced the carcass in its toffee-tin which he wrapped in newspapers and slid below his bed.

The next day, he instructed one of the labourers to dig a hole by the pond beside the mutilated statue of Sir Maneckji, interring the remains of the child that night. He resolved never to share his discovery of Byramji's son, nor show the photographs he'd taken of little Ardeshir to anyone. This would be, he considered, as his father would have wanted the matter resolved. A sacred family secret.

But one night, not long after the incident, he had a dream in which he saw the banjaras digging up and eating the body of Ardeshir, crunching the infant's bones in their powerful jaws. In the dream, he saw himself walk out into the moonlit compound to investigate. When he found a tiny, half-consumed foot by the Krishmachura tree, he screamed himself awake. Finding his torch, he went outside to check the grave. It had not been disturbed.

The next day he asked his Aunt Kety who Freni Kapadia was. She stared at him with dull, uncomprehending eyes. He explained that it was probably somebody old Byramji was friendly with fifty years ago or more. She did not know but put the question to Soli when he came in. He replied without hesitation.

'Freni Kapadia,' he declared, 'was the unmarried name of Friski Dalal.'

Chapter 25

On Saturday afternoons Minoo went to the races with Pythagoras. They travelled in the Chutrivala Buick, chauffeured by Chakramkhan. Pythagoras had the knack of winning small amounts and losing large ones. Minoo, on the other hand, was lucky, rarely leaving the course without showing a profit.

'I have a gift for it, Sir,' he explained to the lugubrious Pythagoras, 'my grandfather being a Wadia and one of the greatest gamblers Bombay has produced. His mare Syncopation won the Bombay Arab Derby three times.'

'I remember Syncopation running when I was a boy,' Pythagoras recalled.

'Sir, how does Mahaluxmi compare with Ascot or Long-champs?' Minoo asked.

'Mahaluxmi is, without any shadow of doubt, the finest racecourse in the world,' Pythagoras asserted gravely. 'For where we have nine races on our card, those other places usually have six.'

'Only six?'

'Furthermore,' Pythagoras said, 'while racing in most parts of the world is not entirely straight, racing at Mahaluxmi is completely dishonest. Many of the horses are doped, all the jockeys pull their mounts to instruction and our stewards rarely embarrass the crooked connections with a serious enquiry.'

Minoo gave his master a searching look.

'If the result of a horse-race depended upon form, favourites would generally win,' Pythagoras pointed out. 'And since most gamblers are looking for outsiders, they would find the predict-ability unbearably boring. It's uncertainty that keeps the grand-stand packed with madmen like us and that can only be ensured by well organised corruption. Racing, my boy, is no more than theatre.'

He entertained Minoo with stories of men who mortgaged their estates and risked everything on one horse putting its snout in front of another.

How, Pythagoras demanded, did a mediocre animal like Why beat the great Finalist in the Gold Cup at even weights?

'How, Sir? How?'

Pythagoras gave a bitter laugh.

'Not on form, Minoo. Not on form.'

It was an auspicious day for buyers of money. Thousands had come to see Golden Fawn, the placid son of the great Bahram take the local version of the Eclipse Stakes. The Tote guarantee of a 10–1 On minimum dividend for a place had induced speculators to plunge fortunes on Golden Fawn finishing in the frame. Golden Fawn, bearing the terracotta silks with crimson chevrons and cap of the Maharaja of Baroda, and ridden by Edgar Britt the Australian, was already a legend in Bombay. Not only had the crowds come to buy easy money but they were there to witness the tamasha of Britt's disdain for the opposition, riding his mount from the back, chancing all on a late burst of acceleration. Pythagoras and Minoo were parted in the tumult of people pushing and climbing to get a view of the race. Minoo, his throat parched by the dust and his heart pounding with the expectation of the race, had climbed onto one of the grandstand supports. He lifted himself onto the sloping wall, clinging to a wooden post and peering at the ten furlongs start. Below him, a lady with hennaed curls, in a white silk trouser suit, looked up at him as she tried to balance on the back of a bench. He was half-minded to offer her his leg to hold but the idea seemed preposterous. Her perfume drifted up to him, distracting his concentration, and he sensed that she was unsighted and restless.

'What's happening?' she called, her face craned enviously in his direction.

'They're coming in,' he replied.

There was no need to say more. The electric bell, the commentary on the crackling tannoy and the boom of the crowd indicated that the horses were running. He looked down at her, estimating her to be elderly. Past forty perhaps. But the aroma of her expensive body could not be ignored. Suddenly and without warning, he felt her hand around his leg. He looked down and saw the tight, white knuckles and clusters of rings.

'I'm sorry,' she laughed, steadying herself.

The feel of the strange woman's hand on his leg excited him. He erected slightly.

'What's happening?' she demanded again, tightening her grip around his ankle.

'Golden Fawn is last,' he said, looking down at her fine-spun russet twists of hair.

As the horses swung around the final bend, Golden Fawn was three lengths behind the field. Approaching the two, the prospects of the favourite winning seemed dire. For a moment or two, a panic-stricken silence that sensed an impossible defeat stupefied the crowd. With one to go, all seemed lost. Then, almost too late, Britt shook the little grey. In a few bounding strides, Golden Fawn sailed past the field, almost floating to victory by one and a half lengths.

Tears filled Minoo's eyes. He stared down at the lady in disbelief.

'Golden Fawn has won,' he said emotionally.

She did not reply. And if she had done, no single voice could have been separated from the screams of delirious excitement around them. He climbed down awkwardly, tearing his trousers as he joined her. He now saw that she was older than he had at first imagined, with the fine lines of age around her red mouth and purple-shadowed eyes. But she had a tranquil and handsome face that did not appear to be happy with the result.

'I lost,' she shrugged glumly.

'I'm sorry,' he replied.

By now the pressure of the crowd had pressed them closer. He lusted for her, wanting to crush her fragility and kiss the whiteness of her slender, blue-veined neck.

'Have you got a car?' she asked, making a quick and desperate assessment of her situation.

'Yes,' Minoo said.

'Do you want to come back to my place?' she whispered.

The unexpected invitation first astonished and then made him breathless with goatish need as he looked hopelessly around for Pythagoras.

'I have a friend,' he explained woodenly.

Once more the crowd pressed them together. Her hand found and slyly touched his swollen cock.

'I can be your friend too,' she said gently.

He stared into her ice-blue eyes and found a look of faded futility there that gave him the confidence to reach for and take her soft and pampered hand. They edged down the stone steps and made their way past the paddock towards the entrance. It was, he realised, only the end of the sixth race. There were three more events on the card and one and a half hours before the meeting ended. How, he wondered, would Pythagoras get home?

Chakramkhan was asleep when Minoo tapped on the window. The driver, trained in the ways of young gentlefolk, did not betray his surprise at Minoo's appearance with an elderly European lady with glittering turquoise eyes and carmine hair. She gave an address which she told the driver was at the back of Green's Hotel. Inside the car, she restored her lip-paint and dabbed a strong perfume on her earlobes and neck. Now he could see that there was grey below the amber sheen of her hair; her teeth were too flawlessly white to be authentic and her lips trembled a little in repose.

'I'll do you a special rate of three hundred,' she suggested, squeezing his hand.

He looked sideways at her in surprise.

'Three hundred?'

She seemed slightly hurt by the intonation of his voice.

'It's five hundred usually, darling,' she assured him. 'I only go with diplomats and the better class of maharajas, being a frightfully close relative of the Governor of Bombay.'

It was not a revelation Minoo readily believed but he felt that the story had a harmless charm and already imagined re-telling it to his friends at school. They left the Buick in a side-street and as Minoo made to follow her Chakramkhan restrained him with a hardly perceptible tug on the sleeve.

'Take care, Minoo Sahib,' the Pathan whispered.

They passed along a vaulted arcade of steps past a mercer's display of vivid silks chatoyant in a tumble of columns caught by the falling sun, assailed by the smell of new leather, bhujjas sizzling in oil, graveolent drains and fresh pistachios. Turning down a gully between a jeweller's and a money-changer's, they

215

passed through an entrance to a foyer warm with the aroma of sweet limes, entering a narrow brass lift that carried them slowly to the fifth floor.

What confidence, assurance and lechery had sustained him until now evaporated as she let him into her hot and shuttered apartment, cluttered with palms, brassware and Turkish wall-rugs. She switched on the ceiling fan and adjusted an upper venetian blind, catching the evening sun in the trickling water of a clepsydra that took Minoo's interest. He turned to catch her patient but slightly weary gaze.

'It's a gift from the Chief Presidency Magistrate,' she murmured, 'not terribly accurate but comforting at night.'

She paused as she heard a sound from another room.

'I'm home, Dulcie,' she called. Then, walking towards a half-opened door, warned, 'I have a friend with me.'

There was much in her collection of ivory objects and wooden figurines that reminded him of Peccavi and he was suddenly depressed by the twilight feeling of sadness in these rooms. They passed the door of the room that was occupied by Dulcie to one that opened to disclose a large bed covered in a black cashmere counterpane. She sat on the bed and, drawing him to her, unbuttoned his flies; then, stooping, gave his semi-erect cock a perfunctory kiss. It seemed very much in the nature of a cheerful greeting.

'As you can see,' she said, 'I'm not prejudiced. There's not many memsahibs in Bombay who'll kiss an Indian down there, but I'm a very enlightened lady. Something like Annie Besant. Have you heard of her?'

Minoo remembered that she was somebody famous but couldn't recall what she was famous for. As she played gently with his genitals, she informed him that he was the first hunchback who'd had an opportunity to make love to her and reflected that it might change her luck. Minoo smiled. She admitted that when she had noticed at Mahaluxmi that he was a hunchback she'd gripped his ankle for luck but it didn't work. Maybe, she observed, she should have held something else.

'How old are you?' she asked, stroking his curved back.

'Eighteen,' he lied.

'You look younger,' she murmured, 'despite your fine moustache.'

She chattered brightly, informing him that she was from Redhill in England, but had lived in India previously with her husband, who'd been a Deputy Commissioner of Police. She had returned to Bombay after his death to stay with her best friend, Dulcie.

'I've always taken Indian lovers,' she confessed with a giggle. 'Even when I was an important memsahib and the wife of a senior policeman.'

Pointing to the bathroom beyond, she asked him for the money and instructed him to use the bidet, an appliance he had never seen before. She followed him in and ran the taps in a businesslike manner, miming the way the bath should be used.

'Soap, water and towels, darling,' she advised sweetly, returning to the bedroom to disrobe.

Minoo undressed down to his muslin vest and, after dutifully washing himself, draped a towel around his lower body to join her. She was naked and appeared to have shrivelled to a pale, etiolated pixie, the platinum wisps almost invisible between her spindly shanks. As he approached her, he noticed that she was curiously wrinkled around her belly and thighs. She pulled his towel away and grasped the semi-erect cock, arousing him with her genial acceptance of the rubbery black object.

'Have you ever had fun with a European lady before?' she asked mischievously, like a maiden aunt who was enquiring whether he'd like a game of musical chairs.

'No, Miss,' he mumbled, subdued by the unexpected spectacle of her antiquity. She parted her thighs, drawing back the pale, ham-like folds of her pearl-pink ostiole.

'Doesn't Brer Rabbit know where the front door is?' she coaxed, massaging him with an urgent hand. He came almost instantly as he crouched on the bed waiting to mount her, shamed by her tolerance as she cleaned up the mess and wiped his flaccid cock. From outside came the sounds of a phthisic cough.

'You're a very excitable fellow,' she reproved, swinging herself out of bed and making for the bathroom. 'I thought you had the makings of an agreeable fuck.'

She asked him whether he'd care to put his clothes on again and he sensed that she was offering him no alternative. He dressed reluctantly.

'I'm sorry,' he mumbled when she rejoined him, wrapped in a

white bathrobe. He ventured an arm around her shoulders and sought her lips but she moved her head away with a fastidious jerk.

'No kissing, darling,' she scolded, 'there's far too much pyorrhoea around.' She allowed him however, a compensatory nibble of her throat.

'We'll try it again some other time perhaps,' she offered, lighting herself a Turkish cigarette. 'Vanessa always gives her friends a fair crack of her whip. Which is more than you boys will get when we really quit India.'

She seemed to like her joke giving him a droll look. Then brooded wryly on his inability to consumate the act, reflecting that failure with a hunchback was probably the same as breaking a mirror.

'I'll probably get knocked down by a bus tomorrow,' she sighed. Parting her bathrobe he kissed the flat mamillas on her soft wrinkled paps and pressed ruefully into her.

'That, you naughty boy,' she reproved, pushing him away, 'is against the rules of engagement. Whatever would the Duke of Wellington have said? You can't fire your cannon twice, on a one-shot ticket.'

She told him that, had she not had a prior appointment at Government House that evening, he could have stayed, rewarding him with a walnut toffee from a stoneware gourd vase by her bed.

'Do you like Parsees?' he asked shyly as he edged out.

'I adore them, darling,' she enthused, then remarked upon the brooding limpidity of his big, black eyes. She gave him a card on which was inscribed a telephone number and address above a gothic *Vanessa*.

'I give discounts on Monday afternoons,' she called from the door.

On his way back to the car he recalled all his inventions. That he was an extremely rich Parsee who owned two cotton mills and a cinema.

'Which cinema?' she'd asked with interest.

'The Pathé,' he lied.

It had seemed to impress her. And she had swallowed the story that he was eighteen, never apparently suspecting that he was not yet seventeen. He, on the other hand, was dubious about her advertised thirty-nine. Forty-nine, he imagined, even older. Perhaps his cock-kissing memsahib was indeed related to the Governor of Bombay. It was an aspect of the Raj that might have surprised the enclopaedic Barton Fry but not one Minoo dared discuss with him. Pythagoras was a different matter. In the car, he ordered Chakramkhan to return to Mahaluxmi, telling him that they had to find Mr Pithers. On the way, he confided in the chauffeur.

'I've had my first whore,' he boasted lightly.

The Pathan beamed.

'Was she all right?' he enquired.

He assured him that she was as sweet as a ripe jackfruit. And Chakramkhan, who had had many boys of that description, knew exactly what Minoo meant.

The racecourse was almost deserted when they arrived. Minoo walked briskly around the paddock and looked up at the grandstand. No more than half a dozen people sat there ruminating in the confetti of a million losing tickets. Deciding that Pythagoras must have walked, he instructed Chakramkhan to drive slowly towards Byculla. They recognised the despondent figure of Pythagoras not more than a few hundred yards from his home. He looked sideways at the Buick as it drew alongside him.

'What happened?' he asked, climbing in beside Minoo.

Minoo explained that he'd had to drive a lady friend home as she'd lost her taxi-fare.

'Like me,' Pythagoras laughed, flapping the leather soles of his dusty shoes. 'The Pats will have me tonight,' he grunted, looking out of the window for the two Pathan moneylenders he feared might be waiting for him.

'Will they hurt you?' Minoo enquired gently.

'A little, maybe,' Pythagoras replied, opening the door and preparing to run towards the entrance of his apartment block.

Minoo allowed himself the impertinence of holding Pythagoras's arm, a familiarity he might not have perpetrated before that afternoon. Pythagoras, mysteriously aware of the slight change in their relationship, looked vulnerable.

'How much do you need, Sir?' he asked, half tempted to address the man as Wesley but losing his nerve at the last moment.

'Two hundred should save my skin.'

Minoo handed Pythagoras two notes. The master screwed them up and thrust them into his trouser pocket.

'I'll settle up next month,' he promised, suggesting that they take some tea at the Evergreen Café.

They got out of the car and walked slowly along Clare Road, past accusative shouts from Prakash the secondhand bookseller.

'I'm owed for books,' the little man called with cheerful resignation.

'Next month,' Pythagoras winked, moving on.

He confessed to Minoo that the baker, whose shop was on their way, was owed for bread, and the dairy next door for milk. Minoo laughed at these confessions. Pythagoras kept glancing back as they walked. At the corner, Minoo turned his head, expecting to see the two Pathans Pythagoras feared. Instead, some fifty yards down the road, he recognised the slight figure of Mrs Fernandes.

'I think it's your friend, Sir,' Minoo murmured.

Pythagoras stopped and, wild-eyed, signalled to the timorous woman who was half-concealed by a tree. It was a theatrical gesture of rejection, instructing the woman that her company was not required. She stood and stared sadly. There was another dismissive wave. Minoo was surprised by the submissive manner in which she accepted Pythagoras's command. The moment she was certain of his wishes, she turned and set off, walking briskly in the opposite direction.

Although he had never discussed Mrs Fernandes with Pythagoras, Minoo often wondered at his cavalier treatment of the woman. In his opinion, there were few kinder and more considerate men than the science master but his cold and calculating attitude to his mistress appeared to betray that estimation. Then, over a saucer of steaming tea, Pythagoras mentioned Josie Fernandes for the first time.

'She wants to leave her husband to live with me, Minoo,' he brooded. Minoo did not speak. He felt privileged to have been taken into the master's confidence. To hear admissions of such intimacy from the man he most admired in the world brought tears to his eyes. Glancing quickly at Pythagoras, he noticed that his eyes were also moist and unhappy.

'It would be an imprudent thing for her to do,' Pythagoras

continued. 'You see, I'm being very slowly consumed by a female serpent, Minoo.'

'A serpent, Sir?'

'Her name is cancer,' Pythagoras said simply, blowing thoughtfully over his second saucer.

'Have you been to the hospital, Sir?' Minoo asked.

Pythagoras laughed. When he was struck by an amusing thought, his lean, protean face was transformed into that of a guileless child.

'The joke is,' he said, 'that the serpent is gobbling up what really belongs to the Pats. I would give anything to see their faces when she takes the last bite of their investment.'

Minoo was now weeping without restraint.

'Don't die, Sir,' he pleaded.

'Chutrivala,' the master said, 'you're a blockhead. Can't you see that the serpent is protecting my interests? Where is all the logic I've tried to knock into that stupid noddle of yours?'

Minoo stared at the lights of Byculla despondently. Ever since he was a small boy he had always suspected that his father would die suddenly, so that in a strange way the terrible event was a consummation of his innermost certainty. As for his mother, she had always been a beautiful and remote figure whom he had once feared losing. But he was now inured to her long absences. Even when she visited Bombay she never slept at Peccavi but stayed at the Taj, where she occasionally invited him for tea, a fearsome ordeal for a young boy that not only involved a suit, tie and polished shoes but critical looks and dreary questions.

'And how is your Aunt Kety's failing eyesight?'

'And does Uncle Soli still scream at the moon?'

She had informed him that after the cursed war, Jimmy and she would probably live in Paris. It was a city Minoo had always wanted to visit with his camera but the news that his mother and her husband would be there tempered his enthusiasm. He had not seen her for a year and sometimes dreamed that he would one day receive a message that the Rani of Pinjrapore had died in the twisted metal of a smoking Bugatti. A quick and painless end, he hoped. He would not want his glamorous mama to suffer.

So, he had put the sadness of losing his parents behind him. But Pythagoras? He had always imagined his friend would live forever, for, despite his spare frame, the science master was an accomplished gymnast with a dazzling repertoire on the rings, parallel bars and ladder. That such a man was terminally ill was unthinkable. Pythagoras asked him not to repeat the story about his serpent, declaring that its presence might infringe the conditions of his tenancy as it was not permitted to keep pets. They took a third cup of tea and some kheema together.

'What horse did you back in the Eclipse?' Minoo asked Pythagoras.

'Nebleaux III,' the master replied.

'To beat the great Golden Fawn? Why, Sir?'

'Because,' Pythagoras laughed, 'the bugger had no obvious chance.' Minoo confessed to Pythagoras that he had behaved improperly, going to the rooms of a whore and leaving before he'd managed to penetrate her. Pythagoras nodded and pointed out that a person's first sexual transaction was often quite unsatisfactory. It would have been nothing short of miraculous if things had gone really well.

'I told Chakramkhan that I'd done it, Sir,' he said. 'Should I admit my lie to him?'

Pythagoras shook his head.

'When a man inflates his sexual experiences it's usually nothing more than a statement about his self-esteem. I'm sure Chakramkhan wouldn't seriously expect honesty in such matters. Most men, when speaking of sex among themselves, are guilty of deception. Generally speaking, only women are mature enough to articulate and receive sexual truths.'

Chapter 26

When Pythagoras was passed over for the vacant Headship of Christ Church, his claims of a master's degree and seniority failing to outweigh his shabbiness, questionable character and general non-conformity, there was a small but vociferous demonstration by some ex-students. Pythagoras himself had half hoped for promotion and indeed impressed some of the governors with his foxy replies to their questions during the interview. As a generous compromise, he was appointed Deputy Head, a post that provided a modest increase in salary and the responsibility of presiding over morning prayers every other day.

'You are aware,' he said anxiously to the governors, 'that I'm an atheist of sorts.'

They reminded him forcefully that the school was a Church Trust, and membership of the Anglican communion was a condition of service.

'But I am,' Pythagoras protested, 'a Christian atheist.'

In response to the view that this was a contradiction in terms and that, although a degree of doctrinal agnosticism was acceptable within the Christian dispensation, atheism clearly was not, Pythagoras stated, 'My atheism reposes in a sincere belief that God does not exist. However, I am proud to line up with my friends who take the contrary view, preferring in essence to be a failed Christian than a successful Moslem, Jew or Hindu. I am captivated by the romance of the Virgin Birth, witness, crucifixion and resurrection of God incarnate, while the redemption of sin that is central to the Christian mystery has always excited my mind. I am a regular communicant in the mad hope that credulity will possess me, yet certain that my scepticism will instantly extinguish the tiniest threat of faith.'

'Do you believe in the possibility of a personal God?' demanded a bishop on the committee.

Pythagoras shook his head.

'I am, alas, irrevocably contaminated by reason.'

In the closed discussion that followed, it was the bishop who gave a ruling on the quality of Pythagoras's faith and his eligibility to continue as a master of the school.

'Any man who takes the sacraments of the Church,' he declared, 'must *ipso facto* be accepted as a Christian, whether he protests the fact or not.'

It was a view that alarmed some members of the committee, but the bishop pointed out that as the appointment was not sacerdotal, morning prayers not having the status of an ecclesiastical assembly, there was no impediment to Mr Pithers's selection.

'Will you lead in the hymn singing?' asked an anxious lady missionary who had visceral views on the choral component of faith.

'I'll bawl my head off,' Pythagoras promised cheerfully.

'And be seen by the assembly ennunciating the Nicene Creed?'

'As an atheist,' he declared solemnly, 'I will discharge that responsibility with particular sensitivity.'

Pythagoras appeared to glow with a new incandescence when he was appointed Deputy Head. He was given a private office to read his racing papers and a rack of canes to whack recalcitrant boys, a responsibility he chose to evade. The peons passed in and out of his office with endless cups of tea and Mrs Fernandes became a regular visitor after he'd arranged for an inner bolt to the door, the replacement of twin armchairs for a chaise-longue and venetian blinds for the windows. Mr Kismet and Miss Flinto were outraged by Mrs Fernandes's visits, Kismet rushing to Miss Flinto's classroom whenever the little woman was seen passing his door. And, as the blinds were slatted shut, they stood together in the corridor watching Pythagoras's office window, reflecting on the grave error of trusting him with the Deputy Headship. Miss Flinto reminded Kismet of Pythagoras's other notorieties, like pissing in empty sulphuric-acid jars when taken short in the laboratory and leaving the liquid to confound the experiments of chemistry classes, or demonstrating the splits on the parallel bars with no buttons on his flies, oblivious of the fact that his brown mouse kept popping in and out of his trousers, or running out of a class halfway through a lesson to place a bet at the barber's shop several hundred yards away.

Sometimes, Kismet entertained Miss Flinto by rapping on Pythagoras's door about five minutes after the windows were shuttered. But the door was never opened until Mrs Fernandes had left. Miss Flinto, who felt that as Head of the Junior School she had a duty to protect the morals of her pupils, raised the matter of the bolted door and shuttered window with Mr Baig, the new Headmaster. He pointed out that as Mrs Fernandes had a daughter in the school, a meeting behind closed doors was available to any parent who so wished, and affirmed his absolute trust in Mr Pithers's sense of propriety. Kismet, offended by Baig's dismissive attitude, privately questioned the new Head's Christian commitment in the Common Room, arguing that a proselyte did not have quite the nice perception as a man Christian-born.

Curiously, this not excessively abrasive opinion initiated a train of events that changed both Kismet's and Miss Flinto's lives. It started with Barton Fry's mild exception to Kismet's disparagement of the new Head and escalated grotesquely to a scuffle between the two men that came to no more than cracked glass of a hymn-book cabinet and a scratched cheek for the English master caused by the wildly negligent use of Kismet's fingernails. Fry retreated, Miss Flinto wept and Kismet comforted her, something he had longed to do for many years.

The painful subject of Pythagoras brought them together, allowing his hand to caress her breasts and his mouth to take hers. He confessed that his wife had at last abandoned him.

'Bunty?' Miss Flinto murmured, dabbing her eyes.

He informed her that she had left a week before, with an engineer in the Merchant Navy.

'Not Bunty?' Miss Flinto declared in disbelief.

Kismet nodded, ravaging her mouth greedily once again. He invited her home for a poached egg on toast and a pot of Selimbong, the significance of which did not entirely escape the thirty-eight-year-old spinster.

He entertained her on the way by walking up two flights of stairs on his hands, cascading, as he progressed, small coins from his coat that she tried to retrieve, giggling with amazement at his prodigal strength. At the door of his apartment, he kissed her once more, slipping an experienced hand up her skirt.

'Not here, George,' she squealed.

The noise of somebody clearing their throat alarmed Miss Flinto, who drew away from Kismet and looked up in the direction of the sound. The owner of the throat clumped down the stairs to show himself, a Leica around his neck.

'Chutrivala,' shouted Kismet angrily. 'What are you doing in my building?'

Minoo explained that he had been visiting a Miss Dementa Fardel, a lady who modelled for him. He did not disclose that he'd also taken several shots through the stairwell of Kismet balanced on his hands and one of Miss Flinto in his arms.

'Does Miss Fardel pose in the nude for you?' Kismet asked sternly. Minoo felt that Kismet and Flinto were hardly the people to entrust with that sort of information. Besides, they were Pythagoras's enemies.

'No, Sir,' he replied, trying to edge past the teachers.

Kismet warned him that he did not want to see him in the building again as the African lady he had been visiting was not a suitable person for a pupil of Christ Church to know.

'Consider this place out of bounds, Chutrivala,' he snapped.

Minoo nodded and continued down the stairs.

As much as anything, it was the restriction of his artistic freedom which being a schoolboy imposed that made him decide to leave school. Dementa Fardel had been his first assignment for *Chic Chic Cuties*, an adult magazine that was a best-seller among the Tommies. His art shot of Miss Dementa's well-oiled, black arse featured in 'The Bums of Bombay' centrefold would soon be pinned inside hundreds of army lockers around the province. He had arranged for his photos in the sex magazine to appear under the pseudonym M. Parapluie, this being a part-translation of his name, a tribute to his favourite painter Renoir, and a small bouquet for his beautiful mama who looked uncommonly like the girls in the painting that celebrated umbrellas.

Safely in his apartment, Kismet induced Miss Flinto to punch his stomach, feel his biceps and sit astride him as he did press-ups. Stimulated by this demonstration, he mounted her on the settee, occupying her without significant resistance or distress apart from a severe cramp in her left thigh, the fleshy limb suspended over the Rexine armrest being denied an adequate supply of blood during Kismet's exertions. There were implorations to take care, avocations of love, expressions of anxiety, assurances of responsibility, professions of pleasure, sobbing, biting, licking, kissing and finally quiescence.

Before the poached eggs and Selimbong, he jumped onto the floor, falling eighteen inches into a handstand, quivering as he held the position for half a minute.

'You're unbelievable,' she laughed.

'Live with me,' he pleaded.

'It's so unprofessional,' she reflected doubtfully.

But after they had made love for the second time, Jenny Flinto agreed to move her possessions into George Kismet's apartment. Her acceptance, he felt, was worth a celebratory one-armed handstand on a chair balanced on two legs at the edge of the kitchen table and the elevation of a five-pound bag of sugar on his erect phallus.

'Now there's something for young Chutrivala to immortalise with his Leica,' he panted proudly.

Jenny Flinto clapped her hands happily, before brushing away an unexpected tear. She entertained him with an extempore parody of some remembered lines, intoning them in a thin, sing-song voice:

'In the evenings, mornings, afternoons, I will measure out my love with sugar spoons.'

'What?' he grunted, giving her a wild and anxious look.

Pythagoras asked Minoo if he would help with a charity football programme in aid of the dependants of those killed in the Bombay Explosion. It entailed taking photographs of the Indian team, the European team having made arrangements with an English photographer. The assignment brought Minoo to the Cooperage, the ground where his grandfather Bert Sweetwater had been groundsman and where his mother used to cheer the Tommy teams that had dominated football in the late twenties and early thirties.

Minoo took a hundred shots of Kadirvelu the flying goal-keeper, the player he felt symbolised the spirit of the Indian team. He finally selected a picture of the acrobatic South Indian twisting through the air with his legs a metre higher than his outstretched arms. The photograph showed the intensity in Kadirvelu's eyes and the pliancy of his eel-like body as his fingers reached for the ball. His other photographs were equally as dramatic, high-speed action shots that incorporated theatrical urgency with meditative calm, recording as much about the nature of a player's genius as making a statement about his character. The pictures of Rashad, a tall, loose-limbed African inside forward, left one in no doubt about his ball-playing skills, the stylish eccentricity of his loping deceptions and elusive angles as he leaned away from the ball he still controlled. And the inimitable nature of his whimsy was captured in the slack-mouthed look of wonder his protean features reflected as he tacked around a defender's boot. But whether it was the evocations of the muscular, right-footed, bent shots of Thomas the centre forward or the speed of the winger Dhakuram, Minoo's pictures astonished all who saw them. Nobody had ever before made footballers look like soaring birds, ballet dancers and leaping gazelles. Compared to the archaic images of the stocky European team taken by a professional British Army photographer, Minoo's pictures were high art. He had asked his subjects to assemble just before dawn so he could photograph them running out of the morning mist and silhouetted against the rising sun. The original collection was exhibited first in the boardroom of the Western India Football Association and later at a public showing in the Cowasji Jehangir Hall.

'Your photographs will win us the match,' Kadirvelu predicted. He was correct. The gifted, wheeling, swerving, ball-juggling Indian amateurs beat the solid British professionals by two goals to one.

It was at his photographic exhibition at the Cowasji Jehangir Hall that Minoo met Bill Jolly, a prominent member of the Progressive Group of the European Association. From this chance meeting, Minoo was invited to Jolly's house for dinner, met young Indian nationalists who associated with the Progressives, and received so many photographic assignments that he could hardly cope with the growing business.

'The Jollys,' he informed Pythagoras, 'are liberals. People who treat Indians with courtesy and respect. They are my twenty-four carat friends.'

But Pythagoras warned Minoo that friendship with even the nicest English people was rarely better than the nine carat sort.

'You charge far too little,' Mabel Jolly advised Minoo, who was persuaded to treble his prices.

In the year the war ended, Minoo left school, was seen in his first dress-suit, heard Gracie Fields sing at the Cooperage, had a photograph of the Jolly's daughter Sally accepted by the *Illustrated Weekly of India* and secretly fell in love.

It seemed quite hopeless of course, for Sally the object of his passion, was only thirteen. As the taboos of age and culture prohibited him from demonstrating his affection in any recognisable way, he photographed her again and again. And he could not sleep unless he carried her image with him into his dreams. Fortunately, Sally enjoyed posing as much as Minoo delighted in posing her. Although none of the family suspected his interest, Sally knew. He rapidly became her creature, organising picnics for Bill, Mabel, Sally and her friend Alice to lakes, forests, parks, beaches and caves, where the girls would generally disappear, leaving the disconsolate Minoo with the older Jollys, playing Lexicon, Three-Handed Whist or Monopoly.

Sally had loose, nut-brown curls, a moist petulant mouth and grey, circumspect eyes. She was slim and honey-skinned with firm well-formed limbs covered in golden down. Her flowering was revealed in her curving hips, slinky tail and small, rounded breasts. She ran with grace and fluency, balanced on her hands, skipped tirelessly and glowed when she perspired, exuding an aroma of caramel, lavender talc and fresh, warm sweat. One day, on a rare occasion when Minoo was alone with her and the russet-haired Alice, Sally asked him if it was heavy. At that moment he felt that it was five times as large as it was, imagining it towering up above his head like a washerman's bundle.

'Of course not,' he whispered, averting his eyes from her curious gaze.

He had told her on another occasion that his condition was congenital and irreversible but that he did not find it a serious impediment or suffer any pain.

'Can I touch it?' she asked suddenly.

He allowed her to run her warm, damp hand under his shirt over his back. Her nearness made him catch his breath, as he felt her curls brush his neck and the slight pressure of her breast against his arm.

'It's bony,' she concluded, 'like the breast of a large bird. A turkey perhaps?'

She smiled, wiping her hand on her handkerchief. It seemed an action of rejection and caused him pain.

'Can I touch it too?' asked Alice.

Minoo submitted himself for a second examination, looking up to see that Sally had already wandered away, uninterested either in him or his loathsome hump. But after that she always alluded to his hump in private as her turkey. It was the only secret they shared.

She learned, in the brief times they spent together, to make him unhappy with talk of her boyfriends in Naini Tal and the hope that they would soon be on their way to England. Bill and Mabel Jolly, however, always spoke of staying on as long as they could, although the approach of Independence made their future uncertain.

Minoo had compiled a large album of Sally's photographs. He often returned to one of her in a black bathing costume, taken with the shape of her slim thighs and faintly discernible nipples under the clinging, wet wool. The realisation that any ambitions he had with regard to Sally Jolly were impossible gradually caused less and less pain. In time, he hallowed his secret love with an impetuous resolve to be celibate. It was a fearful decision for he was tormented by priapic reveries and nocturnal emissions, rising in the night to walk around the compound of the ice factory, murmuring the name of the person he loved like a tormented creature. He even investigated the possibility of becoming a eunuch but, terrified by the grisly finality of emasculation, wrote his half-sister Meroo a letter asking her advice. Since he had never met her or ever corresponded with her, he did not seriously expect a reply. But within seven days he received a postcard from Lahore.

My dear Minoo,
    I too am a hunchback but of a less exotic kind. Grow a beard. I would if I could. Keep your penis. You never know when it will come in handy. By all means be celibate for a while. There is nothing wrong with self-

denial. Under no circumstances reveal your true feelings to the thirteen-year-old. No good can come of burdening a pretty child with your ugly dreams. Incidentally, if it is any comfort to you, the Chutrivalas were all hunchbacks of one sort or other.

Love to Uncle Soli and Aunt Kety.

Warm regards,
Meroo

Chapter 27

The fire at Peccavi damaged most of the upper floor, making it necessary for Soli and Kety to live downstairs in an area that had once been used for billiards and, for a while, during the time of Kety's special interest, table tennis. Soli had stopped coming to the ice factory, leaving Minoo to supervise the day-to-day running of what had now become a food storage plant. Soli's long white beard and hair down to his shoulders dramatised his size. He started to go out with Chakramkhan in the Buick every evening, returning at nightfall. Eventually Chakramkhan spoke to Minoo. Soli, he complained, progressed down the Marine Drive feigning blindness, placing one foot carefully before the other as he shouted, 'Mother, Father, I am the lost child.' He would return to the car with his begging-bowl filled with copper coins.

Minoo remembered that when his father was alive Soli had behaved in a similar manner. He telephoned Dilduktha, who arrived the next day. Soli was outraged when he recognised the doctor, guessing that he had called to examine him.

'What do you want, you miserable mothercunt?' he screamed from the window.

Dilduktha was inured to aberrant conduct.

'I'm here to cut your balls off, my friend,' he joked, following Minoo into the house.

'Mothercunt,' shouted Soli, glaring at Dilduktha.

Theresa brought in a tray of tea and biscuits and everyone, with the exception of Soli, tried to pretend that nothing was amiss. Kety, who was now almost blind, was struggling to acquire Braille. She complained that her fingers were too insensitive to identify the letters and was using her toes instead.

'I've always had intelligent toes,' she claimed.

'Mothercunt,' snarled Soli, watching Dilduktha warily.

After tea, Dilduktha, Minoo and Kety made their way across the compound to Minoo's studio. Dilduktha informed them that his clinic would be an inappropriate place for Soli and asked Kety to seriously consider Soli's certification. The suggestion distressed her and she pleaded to be allowed to look after her brother. The proposal to send him to the Thana madhouse was unacceptable.

As a compromise, Dilduktha offered Kety and Soli 'Cheelchinar', his bungalow at Lonavla.

'It's fairly remote and you would be obliged to incur not only the cost of renting the premises but the additional expense of hiring a pair of trained keepers.'

He suggested a figure of at least a thousand rupees a month. Minoo looked glum but Kety insisted that money was no object.

'Is he likely to hurt Aunt Kety?' Minoo asked anxiously.

Dilduktha nodded. 'It's a possibility. In my opinion, Soli Chutrivala is not responsible for his actions.'

Kety's face was set in defiance.

'I would rather run the risk of being killed by Soli than allow him to be locked up in a padded cell by strangers,' she declared.

So it was arranged that Soli and Kety would move to the bungalow at Lonavla. They left Bombay a few days later in the Buick, sitting calmly together in the rear with Katarsingh, one of the two keepers Dikduktha had hired, beside Chakramkhan. It was just as well. Suddenly, when they had presumed his placidity for the journey, Soli became alarmed when they stopped for petrol. He jumped out of the car and ran down the road. Katarsingh pursued, captured and frogmarched him back.

'Don't hurt him,' implored Kety.

Soli was panting with the exertion but cheerful at what he saw was a not unpleasant diversion.

'I am the lost child,' he informed Kety, sandwiched now between her and the vigilant Katarsingh.

'Of course you are, my darling,' Kety said, kissing his hairy cheek.

After the first week she wrote to Minoo that things were going well. Soli's occasional escapes were accepted as a kind of good-humoured paperchase. He rarely ran away in the dark and never travelled more than a mile from the house, returning happily whenever the keepers found him. 'I think he's showing signs of improvement,' she added in a postscript, a diagnosis that Dilduktha did not entirely accept.

*

When Soli and Kety had been gone several weeks, Theresa came to see Minoo. He received her in his studio.

'Sit down,' he said.

Theresa looked uncomfortable and reminded Minoo that she was a servant.

'You've been like a mother to me,' he observed, insisting that she sat down.

'It's Angelica,' Theresa said. 'She's expecting Soli's child.'

Minoo stared at her wide-eyed.

'She's not a young woman,' he said anxiously.

'I think she's nearly forty,' Theresa replied.

'I'll arrange for a doctor to examine her,' promised Minoo, 'and of course make provisions for her to be admitted to hospital when the time comes.'

Theresa informed him that Angelica was concerned about her job. Minoo reassured her that nothing would change.

'But she'll have nothing to do now Soli and Kety have gone.'

'I'll think of something,' said Minoo with a frown.

Theresa's eyes flooded with tears as she got up to leave.

'You're like your father,' she sobbed. 'He looked after us all when he was alive. Unlike Soli, who's a thoughtless man.'

'He's unwell.'

'He used to fuck us every night,' she blurted out in despair. 'Oh Jesus, he had such a big, long truncheon. And it felt as though there was a bone in it as he jig, jig, jigged like a demented beast.'

'I'm sorry,' Minoo said bleakly.

Minoo had Peccavi boarded up. He consulted several builders about restoring the old house. The estimates ranged from fifty thousand to a lakh and a half. It seemed beyond the resources of the business. He spoke to Friski Dalal, Dilduktha, Mr Fazal, the Jollys and Pythagoras, eliciting their opinions. All of them were in favour of demolishing the property and selling the plot for industrial development. Bill Jolly, however, who was fascinated by the history of the house, considered that part of the cost of restoration could be met by subscription from wealthy Parsees. He saw its future as a Parsee museum. Mabel Jolly drafted a prospectus which she felt could be illustrated by Minoo's photographs of Peccavi. She planned the printing and the circulation of the appeal to potential subscribers.

What at first appeared to be a minor impediment delayed

Minoo's final judgement for he realised with trepidation that, whatever his decision, until his majority the contract would have to be signed by Soli and Meroo, an undertaking even more formidable than any envisaged solution.

'Well?' Pythagoras enquired, as he strolled around Peccavi with Minoo. 'What conclusion have you reached?'

'To wait,' observed Minoo.

'That does not seem excessively rash,' agreed Pythagoras.

The birth of Angelica's son was an uncomplicated event, the mother being transported to the Jamsetjee Jeejeebhoy Hospital in the Buick as labour commenced and returning ten days later with Byramji's grandson.

'He looks like a Wadia,' proclaimed Minoo. Theresa and Chakramkhan agreed. Angelica had decided to name him after her favourite film star, Tyrone Power, and Minoo felt that she should use the Chutrivala name if she so wished. But the idea did not commend itself to her, and she elected to use her own family name of Braganza. She pointed out that, as she'd been raped, it was hardly appropriate that the child should bear the stigma of the rapist. Besides, she did not feel that Chutrivala had the right sort of ring for a Goanese Catholic.

Minoo smiled.

'Tyrone Power Braganza, then,' he said.

The last of Fram's cache of champagne, eleven bottles of Pol Roger 38, was fished out of the Peccavi cellar, an iced cake was ordered from Carnaglia's and the baby was christened up the road at St Mary's, after which there was a modest celebration in the ice factory, Minoo's studio being too cramped for the occasion. The guest list included Pythagoras, Barton Fry, Archdeacon Cecil DeLisle, Father Pontius, Theresa, Chakramkhan, Dagroo and Pandu Kandu, the last two representing the entire workforce of the ice factory. Tyrone Power cried when they toasted him, which Theresa declared to be an auspicious omen.

Later, when everybody had gone home and Minoo had retired to bed, he heard the cries of a baby in the distance. They sounded uncommonly like the other baby that he had prised from the wall of the freezer room. And although he was fairly certain it was Tyrone Power, he had the passing fancy, as he slid back into sleep, that it might have been the ghost of little Ardeshir welcoming the newcomer.

Chapter 28

Minoo saw less of the Jollys than he had in the year the war ended. It was not that they didn't greet him cordially and talk to him with animation when he called at their apartment in Churchgate. But on one occasion their servant informed him that they were out when he imagined he heard Mabel's laugh from an inner room. And it was always he who made the effort to call on them, they never contacting him. Sally was hardly seen during the summer of 1946 and never accepted his invitations to picnics, concerts, exhibitions or football matches. Then, when he was convinced that the Jollys were deliberately freezing him out of their lives, he would meet either Bill or Mabel or both together when shopping or in a restaurant. Their pleasure at these encounters hardly seemed simulated. He would be introduced to whomever they were with, as their good friend the gifted photographer, and urged to call on them whenever he was free to do so.

'Ring me,' Bill would plead. And he would. But it generally took half a dozen phone calls before a date could be arranged. When he arrived, there was always the suggestion that they were expected somewhere else, although this was denied when he rose to leave.

'It wasn't very important anyway,' Bill would protest as Mabel made several phone calls changing their obviously planned arrangements. It seemed that no sooner had he arrived than it was time to depart. He always enquired, out of courtesy, how Sally was. In the year of their close friendship, the question would have provoked a detailed reply about her prowess at swimming, netball and athletics. He would have been informed about how well she was doing at school and how she was looking forward to being photographed by him. But now, he received the most cursory reactions. 'She's fine,' was as much as he could expect from either parent.

Minoo soon recognised that the coded message these almost dismissive responses carried was that the Jollys did not wish him to talk about their daughter. The briefest sight of Sally now cast a shadow over him. He felt alien and unclean in her presence. He could hardly bear to open his album of her photographs or think about the happy times when he had been her friend.

Just before Sally was due to return to Naini Tal that summer, he met her in the foyer of the building where the family lived. He felt sick with apprehension as she approached him.

'Hello, Minoo,' she said, in her old friendly voice.

'Hello, Sally,' he replied cautiously.

They went up to the third floor together, the lift filled with the fragrance of her body. And then, quite unexpectedly, she kissed him at the side of his mouth. She told him that she was returning to school the following day and hoped he'd write to her. He promised that he would and she placed a palm on his hump.

'Are you my very own hunchback?' she demanded.

He searched her face for a meaning to the question that both hurt and excited him.

'I'm anything you say I am,' he whispered.

Minoo didn't see her to say goodbye properly before he left the Jollys' flat. She was, he suspected, taking a bath. And although he ventured a wish to be remembered to her as he left, his request was ignored by her mother and father as though it had never been articulated.

The letter that she had requested from him was written and posted. She did not reply. He wrote a second, shorter and rather cheerful note, which again was not acknowledged. Then, two months later, he ran across Mabel at Mongini's where she was taking tea. He received a painful rebuke.

'I would rather you didn't write to Sally at school,' she said to him. 'She's finding it terribly difficult to get down to serious business this term.'

How, he wondered, had Mabel found out about his letters which fortunately were quite innocuous, indeed almost Victorian in their propriety? They started 'Dear Sally' and ended 'Sincerely,

Minoo'. He had deliberately chosen not to use the more common 'Yours', deeming it vaguely suggestive, and he had been scrupulous in avoiding the most harmless innuendos. Either Sally had written to her parents about the letters or they had been intercepted by a teacher. Some girl's boarding schools were particularly sensitive about letters from non-familial members of the opposite sex. He felt resentful and then extremely angry. His anger led rather irrationally to an anti-British letter to *The Times of India*, a whimsical and immature piece of vituperation about how much more enlightened and symbolically potent it would have been if the job of last Viceroy had been offered to Gandhi instead of yet another effete member of the British aristocracy. To his surprise, it was printed and drew a number of serious replies. Barton Fry telephoned his congratulations but Pythagoras laughed.

'You're joking, of course,' he hooted over the phone.

'Of course,' Minoo agreed, but for some unaccountable reason, wept when he'd replaced the receiver. The tears were for himself and for the girl he could never have. But he was, he remembered with gloomy satisfaction, her very own hunchback.

He avoided Bill and Mabel Jolly after that, crossing the road or ducking out of view until they had passed. He achieved another minor revenge when Gospie, an Englishman who managed the storage of game for the Bombay Gymkhana and Bombay Yacht Club, mentioned Bill Jolly.

'I don't think I know the man,' Minoo murmured.

His answer appeared to perplex Gospie, who seemed to have thought otherwise. Nothing more was said, but Minoo hoped his remark might have been carried back to the Jollys. But old Gospie was a deep bastard, a Wykhamist and ex ICS man. If he'd perceived Minoo's comment to be a barb intended for one of his fellow countrymen, it was possible he would not inflict the intended damage. He was not the sort of man who would give a wog that sort of psychic satisfaction, for he was perceptive enough to see that Minoo didn't possess the balls or authority to do the job himself.

Chapter 29

Minoo found the July of Independence Year extremely depressing. Dilduktha had phoned him with the news that Kety was completely blind and that Soli had become increasingly troublesome, running around the wooded slopes of the Western Ghats completely naked. He was warned that it was almost inevitable that he would have to be certified. Then there was Meroo. He had, after that first letter, sent her several more. In his latest one, he hinted that he hoped in the near future to visit Lahore, which he pointed out would soon be incorporated into another country. 'I can't take this notion of Pakistan seriously,' he wrote, deploring the creation of what was clearly a theocratic state.

Meroo ignored all his letters with the exception of his threat to call on her in Lahore. She replied on a postcard depicting the tomb of Anar Kali. It was to the point and read:

> Dear Minoo,
>   I do not wish to see you.
>
>   Cordially,
>   Meroo

He was hurt by this card and showed it to Pythagoras. His friend did not consider if unusual, pointing out that she was probably ashamed either of her appearance or her living conditions and possibly needed time to prepare herself for his visit. If her decision to exclude him from her life was irrevocable, she would hardly have used the word 'Cordially'.

'It resonates,' Pythagoras concluded, 'with covert optimism.'

The opinion cheered Minoo and he sent Meroo a book of sonnets by Christina Rossetti to demonstrate that he was not

239

offended by her asperity. She did not acknowledge the gift. Again, Pythagoras shrugged off what Minoo interpreted as contempt.

'It may be,' he pondered, 'that your half-sister finds Christina Rossetti's work singularly disagreeable.'

'But how can any educated woman consider Rossetti's work disagreeable?'

'Easily,' retorted Pythagoras, 'as she is averse to sentimental religiosity.'

'She could at least have thanked me,' complained Minoo.

'She will,' predicted Pythagoras.

'When?'

'That's almost a metaphysical question,' reflected Pythagoras, drawing a loose thread from his flies.

Melancholy began to seep into Minoo's marrow. His gloom, he suspected, was three parts his unrequited love for Sally Jolly and the rest, a sense of suddenly being alone, without people of his own blood to love or to laugh with. In a way, this diminishing of the world into which he'd been born was symbolised by the decay of Peccavi and the twilight of British rule. Of course, like Barton Fry and Pythagoras, he was pleased about Independence. But seeing the pink Tommies and their patrician masters off the premises was very much like saying goodbye to irascible tenants whose eccentricities, bloodymindedness and desperate behaviour he would, in a perverse way, miss.

There was a wonderful madness about grown men hauling down pieces of cloth at sunset, screaming orders and stamping their boots until sparks flew. And there were those who would miss them even more than he would.

'Hello, Johnnie. You want short time with clean girl? You wanna virgin? Whisky soda? Ham and eggs? Player's Please? This way Johnnie. Only two rupees. You wanna three girls same time? You wanna chicken sandwich? Very young pussy? No bugs in this place, Johnnie. All girls fourteen, Johnnie. Very nice. Very clean. Brandy pawnee? Mutton chops? You need big breasts? You wanna see lady with two dogs? Donkey? Sure Johnnie, real donkey. You wanna see naked dancing girls? Everybody very tight in this house, Johnnie. God Save the King, Johnnie. You wanna lady with Union Jack on arse, Johnnie? Fat girl, Johnnie? Thin one, Johnnie? Very small girl? Cold beer? Very friendly place, Johnnie. I make you special price, Johnnie. All night jobs, Johnnie. You wanna suckoff? Roast beef and Yorkshire pudding, Johnnie? All girls speak English, Johnnie. You need music, Johnnie? Rule Britannia, Johnnie. My sister needs to fuck with you, Johnnie. So glad you could come. This way, Johnnie. This way . . . this way . . .'

He half wished that, at the last minute, there would be a change of plan so that the British would stay, not as rulers but as friends. He saw Peccavi restored to its former glory and filled with tattooed men who shouted, drank, made jig-jig and sang. Tommies, when drunk, loved singing. Fighting too. Minoo didn't mind as long as they didn't hurt anyone.

'Get your small pack off, you silly little bastid.'

'Wish I could, Johnnie. Wish I could.'

The thought of Sally Jolly disappearing forever was so painful that he tried not to consider it. He had always realised that some other man would marry her and become the father of her children. He dreamed sometimes of his magical transformation from a beast to a dashing boulevardier. Marcel Parapluie, he called himself. Marcel had something of Minoo Chutrivala about the eyes, lips and moustache, but he had a tall, strong body that was fit for his Beauty.

Sometimes, he would plan his marriage to a quiet, Parsee girl. Someone who was plain, ugly even, but gentle. He craved gentleness. But as the idea caught hold of his mind, Sally's face would appear before him and he would weep. These strange thoughts he did not disclose to anyone, not even Pythagoras.

Early August, however, was redeemed by a postcard from Paris. The message from the Rani of Pinjrapore was genial enough and the news that she had a runner in the Arc excited Pythagoras. But the picture on the card did not depict any one of the more usual visual clichés for which Parisian cards are celebrated but showed the entrance to 9 Boulevard Malesherbes. Pythagoras, for once, could not provide an instant solution but sensed that it probably had some literary allusion. Barton Fry's help was sought. His eyes lit up.

'It's the house where Proust was born,' he said simply.

'The great writer?' Minoo asked.

'Well,' mused Fry, 'that depends on your point of view. The

man to whom I refer is Robert Proust, younger brother of the more celebrated Marcel.'

'But what does it mean?' Minoo demanded.

'Robert,' said Fry, 'wrote about a subject that is hardly my special interest.' He smiled at his private joke.

'What?' asked Minoo.

'He was the author of a book called *The Surgery of the Female Genital Organs*. Since the writer of the card was your mother, perhaps she is indicating that she's undergone or is contemplating an operation in that area.'

'How outrageously elliptical,' laughed Pythagoras, clasping himself around the shoulders with delight.

Minoo trembled with excitement. He resolved to write to his mother immediately, disclosing the information they'd deduced and enquiring after her health. He would not, of course, mention Barton Fry, but would claim the perception as his. It would, he was convinced, induce her to admire him. He dared not hope for love but her admiration was assured.

'Do you mind me filching your brilliant deduction?' he asked Fry.

'I could be wrong,' Fry warned. 'It could mean nothing at all.'

'Never,' exulted Minoo, madly jubilant, 'never. I feel it in my bones that I will amaze her.'

When Pythagoras and Fry had left, he was more elevated in spirits than he had been since the happy year with the Jollys. He had an uncanny feeling that his luck was going to change for the better. There was no explaining the feeling. A faster heartbeat, a kind of euphoria and suddenly the mad certainty that being in love was a blessing; that unrequited adoration was nobler and purer than carnal fulfilment. He thought of Sally and cried out to her in his mind the way he often did, imagining that they were on adjacent peaks with the mists of an abyss between them.

Then, quite inexplicably, he heard her voice. But when she actually called his name, he chilled with disbelief. He went outside. It was Sally Jolly dismounting from a red bicycle.

'You'll live for ever,' he laughed. 'I was just thinking of you.'

'Do you often think of me?' she asked.

'Yes,' he shouted shamelessly.

'I've come to see your ice factory,' she said, coming to him like an old friend and kissing him noisily on the cheek.

'You're growing a beard,' she remarked.

'I'm trying,' he said, rubbing away at the tufts he had managed to cultivate.

He did not expect the red lips or painted finger- and toenails. Her cheeks were tinged with rouge and she wore mascara. The hair had been cut much shorter and the movement of her breasts was visible under the white cotton dress. At fifteen, she was already a woman. He was stimulated by the lynx-like slyness in her eyes and her mocking mouth that looked more experienced than he hoped it was.

'It's wonderful to see you,' he murmured, daring to touch her bare arm.

She did not appear to mind his slight familiarity.

'Have you been good?' he asked.

'Horribly wicked,' she laughed.

'I can hardly believe that,' he said lamely.

She regarded him with amusement. Poor Minoo, her eyes seemed to be saying.

'Alice is with me,' she said suddenly, pointing towards Peccavi. 'She's fascinated by your giant goldfish.'

He asked after her mother and father in a stilted, sort of way. She made a face and confessed that they didn't know where she was.

'Are you going to photograph me?' she asked, reverting for a moment to childhood as she did a criss-cross step between paving-stones.

'Of course,' Minoo replied, 'you were born to be photographed.' She posed, her golden arms akimbo, staring at him boldly.

'Are you still sweet on me?'

He was shocked by the question and almost stammered, but ended with a self-effacing display of teeth.

'I'll always be sweet on you,' he said, sliding his hands into his pockets to stop himself shaking.

He could see Alice by the side of the house now. She appeared to be more interested in the stump of Sir Maneckji's marble horse beside the pond than she did in joining them. He halloed and waved. She waved back and turned away, disappearing behind Peccavi again. Sally asked about the derelict house and Minoo told her the story briefly.

243

'Will you show me around there?' she asked.

'It's dangerous,' he said.

They walked together into the ice factory.

'Do you photograph girls in the nude?' she asked with a wide-eyed show of innocence.

It was, he sensed, a mischievous question but despite this he blushed, diverted by the smell of a body damp with perspiration as she swished past him.

'Occasionally,' he replied, his voice cracking slightly.

She smiled at him and took his hand as they passed through the door.

'This building,' he droned like a guide, 'is sixty foot by eighty. We have a capacity of ten tons of ice per day.'

'Ten tons?'

Minoo nodded proudly as she squeezed his hand. He explained that in the event of an electricity failure they had four standby 12 BHP oil engines here to power the ice-making plant, extra large condenser equipment and agitators that activated the ice-tank fillers.

'How jolly,' she murmured, leaving him to climb up a pile of filled sacks in the corner.

'Paddy husks,' Minoo said. 'Byramji Wadia discovered that they are cheaper and as efficient as other types of new-fangled insulation like granulated cork or slag wool.'

'And what's that boring smell?' she asked.

'Ammonia,' he said, 'is part of our ice-making process.'

She yawned as she glanced around.

'Is that all you do? Make lumps of ice?'

Minoo laughed and pointed out that some of the past uses included the tempering of high-grade steel, the preparations of anti-toxins and serums, the coating of moving-picture films and photographic papers and the testing of delicate instruments.

He told her of his father's fast friend, Stollmeyer, who helped the business before the war.

'I remember him as a kind and wonderful man. A Swiss.'

'And did this Swiss guy go home?' she enquired langorously.

'Many years ago.'

He led her around the food storage freezers, taking her into the last one.

'This is the poultry chamber,' he said, as they walked between tiers of frosted, pink chickens, ducks, geese and turkeys.

'It's colder than Naini Tal at Christmas,' she shivered.

Minoo looked at her, tormented by her nearness and the strange possibilities that appeared to be unfolding.

'Does Alice want to look around?' he enquired politely.

Sally stalked around the room rubbing her hands, pouting plumes of gelid breath before her.

'Alice is more interested in big fish,' she confided.

'I'm pleased you choose to be with a minnow,' he joked, stooping chivalrously to hide his obvious tumescence.

She did not appear to be amused but turned away to bump past the rows of frozen bodies. He informed her that they had better leave the room lest she catch a chill, warning her that if a person remained at these sub-zero temperatures for any appreciable time, recovery could be protracted and painful. Even death was a possibility.

'Death?' she murmured, rocking a turkey on its hook, then stroking its breast suggestively. She stared at him and he knew what she meant. He smiled, remembering another time.

'How long would it take?' she asked.

'With the door closed, no more than an hour,' he replied.

'And what would happen if I locked you in here?' she enquired in a challenging voice.

'I'd die,' he said amiably, celebrating her with lubricious eyes.

'And would you do that for me?' she asked gently.

He nodded, sensing suddenly the oracular shadow of his affirmation while her face, for a moment, was illuminated with the wonder of the power he had given her.

'Really?'

He nodded again.

'Take your shirt off,' she whispered, investing the seductive request with a playful edge.

She waited for him to respond. He slipped awkwardly out of his black and white speckled braces, then unbuttoned his magenta shirt, exposing a small island of chest hair. Sally came to him, placing her hands on his hump.

'Are you my very own hunchback?' she murmured, caressing his curved spine.

Minoo grunted like a beast, unable to articulate a response to

245

her question. He lowered his head, submitting to the brief pleasuring of her icy fingers before she clattered slowly to the entrance, turning to give him a quick, incurious glance, as though she was finally disappointed with the facility of her achievement.

He crouched, acting the part of her creature, motionless, bared to the waist, observing her transit against the evening sun from the end of the dimly lit room. And he was abased by beastly desire and utterly unafraid when she swung the heavy steel door shut, leaving him alone in a silent forest of pendant corpses.

Sally and Alice cycled slowly away from the deserted ice factory. By the time they got over Nesbit Bridge it was dusk.

'It's just my luck to get a blush before the weekend,' Sally grumbled.

'I'm clear for another seven days or so,' Alice said.

They slowed at the main road, dismounted, then adjusted their dynamoes and checked their lights.

'I didn't say goodbye to your hunchback,' Alice reflected as they rode down Mohammedali Road.

Sally didn't answer, thinking of other things. The splutter of fire-crackers and the stink of gunpowder filled the air. Rockets and coloured trails traced their way across the dark sky. They travelled on for a while in silence, observed with interest from passing trams, enjoying the occasional whistle.

'Are we really going to allow those awful snottys to slobber over us at the End of the Raj party?' Alice asked suddenly.

'Slobbering is de rigueur, dear child,' Sally declared, glancing sideways at her companion; the spoof plummy voice and elegious look sustaining them in modest hilarity for the best part of their journey home.

Luton
November 1991

Glossary

agarbutty perfumed incense stick

anna $\frac{1}{16}$ of a rupee

apheen opium

banjara large Indian dog

Bhagwan God

bhujja fried savoury

bhaji spinach

bhang Indian hemp

Bookh Hunger

Brahmin member of the highest caste in the Hindu caste system

bunder port, harbour

bundersbusth arrangement

bunia Gujarati grocer

chaprassie uniformed attendant

charas heroin

chatty earthenware vessel

Cheelchinar *lit.* Eagle's tree

chinkara deer

chirag oil light

choli short-sleeved bodice

choothia fool (*lit.* cunt)

chowkidar watchman

chunna chick peas

croreputty person who has more than one hundred lakhs

Cupalari spike chisel-edged spike

dharamsala rest house, without amenities

Dilduktha aching heart

Diwana Madman

dursi tailor

firkee special reel on which kite twine and manja is wound

Frere, Sir Bartle Governor of Bombay, 1862. As the Chief Commissioner of Sind in the 1850s, he issued the Scinde Dawke stamp.

gharry victoria

ghat mountain pass

Gidney, Sir Henry famous Anglo-Indian eye surgeon

godown warehouse

goonda malcontent

gulab jamuns sweet balls made of solidified milk fried in clarified butter and covered in syrup

hamal porter, servant

Hanuman chap Hanuman brand of twine

jaggery coarse brown sugar made from palm sap

juldee quick

jungli wild person

kabadi team game

Kali, Kali, Ma/ Indra ki bheti, Brahma ki pali/ Dho dho hath/ Bunjwani tali. Clap hands for Mother Kali, daughter of Indra, nurtured by Brahma.

kanga comb

khadder home-spun cloth

kheema curried mince

Khoja a Muslim sect

koan mystical riddle that is insoluble by the use of reason. It is the basis of Japanese Zen meditation. 'Has a dog Buddha nature?' is a celebrated example.

kulfi ice cream

Kutab Minar ornamental mausoleum near Delhi

lakh one hundred thousand rupees

machan raised platform used in tiger hunting

maharani wife of a maharaja

mali gardener

manja twine coated with powdered glass

maund a variable unit of weight, depending on place. A Bombay maund is 28 lb.

mistry craftsman

mogul-roti tandoori bread

molee spicy sauce made with coconut

nabob a wealthy man

nautch traditional Indian dance performed by professional female dancers

nilgai large Indian antelope

nullah stream

oont camel

paan digestive consisting of quick-lime, areca nut, spices and sometimes tobacco and other ingredients, folded into a betel leaf

Parsee follower of Zoroaster

Pathan one of Afghan race settled in India

pugree turban

Pylee Pyari First Love.

raga variations on a musical theme

Rani wife of a Raja

razai coverlet quilted with cotton

salwar kamize long shirt

sarod musical instrument

Scinde Dawke *see* Frere, Sir Bartle

sepoy private in the infantry

sheekh kebab skewered spiced mutton

shikari hunter

Shurum Shame

sice stable groom

Subudh system of worship and living, founded by the Javanese mystic Pak Subuh (d. 1937)

sunyasi a holy man

talwar curved sword

tamasha show, entertainment

Theri Ma ki Chabook Your Mother's Whip

tiffin light meal, usually at midday

toddy kind of palm tree, the sap of which is used to make an alcoholic drink

Toofan ki Bibi Calamity's Girl

topee pith helmet

utchkan bearer's white frock coat

vakil lawyer